Charles Bridge

Charles Bridge

A novel of the Cold War

Jefferson Flanders

Munroe Hill Press

Lexington, MA

Cover design by Mick Wieland Design

ISBN-13: 978-1-7354805-0-3
eBook ISBN: 978-1-7354805-1-0

Munroe Hill Press
Lexington, Massachusetts

In honor of the courageous men and women who signed Charter 77 and kept the faith

"Both now and for always, I intend to hold fast to my belief in the hidden strength of the human spirit."

– Andrei Sakharov

"Chance and chance alone has a message for us. Everything that occurs out of necessity, everything expected, repeated day in and day out, is mute. Only chance can speak to us."

– Milan Kundera

A Note on Czechoslovakia's History

For much of the 20th century, the people of Central Europe suffered from economic upheaval, the ravages of war, and the horrors of Nazi and Communist totalitarian rule. Those living in the territory that became Czechoslovakia—Czechs, Moravians, and Slovaks—were not spared from these difficult and demanding times.

The fall of the Habsburg monarchy at the end of the First World War led to the creation of an independent Czechoslovakia in 1918. Tomas Masaryk became the country's first president. While Czechoslovakia suffered during the Depression, it nonetheless remained a parliamentary democracy when other European countries turned to dictatorships. Nonetheless, there was tension between ethnic groups, as Slovaks and Germans chafed at what they saw as Czech political dominance.

Then, in 1938, came the betrayal of the Munich Pact. Britain's Neville Chamberlain and France's Edouard Daladier agreed to cede the border area of the Sudetenland (with its large German population) to Nazi Germany. Chamberlain justified the deal by claiming it guaranteed "Peace In Our Time." In reality, it only served to embolden Germany's dictator, Adolf Hitler. In March 1939, Hitler dispatched the Wehrmacht to conquer the remainder of the country.

The German occupation ended in 1945, when the Soviet Red Army liberated Prague and Bratislava. After the war, Czechoslovakia became part of the Soviet sphere of power, and the Communists captured one-third of the vote in the 1946 elections. They controlled the coalition government led by the Communist Klement Gottwald; responding to Soviet pressure, it rejected Marshall Plan aid in 1947.

The Communists took full power in 1948 in what became known as the Czech Coup. One non-Communist remained in the cabinet, Jan Masaryk, the Foreign Minister, and he fell to his death from a second-floor window under suspicious circumstances. Czechoslovakia became a full-blown Stalinist state, nationalizing industries, collectivizing agriculture, censoring the press, and persecuting political opponents. By the early 1950s, the Communist Party began purging its own leaders, a familiar pattern since Bolshevik times.

By the 1960s, centralized planning had produced a stagnant economy which triggered public discontent. In 1967, the reformer Alexander Dubcek replaced the unpopular Antonin Novotny as First Secretary of the Czechoslovak Communist Party. The idealistic Dubcek believed that Czechoslovakia could establish "socialism with a human face." He introduced political and economic reforms, granted the press greater freedom, and proposed autonomy for Slovakia, but Dubcek misread the willingness of Moscow to allow liberal change. In response, Soviet leader Leonid Brezhnev established the Brezhnev Doctrine, which barred Soviet bloc countries from abandoning Communism.

The brief period of liberalization, dubbed the Prague Spring, ended on August 20, 1968, when 500,000 Warsaw Pact troops led by the Soviet Red Army crossed the border into Czechoslovakia. There was no armed resistance by the Czechs—what happened in Hungary in 1956, when the Russians had crushed a popular uprising in Budapest and thousands died, was still a fresh memory. Yet as tanks rolled through the streets of Prague, they were greeted with chants of "Ivan, go home."

Dubcek was spared the fate of Hungary's would-be reformer, Imre Nagy, who was executed by hanging along with many of his colleagues. Instead, Dubcek was detained and brought to Moscow for "comradely" talks. When he returned to Prague, he announced the end of his reform program. In April 1969, Dubcek was replaced by Gustav Husak, a hardliner, who took over as First Secretary, and who also assumed the presidency in 1975.

In the aftermath of the Prague Spring, the Czechoslovak government began a campaign to repress dissent, employing the StB, the dreaded secret police, to harass dissenters and human rights activists. The regime was alert for signs of "decadent" Western cultural influences; in 1976, the government arrested members of a Czech rock band, The Plastic People of the Universe, convicted them of "organized disturbance of the peace," and gave them prison sentences. These repressive policies sparked a response: on the first day of 1977, some 250 intellectuals and former Party members signed a manifesto called Charter 77. It criticized the Communist government for failing to implement the human rights provisions of the Helsinki Accord and other international covenants on political, civil, and human rights.

When the Western press published stories about the Charter, it triggered a harsh response by the Husak regime; many of those who signed the manifesto, including Vaclav Havel, a playwright and dissident, were sent to prison on charges of subversion.

As the 1980s began, what was left of the dissident movement had gone underground. Some who signed Charter 77 had emigrated to the West, worn out after years of harassment, repeated detentions, and imprisonment. Unlike Poland, where the Solidarity movement had emerged to challenge the regime, Czechoslovakia's political landscape remained barren, with the StB poised to crush any renewed resistance.

Part One

One

It began, innocuously enough, with a customer new to Gramercy Antiques.

Claire only took full notice of the man on his second visit to the store. He was older—she guessed that he was in his mid-fifties, perhaps even a youthful sixty. His dark hair was heavily streaked with gray, and he had sharp features, a pointed chin, and a narrow nose. He wore a well-tailored tan suit with a light blue shirt and a striped regimental necktie. A man who had money, like most of her customers.

She remembered that he had spent thirty minutes in Gramercy Antiques the week before, admiring several of the oil paintings and the few antique clocks in the store. He had politely refused any help when she approached him. She had been struck by how gracefully he moved through the store, at ease, very sure of himself. Now, he was back.

She caught him staring at her, and he looked away quickly. Claire was mildly annoyed. Was he attracted to her? He was too old for her by thirty years, but to her continuing dismay, she had found that some men weren't dissuaded by a large age gap. She thought of them as Old Goats, and quickly cut them off whenever they made an advance. This particular Old Goat—if that was what he was—wouldn't get anywhere with her. She was not looking for a father figure in her life. She hoped that he wouldn't proposition her.

Claire wasn't in the mood for romance of any sort. Since her breakup with Hal, she had sworn off men, at least for the moment. She didn't want, or need, anyone in her life. Not yet. She blamed herself for wasting three years with someone who couldn't, or wouldn't, make a commitment. When her friend Bella had pushed her to start dating again, Claire had resisted the idea. She needed more time to let her wounds heal. She needed to be entirely over Harold Lodge Curtiss, and she wasn't yet.

When she glanced up from behind the counter, the man was back to staring at her. This time he didn't look away. "I must apologize," he said. "I don't mean to be rude. It's just that you remind me so much of my daughter. The likeness is uncanny." He paused. "I don't see much of her these days. Rebecca lives in Israel. Ramat Gan. Have you visited Israel?"

Claire shook her head. "I haven't. I'd like to, but I just haven't had the time."

"A shame," he said. "A beautiful country." He cleared his throat. "I'm Benjamin Singer."

"Claire Markham," she said.

"Pleased to make your acquaintance."

"Are you looking for a specific item, Mr. Singer?"

"I collect clocks," he said. "Particularly bracket clocks. Eighteenth century. English. Whenever I'm in New York, I stop by several antique stores in the hopes of finding a Charles Bayles or James Smith of London."

"Wouldn't London be a better place to look?"

He laughed. "Would you rob me of the pleasure of the hunt? It's too easy in London. I scout around in New York, Boston, sometimes even Miami. You'd be surprised what turns up in estate sales or in the dusty corners of a shop like yours." He retrieved a business card from his wallet and handed it to Claire. According to the card, Benjamin Singer was executive director of an organization called the New Exodus Project, based in Washington, D.C.

"Someone will always answer at my phone number," he said. "Please feel free to call if a Charles Bayles or similar clock turns up."

"I shall," Claire said. She didn't know much about English bracket clocks, but she was sure she could find some books on the topic at the Main Branch of the New York Public Library. "I'm curious. What is the New Exodus Project?"

"A charity that helps Jews in the Soviet Union emigrate to Israel," he said, and sighed. "It's still quite a battle. We advocate for them, and hope for the best." He glanced at his watch. "Unfortunately, I have an appointment uptown in a few minutes, but perhaps I can stop by sometime and tell you more about New Exodus. We need all the support we can get."

"I'd like that," she said, puzzled at what she could offer his group—certainly not much of a donation. He seemed like a nice man, and Claire was pleased that she had been wrong—he wasn't a lecherous Old Goat, not in the least.

* * *

Benjamin Singer didn't appear in the store for two weeks, and Claire wondered when, if ever, he might return. She had liked talking with him. She had asked Gramercy Antique's owner, Archibald Galvin, if he had ever heard of Singer, but he shook his head.

"The name doesn't ring a bell," he told her. "See if you can interest him in something other than clocks that we don't have, dear Claire."

"I'll see what I can do," she said. "But I get the sense that he's one of those single-minded collectors."

Then, on a Friday, she found Singer waiting at the entrance to the shop just before she opened at nine in the morning. Claire unlocked the door and invited him inside.

"I don't have a great deal of time, today," he told her. "But I did have a business matter to discuss with you."

"A business matter?"

"I need someone who knows antiques to represent me at an auction in London. There's a clock I have an interest in—a lovely Goddard bracket clock, made in the late 1770s—and I need a bidder to be present. The person I usually ask to substitute for me in these circumstances is unavailable. So would you be willing to take a few days off and fly to London and act for me? I'll compensate you for your time, and for your travel expenses."

14

Claire was surprised, and flattered, by his offer. "I would need to talk to the owner, Mr. Galvin," she said. "I'd have to take some vacation time."

"I understand," Singer said. "I wish I could attend the auction myself, but I have something rather pressing that I must attend to in Washington that day."

"Does it have to do with the New Exodus Project?"

"It does," he said, and smiled. "It has taken priority these days over my clocks."

"I'd like to help," she said. Singer's request made sense—who better to represent him at an auction than an antiques dealer, like herself? Claire wasn't about to admit that she didn't have a great deal of experience at auctions. She was sure she could handle this assignment. She hadn't taken any vacation time in quite some time, and she liked the idea of taking a break. That Singer was willing to finance her trip made the idea even more attractive. "As it happens, my mother lives in London."

"Does she? Well, then, that's even more reason for you to go."

"I could spend time with her after the auction."

He clapped his hands together. "Excellent. I'll stop by tomorrow and we can finalize the details." He paused. "I really appreciate your help on this, Miss Markham."

* * *

Singer watched several seagulls wheeling and diving in the clear blue sky above Battery Park. In the far distance, he spotted a jet contrail moving to the west, most likely a flight from Newark Airport. In the harbor, the ferry to Staten Island churned its way slowly to shore. He waited impatiently, annoyed that Dov had picked such an inconvenient spot to meet. Why not somewhere in midtown? Singer could understand why a Mossad officer might prefer to meet outdoors in a hostile city, but this was New York. Dov was overly cautious, no doubt a function of his occupation.

He had waited fifteen minutes past the appointed time when he saw a young man in a light-colored windbreaker, limping slightly, moving toward him. A summer ago, Dov had been wounded by shrapnel in Lebanon, during the nasty little war the IDF had dubbed Operation Peace for Galilee. That fragile "peace" had come at a high price.

"There you are!" Dov called out to Singer as he came closer.

Singer glanced at his watch. "I've been here for quite some time."

The younger man nodded. "I had an appointment on Staten Island." He waved toward the water. "This is a pretty spot, with the harbor and the river. Historic, they say. And we won't be overheard, will we?" He squinted against the bright sunshine. "Why don't we take a stroll?"

They walked side-by-side. A passerby might think that they were related—father and son out for a walk—but that wasn't the case. The relationship, while intimate, was quite different in nature.

Singer didn't waste any time on small talk.

"I've been working on the problem," he began. "You must remember that it's not what New Exodus does. We've only worked the official channels. We negotiate with the Russian authorities. There are times when we must pay, discreetly of course, for expediting paperwork. Greasing palms. A necessary evil. But never anything clandestine." He paused. "What you've asked us to do is quite different. And very difficult."

"But you've given some thought to it."

"Since we last talked, I have. I've given a great deal of thought to the problem." He paused. "Tell me more about the man involved. Why has he agreed to work with you?"

"Revenge, in a way. A powerful motivation. Dr. Savchenko hates the apparatchiks, blames them for the death of his wife. It's not that he loves us. He has a few demands. As I told you before, he'll help only if we can get his daughter out. Tatiana Savchenko wants to live in Israel. It was a dream of her mother, to see Jerusalem one day. She filled the girl's head with stories of this magical city, *Ir Ha-Kodesh*, the City of Holiness."

"How did she die? The mother?"

"A botched surgery. The doctor involved was drunk, but a long-time Party member with powerful friends. You would think that with Savchenko's prominence as a scientist, this incompetent doctor would at least be removed from practice. Not so. He had more clout than Savchenko. They dried him out, let him return to his clinic. I doubt that he stayed sober for very long, so he's back to butchering patients. As you might imagine, Savchenko is bitter as hell. He blames the corrupt system, the way they cover up their incompetence and negligence. He welcomed the chance to hit back at them, through us."

"How old was the daughter when this happened?"

"Fifteen. She took it very hard. A bout with depression."

Singer took his dark glasses off and rubbed the bridge of his nose. "You've convinced me that he is motivated. Convince me that what he offers is worth the risk."

"Ivan Savchenko has been at the center of their nuclear weapons program for twenty years. He has the keys to that kingdom. Imagine what we can learn, and the value of that knowledge. And there are technical questions that he can answer that will save our scientists time and money. Yes, it's worth the risk."

"You're sure that he will be allowed to attend this conference in Prague?"

Dov nodded. "The conditions are better than we could have expected. It's not far from the border. You can cross into Austria or West Germany. Direct flights from Prague to the major cities of the West."

"We wouldn't chance bringing her out by air," Singer said. He explained what he wanted to do, and the younger man listened without commenting. Singer knew that what he proposed carried with it a great deal of risk, but he hadn't been able to come up with anything better.

When he finished, Dov nodded again. "It's quite clever, your idea. But there's a lot that could go wrong."

"That's true. We need someone willing to play the part. Someone who can pass for Tatiana. I think I've found that person here in New York. By chance, in an antiques store. Her name is Claire Markham, and she could be Tatiana Savchenko's twin sister. And she has a ready-made reason for visiting Prague—she's an antiques dealer. It's plausible that she would be looking for items in Central Europe."

"An American? I don't like that. Can we trust her?"

Singer didn't respond but handed Dov two small photographs. "Here's the Polaroid of Tatiana you gave me. The other is Claire Markham. What do you think?"

Dov scrutinized the photographs carefully. "It's true, they look alike," he said. "Where did you get the one of the American?"

"The photo was in an antiques magazine. I hired a firm to research her background. Discreetly, of course. They did a thorough job."

"The Russian woman has blue eyes. I can't tell from this photo if Claire Markham does."

"She does." Singer took the photographs back from his companion. "They could be twins. There are other advantages to employing Miss Markham. She may live and work in New York, but she's half-British on her mother's side. Carries a British passport. There are enough British tourists visiting Czechoslovakia that she won't stand out."

"Have you approached her? About what she would be asked to do?"

"Not yet. I wanted your approval."

"You know I'd rather recruit from within our own ranks. I could find an officer who looks like this Russian woman."

"There's no disputing that. But if you recruit from inside, you'll have no distance if things go wrong. Your superiors can't want anything that will implicate the government. This way, there's plausible denial."

"That's good. What about her family?"

"Her mother lives outside London. Her parents divorced when she was twelve. The father's a banker. Wealthy. He's living in San Francisco with his second wife. Claire Markham is unmarried. No romantic entanglements at the moment. She had a serious boyfriend, but they broke up."

"Will she help us?"

"One grandmother on her father's side was Jewish. Nothing to suggest that Claire sees herself as Jewish. She does not appear to have strong political views. A quiet life. But I sense that she would help, if approached correctly. I've asked her to represent me in London on a brief trip to bid on an antique clock."

"So an indirect approach?"

"I think that would be best. I believe that she can be persuaded. If she agrees, it will be from conviction. She doesn't need money—she lives in Gramercy Park, rent courtesy of her father I suspect. So I'll have to appeal to her sense of fairness, of justice. I think that she will be receptive."

"Anything concrete? Or just your sense?"

"My sense of her."

"You have a month. If she doesn't agree to work with you, then I'll recruit someone we can be sure of."

"What about the operation itself? How much support can I expect from your people?"

Dov shook his head. "On that side of the border? None. We don't have an embassy there, you know. We'll be stretched thin with handling the connection with Dr. Savchenko. I can't get approval to send anyone else in. After Lebanon, they're worried about public relations. We can't afford an international incident. It's why I approached you in the first place. You have your own people. You have resources."

Singer rubbed his chin. "I understand. There's no one within New Exodus who could manage this. I've asked around and located someone in the private sector. An Englishman with Eastern bloc experience. Formerly MI6. Hates the Reds. Highly recommended by Robert Burrows. Do you know Burrows?"

"I've heard of him."

"I trust his judgment. If I can get this Englishman, then I'll have a professional running the operation."

"If you can get him?"

"He will need persuading, just like the girl."

"That's your skill, isn't it, Benjamin? Persuading people?"

"I'll take that as a compliment."

"It is. You've persuaded me that your crazy idea might just work."

Two

Claire felt excited but slightly anxious on the morning of the auction. After a light breakfast, she took a black cab from the Connaught, her hotel, to the auction house in Chelsea. She checked in at the registration desk ninety minutes before the Goddard clock was due to be auctioned off. The young woman registering her had greeted her warmly, mentioning that Mr. Singer was one of Bonham's favorite clients. That made Claire even more nervous—she worried that she would lose the clock to another bidder and disappoint Benjamin Singer.

She found an aisle seat and tried to enjoy the bidding for a variety of other items—furniture, paintings, an extensive stamp collection. When there was spirited competition with escalating bids, the winner would be rewarded with polite applause. While she waited, she glanced at the day's program: the Goddard clock was "*hand-built by James Goddard of the Goddard family of clockmakers,*" a "*very elegant Georgian twin fusee bracket clock,*" and boasted a "*beautifully engraved silvered dial & blued hands.*" It made her smile—even Bonham's abandoned British understatement when promoting its auction lots. She studied the black-and-white photo—it was lovely, just as Benjamin Singer had said, and when the auctioneer's assistant brought it to the front of the room, she was impressed by how well preserved Mr. Goddard's centuries-old mechanical device appeared to be.

When the time came to bid, she only had to raise her paddle three times. There was only one other bidder, an older man with stringy gray hair and horn-rimmed glasses. He shook his head when Claire topped his second bid. Nonetheless, she held her breath until the auctioneer rapped his gavel and declared her the winner. She felt a sense of accomplishment—she had won with a bid well below the maximum amount that Mr. Singer had set.

After arranging for the shipment of the clock to New York, she returned to the Connaught in Mayfair. She had a drink in the bar and then went to her room and called the telephone number in Washington that Singer had given her. He answered on the first ring, and she quickly told him that she had won the bidding for the Goddard, at a price lower than he had expected.

"It's a lovely clock," she said. "Just as you described it."

"Splendid," Singer said. "I'll drop by the store in New York to pick it up. While I'm there, I have another matter to discuss. A situation where you might be of some help."

"I look forward to that," she said. She wondered what he had in mind—she hoped it might be another auction.

"Enjoy your time with your mother," he said. "I really appreciate your help on this."

She stopped at Fortnum & Mason and picked up a package of Royal Blend tea and a tin of Cornish fairings—her mother's favorite ginger biscuits—before taking a cab to her mother's flat in Richmond. Claire hadn't seen her in more than a year, and they had only talked on the phone sporadically.

Once in her mother's modest living room, Claire found no changes in the decor, nor in the drift of the conversation.

"You look tired," her mother said. "Have you been taking care of yourself?"

"I have," Claire replied, trying not to show her annoyance. "Long flight over, and I'm still a little jet-lagged."

"How long can you stay, dear?"

"It's back to New York tomorrow." Claire paused. "I didn't want to disrupt your routine, so I'm staying at the Connaught. Paid for by my client."

"You needn't have done that," she said. "You're always welcome here."

At dinner, her mother waited until dessert—syllabub, Claire's favorite—before she turned to one of her favorite topics, Claire's love life.

"Are you seeing anyone? In New York?"

"Not at the moment," Claire said. "And I'd rather not talk about it."

"I take it there's no chance of your getting back together with Hal?"

"No chance. Please, I don't want to talk about it."

Her mother sighed. "I always liked Hal. Well, you're still quite pretty for your age. I don't know what the men in New York are thinking."

Claire had often wondered why her mother was so concerned about her marital status. Did it stem from her mother's own failed marriage? Or for her oft-expressed desire for grandchildren? Claire had been twelve years old and living in Rye, New York, when her parents divorced, a divorce triggered by her father's affair with a young attorney who specialized in mergers and acquisitions. "Miss Leah Schulberg's quite skilled in the acquisitions department," Claire once heard her mother say bitterly to a friend. "She acquired my husband, didn't she?"

Claire's life had changed dramatically after the divorce. Her mother had insisted that they move back to London. Claire had to find her footing in an all girls' private school, and it had been a difficult transition to make. She had few friends, and she compensated for her loneliness by throwing herself into her studies. Claire missed seeing her father, who stopped by only when he visited Europe on business once or twice a year.

When it came time for college, Claire had returned to New York, majoring in art history at NYU. Claire thought her mother secretly was happy to see her go, and Claire was delighted with the city. She loved the energy of Manhattan's streets, its canyons of skyscrapers, its distinct neighborhoods, its glittering lights and "open all night" ethos.

Her memories were interrupted by the sound of her mother's voice.

"I don't know how you can live in New York," she said, almost as if she was reading Claire's thoughts. "London is a much more civilized place."

"New York is my home, now," Claire said. "I belong there, Mother. I fit in."

"As long as you're happy. I know I wouldn't be."

When her mother offered her another cup of coffee, Claire demurred. She called a cab, made her farewells, and was happy to be back at the Connaught by nine o'clock.

* * *

She returned to a quieter city, which always seemed the case in the weeks before Labor Day. New Yorkers of means fled to the Hamptons, or Block Island, or Cape Cod to escape August's heat. The store attracted only a handful of customers—many of the regulars were on vacation. Claire enjoyed the slower pace.

Two days after her return, as she was listening to Stravinsky's Basel Concerto playing softly on WQXR, Benjamin Singer appeared at the front door of the store. He wore a blue-and-white striped seersucker suit, with a carnation in the buttonhole, and he seemed in good spirits.

"Thank you for your help with the clock," he began. "You saved me some money with your winning bid."

"I feel a little guilty," she said. "I didn't have to do very much. There was only one other bidder for the clock, and he dropped out rather quickly."

"Long gray hair? Glasses? Looks somewhat like a stork?"

She laughed. "That's him."

"Giles Stanton. A bottom feeder. No doubt scared off by your resolve."

"I want to thank you for the experience," she said. "My first time holding up a bidding paddle at a London auction."

"And how was your mother?"

"She's doing quite well. We had a quiet dinner together and got caught up."

Singer nodded. "There is something else," he said. "The matter I mentioned on the phone. I hesitate to ask you for another favor. It would be a great imposition."

"Nonsense. What is it? I'd be happy to help out."

"Let me be clear. This is quite different."

"Different?" she asked.

"There's some risk involved. Personal risk. All for a good cause, but risky nonetheless."

Claire smiled. "Risk?" The thought that Singer's favor could involve risk seemed far-fetched.

"Then let me tell you a story. It's a sad story. You must first promise me that you will keep this just between us. No one else." He looked at her with a sudden fierceness. "Do you agree?"

"I can keep a secret," she said, annoyed that he would question her discretion.

"Very well then," he said. "The New Exodus Project assists Jews in the Soviet Union make aliyah to Israel, to shake off the 'dust of exile.' We provide funds, negotiate with the Russian authorities, whatever is necessary. There are some poor souls that the Soviets will not allow to emigrate. It is quite tragic. The reasons for this vary. The person in question may have angered the regime through public agitation. You've heard of the refuseniks? The dissidents? The Russians have kept them trapped, imprisoned, because of their political views, or their desire to practice their religion, to worship God in their own way."

Singer paused, looking directly into Claire's eyes.

"Now, the sad story," he said. "A young woman in Moscow has recently rediscovered her Jewish roots. She desperately wants to leave Russia and to live in Israel, but the authorities have rejected her requests. Why? It's political. Her father has rubbed someone in the Party apparatus, the *nomenklatura*, the wrong way. They're punishing the daughter."

"That's terrible," Claire said.

"It is. The New Exodus Project would like to assist this young woman. There is an opportunity to do so, a window of opportunity. We believe that you might be of help in this matter. You're smart, poised. And I would hazard the guess that you care deeply about justice and fairness. I'm correct about that, am I not?"

Claire nodded, curious about where Singer had steered the

conversation. What did she have to offer Singer's organization? She didn't understand how she could contribute.

"I'll not minimize the possible hazards in this work," Singer said. "The Russians are an emotional people, impulsive, and highly suspicious. We're very careful not to provoke them, although sometimes we have to push the boundaries. This is one of those times. This young woman—her name is Tatiana—will visit Prague in a few month's time for a few days. This is that window of opportunity. We think that we'll have a chance to extricate her, then. And that's where you come in. The favor. We need someone to make contact there and provide her with the tickets and papers she will need to leave."

"Why me?" She had been caught off guard—what Singer was asking for was more than a simple favor; she could see how it could be risky, even dangerous.

"You'll have a good reason to travel to Prague. I'll hire you to acquire antiques for me. While you're there, you can pass the necessary travel documents to her." He paused. "I know this is a lot to ask from you, considering the circumstances. You're not Jewish, true?"

"One of my grandmothers was. She wasn't particularly religious, though. Neither am I, even though I was raised in the Church of England. We did sing some beautiful hymns."

"I see. It's a lot to ask of you. Perhaps too much. Why don't you think it over and let me know in a day or so?"

"What will you do if I say no?"

Singer shrugged. "We'll have to find someone else. The show must go on." He smiled. "But you are my first choice. You would be doing a marvelous thing for this poor young woman."

She felt herself tearing up, touched by his confidence in her. Working with Singer would mean she could do something that mattered. It was a way to make a difference, to prove something to herself. If she turned away, if she lacked the courage to say yes, Claire was certain that she would regret it.

"I don't need to think it over," she told Singer. "I want to help. What you're doing is right, and what you're asking me to do is not that much. And I've always wanted to see Prague. I have plenty of unused vacation time." She surprised herself. What had come over her? She wasn't an impulsive person, but she had found herself moved to agree to Singer's proposal.

Singer shook his head. "Give yourself a little time to think it through. Sleep on it. You need to be very sure this is something you want to do."

"My answer will be the same."

"Very well," he said. "Then, there's someone you should meet. He'll decide if you're ready for this sort of work."

"I'm ready."

Singer sighed. "We shall see, Miss Markham. We shall see."

Three

It had been an ordinary London Thursday for Feliks Hawes. A routine day. He only came to the office on Tuesdays and Thursdays, preferring to work from home in Redhill the rest of the week. Charlotte was more than capable of handling any over-the-transom inquiries, and the truth was that he kept the office more for the prestige of the address than for its utility—the clients of Knightsbridge Security expected him to come to them when a face-to-face meeting was necessary.

Charlotte had some correspondence and a few bank checks ready for him to sign, and he spent the morning on paperwork. In the late afternoon, he had a long distance call scheduled with Robert Burrows, an American security consultant who, like Feliks, had a background in counterintelligence. They had never worked closely together when Feliks had been in the Secret Intelligence Service and Burrows at the CIA, but they had mutual friends, and Feliks had been to dinner with Burrows once or twice in Washington.

When Burrows called, they made small talk until the American got to the purpose of his call; he asked Hawes if he would be willing to talk to a potential client about a delicate assignment. Burrows had offered to introduce the prospect to Feliks, but hadn't promised the man anything more.

"His name is Singer," Burrow said. "Benjamin Singer. I don't know him that well, but I do know that he's influential in certain circles. A philanthropist. Made his money with an automated payroll company. He's semi-retired. Lots of big dollar donations to charity. Singer's quite involved in something called the New Exodus Project. They help Russian Jews emigrate from the Soviet Union to Israel."

"Which means they pay ransom to the Russians."

"They wouldn't be the first. Singer's an Israeli, by the way. Lives in the United States most of the time, where he made his fortune, but most of his family is in Tel Aviv."

"So this delicate assignment? Any idea what he's looking for?" Hawes assumed that Burrows knew more about the possible job than he was saying.

"He was vague on the details but said it involved Eastern Europe, which is why I suggested your name."

"Eastern Europe? I thought their focus was on springing Russian Jews."

"I'm not sure what he's up to, Feliks, Singer hasn't been that forthcoming. He said he would explain it all to you. I told him I would introduce the two of you and then bow out. Are you willing to talk to him?"

"I'll talk to him, but I don't like the sound of it. I try to stay away from anything that involves the comrades. I've more than enough corporate work, and I don't need political problems with my former colleagues at Century House. They don't like anyone trespassing on their territory."

"Singer is a likable enough fellow," Burrows said. "Can't hurt to hear him out."

"Can you vouch for him, Robert?"

"He's well thought of in Washington," Burrows said. "Solid. Generous. And I happen to think he and his New Exodus Project are on the side of the angels."

"All right, I'll talk to him. Shall I set up a conference call next week?"

"No need. He wants to meet you, face-to-face, in London."

Hawes was surprised. "He doesn't need to do that."

"But he does. He can be quite persuasive. You'll see."

* * *

Hawes took his time on the long walk to the Savoy Hotel. It was a warm day, and he was winded by the time he reached the Savoy's front entrance. He consulted his pocket watch—he was on time for his appointment with Benjamin Singer. He stood still for a moment, letting his breathing return to normal. Hawes didn't feel any twinges in his chest, which was a good sign, since it meant that he didn't need to take any of the nitroglycerin tablets that Dr. Newkirk had prescribed for his angina.

He found Singer waiting in the hotel bar, a glass of white wine in front of him. Hawes guessed that Singer was nearing sixty years of age. Of medium height and build, Singer had salt-and-pepper hair. They shook hands, and Hawes asked their waiter to bring him a sherry.

They made small talk about the headlines of the day while waiting for Hawes' drink. Hawes found himself warming up to the man; Singer was a good listener, capable of turning on the charm. After Hawes had been served, Singer raised his glass in a mock toast.

"Next year in Jerusalem."

"I'll drink to that," Hawes said.

"Please tell me about Knightsbridge Security and its services. Who hires you? What sort of client?"

Hawes explained that he had started the firm after a decade working for a large private security company. Before that, he had spent time with MI6 in counterintelligence, after beginning his career with MI5 as a young man.

"As to my clients, most of them are companies anxious about protecting their top executives and their families from kidnapping, extortion, that sort of thing. It's not only Africa and Latin America. The Red Brigades and the Baader–Meinhof gang have been quite good for business. Once in a while, a client will ask me to clean up an embarrassing situation. A bank executive caught with hashish in his luggage. An affair gone bad, where the young lady—or young man, for that matter—gets a bit greedy when it comes to a nondisclosure agreement. Thankfully, very little of that. Risk assessment has become my meat and potatoes, seeing the vulnerabilities in their corporate security program and making recommendations on how to close up the gaps. If they want, I'll recommend the right people to provide the actual day-to-day. Former military, SAS. But that's not what you're looking for, is it, Mr. Singer?"

"It's not. I've come to you through a circuitous route, it's true. Friends of mine in Washington suggested I contact Mr. Burrows. He tells me that you're an expert on Poland, Hungary, Czechoslovakia. That's what has brought us here."

"Did Robert also tell you that I'm not looking for new clients?"

"He did. On the other hand, you're here talking to me, Mr. Hawes. Why don't I explain the situation, first? You can decide whether or not you want to take the engagement. I should note that we'll be quite generous. We'll more than compensate you if you need to rearrange your schedule." He glanced over at Hawes, studying him. "Do you do any current work in Eastern Europe?"

"For my private sector clients? No. There's little call for it. In the past, when I worked for my government, I ran intelligence operations in the countries you mentioned. That was many years ago." He took a sip of his sherry, savoring the taste. "I can't say I have any appetite for ever working there again."

Singer nodded. "Let me explain our needs. I'm director of the New Exodus Project. Our mission is to assist Russian and Ukrainian Jews in immigrating to Israel. We work with the authorities on both ends, smoothing the way. Which brings us to today. We've encountered a situation where our normal channels won't work. That's why we've contacted you." He paused. "There is a Russian physicist. Brilliant. Now disillusioned. He wants us to bring his daughter to the West.

His wife was Jewish, and thus the daughter, too. Tatiana Savchenko. Tatiana wishes to live in Israel, to make aliyah. The authorities in Moscow will never allow that."

"And why is that?"

"Her father has worked on a number of military projects. Top secret stuff. Neither he, nor any member of his family, would ever be allowed to leave for the West." Singer paused to gently swirl the wine around in his glass. "Frankly, we had given up hope of that ever happening. But then, a break of sorts. Dr. Savchenko will visit Prague in early October for a conference with some Czech scientists, and he'll bring Tatiana with him. She acts as his secretary; arranges his schedule, types his papers. We have a tentative plan, a very general plan, to bring her out. We need someone with experience to review the plan, revise it, and execute it."

Hawes frowned. "You're talking about a defection. That won't sit well with the Russian authorities, the government officials you work with."

"We don't plan to leave any fingerprints. If the girl vanishes one fine day, they won't be able to tie it to us. No trail. They'll blame someone else. The Americans, most likely."

"And why are you so interested in smuggling out Tatiana Savchenko?"

"It's why I founded the New Exodus Project. To free the persecuted. Every Jew deserves the right to live in Israel if that is their wish."

Hawes waited for Singer to say more, but he remained silent. "The father? Dr. Savchenko? Doesn't he want to defect?"

"No, he's clear on that. He's not Jewish. He wants his daughter to go, to be free. He rarely leaves Moscow, and we know he'll be carefully watched when he's in Prague. But this is our one chance."

"I take it that you are in contact with him?"

Singer nodded. "Through friends in Moscow. That's how we found out about the conference in Prague. We have the dates, where they'll be staying. He and his daughter are committed to this."

"And how do you propose to extract the girl?"

"Do you know the story of Peter Selle? A German. He was separated from his wife when the Wall went up in Berlin back in '61. He was in West Berlin, she was in East Berlin. So in 1966, he found himself a girlfriend who looked like his wife. Took her on a day trip to East Berlin, 'borrowed' her papers, and crossed back over with his wife. Left the girlfriend high and dry, and the Stasi put her in jail for a few months until the newspapers found out and they decided to let her go. The West Germans weren't happy with Selle—they didn't care for his cavalier attitude toward his girlfriend's fate—and gave him a seven-month prison sentence for his stunt."

"I remember it," Hawes said. "Not all the details, but I remember it."

"I thought of adapting the idea as a way to bring out Miss Savchenko. Find a look-alike to travel to Prague, then use her passport for Miss Savchenko to leave the country."

"Assuming you can pull that off, which I question, how do you plan for this look-alike to get herself out of Czechoslovakia?"

Singer scratched his chin. "I'm not sure," he confessed. "Perhaps she brings along a second passport? We create another identity for her?"

Hawes shook his head. "That won't work. If she's stopped and searched when she enters the country and they find two passports, they'll know something is up. False papers are also risky."

"What would you do?"

"I'd have her claim her passport was stolen or lost, and get temporary documentation from her country's embassy. That way, she is traveling with official approval. That might work. How far along are you with this idea?"

"I've found someone who looks very much like Miss Savchenko, and who has a plausible reason to travel to Prague. An antiques dealer."

"Nationality?"

"British, although her father is an American."

"Tell me more about her." Hawes listened intently as Singer talked, his face betraying nothing. He asked a few questions about the woman's background and seemed satisfied with the answers Singer gave.

"So what do you think?" Singer asked. "Would you be willing to help us?"

"I'm a direct man," Hawes said. "I'm going to decline. There are two reasons. First, I think your plan is too risky. It has an amateurish air about it. Cribbed from *The Prisoner of Zenda*. A look-alike? Czechoslovakia isn't Ruritania, and the StB chaps in Prague don't have much of a sense of humor. Then, the second reason. The more important one. You're not leveling with me. This will be a very expensive operation. Whoever is paying for this won't get much of a return on their investment from the defection of one young Russian woman. If you're fronting for Mossad, which I suspect you are, there's more than a simple defection involved. I can't work when I'm being kept in the dark."

"I understand," Singer said. He leaned forward over the table and lowered his voice. "Suppose I could remove your objections? You would have complete say over the plan. Change it, shape it. Do it your way. As for my lack of candor, I'll need to get approval before I say more, before I can be more frank about our motives." Singer paused and moved back in his chair. "Can we meet at your office? Tomorrow morning?"

Hawes shrugged. "I doubt that I'll change my mind, but I'll meet you again." He handed Singer his card. "My office is in Knightsbridge. Ten o'clock sharp, if you please."

He was curious about the true purpose of the operation. Why were the Israelis willing to invest so much in exfiltrating a young woman, an unknown, someone without apparent strategic value? He had his suspicions. It had to be connected to the father, and what he could give them. The Israelis weren't a sentimental bunch, in his experience. Surrounded by enemies, they had to be hard-headed and cold-hearted when it came to security matters. They couldn't afford sentimentality.

He didn't need problematic clients, and there was minimal upside to running any sort of operation in Czechoslovakia. Hawes had steered clear of political work in the past. Moreover, he knew the leadership at Century House well enough to know that they would be furious if they discovered he was working in the Eastern Bloc without official sanction, and even angrier if they learned it was on behalf of Tel Aviv. Relations between the Secret Intelligence Service and the Mossad had become quite frigid, if not hostile.

On the other hand, the more he thought about Singer's scheme, the more intrigued he was. While he had initially rejected the idea as amateurish, it might work if the proper groundwork was laid with a keen attention to the details of the operation. It was daring and risky, but there could be ways to increase the odds of success. All in theory, of course, because Hawes had no intention of taking the job.

* * *

Singer arrived promptly at ten, and Charlotte showed him into Hawes' private office. Singer looked around before he settled into the armchair opposite Hawes' desk, focusing on the large framed black-and-white photograph of the Berlin Wall, an aerial view that included the wide no-man's zone around the barrier at the Brandenburg Gate.

"An interesting choice of art," Singer said.

"A reminder," Hawes said. "I was there the night they began building it. At the time, I thought we should have torn the thing down when it was simple barbed wire and fencing. I didn't understand then that the Wall worked for both sides. A modus vivendi. It removed Berlin as a flashpoint. At the cost of the freedom of everyone in East Berlin, of course."

"And that bothers you?"

"It does. When you give the Russians an inch, they take a mile. Like all bullies, they retreat when you punch back. Kennedy failed the test at the Vienna summit, where Khrushchev treated him like a headmaster lecturing a schoolboy. Nikita sensed weakness, and that led to Berlin and the Cuban Missile Crisis where we came too damn close to a nuclear war."

"You have strong political views, then."

"I'm a Tory. I think Maggie's the best prime minister we've had since Churchill."

"And Israel? What do you think of Israel?"

"I'm no Arabist, if that's what you're driving at. The Sabras I've met professionally, I've liked. Tough. Smart. They do their homework."

"You said yesterday that I hadn't leveled with you. That's true. It's best if you ask me whatever questions you have. I'll answer those that I can."

"For starters, are you working for the Mossad?"

"I won't deny that they have an interest in this," Singer said. "They don't employ me. They can't have any direct involvement, but I've offered them an alternative."

"This is about her father, isn't it?"

"Yes. Dr. Savchenko is willing to share certain information if we help his daughter gain her freedom."

"I see," Hawes said. "Information of a technical nature? Helpful for some of your scientists working at Dimona?"

Singer remained silent. While the Israelis denied that they were working on nuclear weapons at their Dimona facility, few observers believed them. It was a logical course to pursue for a country surrounded by enemies who had vowed its total destruction.

"And I imagine Dr. Savchenko's information might be of great interest to the Americans in arms control negotiations," Hawes continued. "The equivalent of being able to see your opponent's cards."

Again, Singer didn't say anything, but Hawes regarded his silence as confirmation.

"I'm curious," Hawes said. "Why approach me for the job? Why not one of your own? Aren't there plenty of security consultants in Tel Aviv who would jump at the chance?"

"You come highly recommended. You know that part of the world."

"And I'm not Jewish or Israeli. If it goes awry, then you'd prefer to have someone else's fingerprints on the operation. British fingerprints. A private operation."

"A private operation," Singer said. "That's how it must be characterized, if ever exposed to the light of day. No overt connections to our respective governments."

"You know that you wouldn't fool anyone with that fiction. Certainly not Moscow Center."

Singer shrugged. "For appearance's sake, then."

"It would be awkward to operate in the East without letting my former colleagues know."

Singer shook his head. "That's not possible. There can't be any communication with them. No connection."

Singer didn't trust the British intelligence services to keep his secrets, and Hawes couldn't blame him for that. Who could say with any confidence whether MI6 had been cleansed of Soviet penetration agents? The only way to safeguard the operation was to keep it in private hands.

"If your idea works, it will make a lot of people in Moscow very cross," Hawes said. "They'll eventually figure out who is behind it."

"They may," Singer said and shrugged. "There may be repercussions. On the other hand, it wouldn't represent anything new. They don't wish us well. The Soviets have encouraged the Czechs and East Germans to train and fund the PLO. They don't do it directly themselves, of course. But every time there's a Palestinian terror attack in Israel, there's Jewish blood on their hands."

"An operation of this sort will be expensive. A premium for operating in Czechoslovakia. Their secret police, the StB, have a well-deserved reputation for brutality."

"We understand that. We have the funds set aside. Within reason, of course."

"I've been thinking about how to do this. Do you know the joke about the worker in the Russian gold mines? Every day he leaves with a wheelbarrow full of sand. The guards at the gate sift through the sand, but they find nothing. One of the more canny guards approaches the worker and says, 'Look, I know you're stealing something. I won't tell anyone. I've got to know. Clue me in.' The worker laughs and says, 'What the hell, I've been stealing wheelbarrows.' And how did he pull it off? He had conditioned the guards to his routine. A wheelbarrow each and every day. We don't have the luxury of time, but we can make use of that same principle.

"A month before the actual operation, we send your antiques dealer across the border on a business trip. She doesn't go in alone. She needs someone traveling with her. Someone we can trust, someone who speaks Czech. I'll need to find a man who knows the terrain. They spend a few days in Prague, buy some antiques, and then return to London. When we send them back to Prague for the defection, they're already on the radar of the StB. A known quantity. At the appropriate time, Miss Savchenko takes the place of the English girl. Our Czech-speaking guide runs interference at the border for her on their way out."

"Does this mean you'll take the assignment?"

"I would need to meet the girl, first," Hawes said. "I'll only take the job if I'm convinced she's up to the task."

"That's fair," Singer said. "We'll fly you to New York to interview her. We'll pay you your day rate for the trip. If you think she can handle it, we can settle on terms for the assignment then. By the way, her name is Claire. Claire Markham."

Four

Claire closed the shop early on the Thursday of her next meeting with Benjamin Singer. Thursdays were typically slow at Gramercy Antiques, and she was confident she wasn't forgoing any sales. She was excited at the prospect of meeting whoever it was Singer wanted her to meet. What sort of questions would this man ask? How would he judge whether she was up for the task? Would they choose her to help the brave young Russian woman? Claire wondered what he would be like. At least she could learn what was expected of a courier for the New Exodus Project.

She was confident that she could pass whatever test they had for her. But did she want to take on the assignment? When she learned more, it was possible that she might want to back out from the job. She had said yes to Singer impulsively. Who could blame her for wanting to reconsider?

Claire walked to Sixth Avenue and hailed a yellow taxicab. The meeting was set for the Oak Room at the Plaza Hotel, and she was amused at the location—hardly the spot she would have chosen to discuss a covert operation behind the Iron Curtain. She was dressed conservatively, a tan skirt, simple white shirt, blue blazer, and her favorite strand of Mikimoto pearls. She touched up her lipstick as the cab hurtled up Sixth, darting in and out of traffic, before braking sharply to turn onto 59th Street.

Once at the entrance to the Oak Room, she immediately spotted Singer, who was sitting at a table by the window facing Central Park. Another man sat across from him. Singer waved her over and introduced his companion, Jack Townsend, and both men stood until Claire had taken a seat. Townsend must have been quite handsome in his youth, she decided, what her mother would have called a lady-killer. Now, he had close-cropped gray hair, a widow's peak, and deep lines in his face. There was something faintly exotic about him—something about the eyes and cheekbones. She decided that he was Eastern European, and there might very well be a Mongol warrior from Genghis Khan's invading horde lurking somewhere in his ancestry. But when he spoke, it was with the clipped British accent of a Cambridge or Oxford man.

"Miss Markham, a pleasure to make your acquaintance," he said, not taking his eyes off of hers. She found it disconcerting but didn't look away. Claire didn't like being stared at—first Singer in the shop, and now this man. She wasn't going to be intimidated.

"Please call me Jack," he continued. "I'm assisting Mr. Singer in this matter. As a consultant."

"Jack has a world of experience," Singer said. "Security experience. I told him how helpful you had been in acquiring the Goddard for me, and how you were willing to help us on this other matter. If you don't mind, he has a few questions he'd like to ask you."

"I don't mind," she said.

Hawes glanced over at Singer, who nodded at him. Hawes asked his first question in a conversational tone of voice. "You've volunteered to help the New Exodus Project in securing the release of a young Russian woman? That's so?"

"That's so," she said. "And here I am."

"This sort of work is not for the faint of heart. You understand that as well?"

"I understand."

"Why would you agree to do this, Miss Markham?"

She didn't like the way he was pressing her, challenging her. "Mr. Singer explained the situation and asked me to help. I said 'yes' because it's the right thing to do, and I liked the idea of making more of a difference. In the world, I mean."

"And this is how you think you can make a difference?"

"Mr. Singer approached me, Mr. Townsend."

"Would you describe yourself as a thrill-seeker?"

"Hardly."

"Or a rebel? How would you describe your politics, Miss Markham?"

"I'm a Democrat. A liberal. This is New York, after all. I was quite disappointed when President Carter lost to Reagan."

"And are you politically active? Attend party meetings? Demonstrations?"

She shook her head. "No, I'm not political in that sense. I vote, of course."

"That's more than many can say," Townsend said with a slight smile. "A different question. Would you break the law if it was necessary to do the right thing, to prevent an injustice from occurring?"

"I imagine that it would depend upon the circumstances. One shouldn't go breaking the law, willy nilly. But if I were convinced it was the only way to stop something that was clearly unjust or immoral, then, yes, I would."

He nodded. "Very thoughtful. So, the matter of Tatiana, our would-be emigrant. The reason we're all here. Mr. Singer—Benjamin—has asked me to assist in the planning stages for her trip to Israel. He suggested that you might help by passing tickets and travel documents to her in Prague. That is so?"

"That is so," she said, now thoroughly annoyed, hoping that Townsend caught her mocking tone. It was as if he didn't believe she understood what she had agreed to.

"Excellent."

"I haven't changed my mind," she said. She wasn't going to falter in front of him. "As I said, it's the right thing to do."

"We appreciate that greatly," Singer said. He turned to Townsend. "Why don't you proceed as we discussed?"

"Certainly. We're in the midst of revising our plans. It turns out that there's a bit of a wrinkle. We do need you to pass the papers to Tatiana, but there's something more required."

"Something more?" She felt herself tensing. What did they want? Wasn't acting as a courier enough?

"You can say 'no'," Singer said. "There's a tad more risk involved."

She felt a twinge of anxiety. "What do you need me to do?"

"It's quite simple," Townsend said. "You happen to bear a remarkable physical resemblance to Tatiana Savchenko. That's her full name." He unlatched his leather briefcase and retrieved a color Polaroid of a young woman. He handed it to Claire. "It's quite fortuitous. A stroke of good luck. Our idea is to make use of this uncanny resemblance. We propose that you give her your passport, so that she can travel to the West under your identity. The train to Vienna. She would pass through border controls as Claire Markham."

"And how do I get back?"

"We've planned for that," Townsend said. "You'll remain in Prague for one night until she's safely across the border. The next day, you turn up at the British embassy and report a stolen passport." He paused for a slight cough. "My friends in the Foreign Office will make sure that their colleagues in Prague expedite the paperwork. The embassy will provide you with an emergency passport, and you'll catch a flight to London. We can have you back in New York the following day, or you can stay on in London and visit family. Benjamin mentioned your mother lives in Richmond."

She looked at the photograph Townsend had given her. There was a strong resemblance. She felt herself flushing with anger. Her value to the New Exodus Project was not as a courier, but as a look-alike—she had been chosen because Tatiana Savchenko could assume her identity.

She turned to Singer. "And how many young women who fit the part have you approached for this?" she asked.

"You're the first and only," Singer said. "I apologize for springing this on you. It was pure chance that I walked into Gramercy Antiques and found you." He glanced over at Townsend before returning his gaze to her. "I apologize if you feel you've been misled. If you don't want to proceed, we'll understand."

"What if Miss Savchenko is stopped at the border?" she asked. "If they arrest her? They'll have my passport, and it will be very obvious that I'm complicit."

"Perhaps, perhaps not." Townsend cleared his throat. "If you're questioned, you can say that you lost your passport in Prague. Perhaps it was stolen."

"Why don't I bring her a new passport, instead? A new identity?"

"It's not as easy to forge a passport and visas as the spy novelists would have it," Townsend said. "The real thing is always better. We're going to a great deal of trouble to assist Miss Savchenko. We want to give her more than a sporting chance."

"You don't have to agree to do this," Singer said. "It's completely up to you. But we need your help."

"Only if you are willing," Townsend said. "No reluctance or hesitation."

"And why are you doing this, Mr. Townsend?" Claire asked. She had decided she wasn't going to call him by his first name.

"Mixed motives, Miss Markham. Benjamin has been very generous, compensating me for my time and trouble. And there is no love lost with the Russians on my part. I welcome a chance to put a spoke in the wheels of the socialist revolution."

"Are you Jewish?"

"Can't say that I am, but I make it a practice to side with the underdog."

Claire was surprised; she had assumed that anyone working closely with the New Exodus Project would be Jewish. But then again, she didn't consider herself Jewish, even if she had a Jewish grandmother.

"Is this the sort of thing you do, Mr. Townsend?" she asked.

"This engagement is a bit out of the ordinary. But I've run similar operations in the past when I worked for the government."

"Will you be there? In Prague?"

"No, that's not possible. I've worn out my welcome on the other side of the border. I'll be in Vienna with you at the start—the plan is for you to catch the train to Prague from there. Should you agree to help us, we'll explain all of this. We'll have you spend a few days in London where we can go over the plans and your role in detail."

"Can you take some vacation time for this?" It was Singer. "We may ask you to make a preliminary visit to Prague in September. Get a sense of the lay of the land."

"I can take the time," she said.

"Marvelous," he said.

"What happens now?"

"Mr. Townsend and I have a few matters to discuss," Singer said. "I promise that I'll call you tomorrow."

As she rose to her feet, Singer and Townsend followed suit. "A pleasure to meet you," Townsend said.

"The pleasure was all mine," she said.

* * *

Hawes watched Claire Markham as she left the room, noticing how she attracted the attention of two businessmen sitting near the front of the Oak Room.

He felt a sudden pressure in his chest and excused himself and went to the men's room. He took one of his nitroglycerin tablets and placed it under his tongue. After a few minutes, he felt the pressure in his chest easing.

When he came back to the table, Singer was writing in a pocket diary. He put the diary in his jacket pocket.

"So what do you think of Miss Markham?" Singer asked.

"She's an intriguing young woman." Hawes paused. "Quite poised. Very attractive in an understated way. I found her accent very interesting—a mixture of London and Connecticut. She sounds a bit like Grace Kelly, the actress. What I don't fully understand are her motives for signing on."

"You heard her. She's an idealist. Wants to do the right thing. I've had her background vetted. She's coming off a failed romance and I think she's eager for something new, something exciting, in her life."

Hawes frowned. "She's a lovely young woman, and my mother would have called her quite well-bred. I'm sure she represents her firm well when dealing with clients. But I don't think she's right for this, Benjamin. No experience. She'd be a babe in the woods."

"Isn't that the beauty of it, though? She's an antiques dealer, not an intelligence officer. She doesn't need an elaborately constructed cover. She has a plausible reason for visiting Prague. If the StB were to probe further, they'd find she's exactly who she says she is."

"And if things go wrong? Will she panic? Freeze?"

Singer shrugged. "I don't think so. Do you?"

"No," Hawes said, surprising himself. "I don't think that she would panic."

"We can look for someone else, if you believe that she's wrong for the job. It will compress the timetable. Unless you want to change the plans, take a different approach."

Hawes shook his head. "No, the plan is sound. For Miss Markham, we'll keep it simple. One task. Changing places with the Russian woman at the train station. Then we'll have her lie low. Pick up the emergency passport and fly back to London. I think with some coaching, she can handle her part. I'll need to find someone in England we can trust to accompany her. Someone who speaks the language, and can help get Miss Savchenko through border control. Two British passports on the way in, two on the way out. Clean."

"Does this mean you'll take the job?"

Hawes nodded. "I imagine that it does."

Singer reached across the table and extended his hand. Hawes reluctantly shook it, not sure he was making the right decision. He didn't need Singer's money—he had done well enough over the years that he could pick and choose his jobs. He had agreed because it was a chance to prove that he could still do something of significance.

"I'll have Charlotte, my assistant, prepare a letter of engagement," Hawes said. "There will be some added expense. A fallback plan for getting Miss Markham out of the country if the initial arrangements should come a cropper."

"And what should I tell Miss Markham tomorrow?"

"That we expect to see her in London in a few weeks."

Five

When Hawes arrived at the Danube on a rainy Tuesday morning, he found the pub looking somewhat worse for the wear, smelling of beer and stale cigarette smoke. He hadn't dropped by in more than a year, and he wondered whether Viktor realized how dingy and worn the place had become. The window curtains were fraying and dusty; the floor was stained; and the dark wood surface of the bar needed a polishing. The decor hadn't changed since his last visit. Polish and Hungarian flags still hung prominently on the pub's walls next to the Union Jack. The red, white, and green Hungarian flag had a circular hole cut in its center—removing the hated hammer and sickle—just like the ones carried by the insurgents in Budapest nearly thirty years ago, when Feliks first met Viktor Toth, then one of the rebels battling the Russians.

When Viktor escaped to London after the Soviets crushed the revolt, Feliks had lent him money to open the Danube. Much to Hawes' surprise, Viktor had proved to be a canny businessman and had made a success of the pub, turning it into a gathering spot for displaced Eastern Europeans—Hungarians, Poles, Czechs, Slovaks, and even an occasional Romanian. Viktor had side business interests as well, some of which probably wouldn't hold up under close scrutiny. He had a checkered past, with a prison stint in Hungary and trouble with the law in the United States, and Hawes didn't ask too many questions about the nature of Viktor's other sources of income. One thing seemed clear to Hawes—Viktor hadn't reinvested any of his recent profits in the Danube, which would explain why it had grown so threadbare.

Hawes spotted Viktor immediately when he stepped into the Danube that Tuesday. His friend sat in a corner booth with a mug of beer on the table in front of him. Viktor had put some weight on, and his dark hair had thinned. He grinned when Hawes joined him at the table.

"How are you, Feliks? Business good?"

Hawes nodded. "How about you? The Danube doing well?"

Viktor looked around the pub—there were only two older men at the bar—and smiled. "It picks up at lunch," he said. "And how is Nigel? Still at Oxford?"

"He is. Still making speeches about the evils of Margaret Thatcher. He took the election quite hard. Who would have thought that my son would want Labor back in power?"

"What do the kids today know? They're ignorant, I tell you, but there's always hope. Send him to me, and I'll make a Tory out of him."

Hawes shook his head. He doubted anything would change Nigel's politics. His son had been a stubborn child, and after Anna's death, he had gone his own way. Anna had always mediated between her two headstrong men, and with her gone, they had grown apart. Nigel had been drawn into Labor Party politics at Balliol College and had rapidly moved toward the left, all to Hawes' dismay. After several bitter arguments—with a particularly bruising one over the Falklands War—they had called an uneasy truce. Hawes tried to avoid talking about politics when they saw each other.

"You said you were recruiting for a job," Viktor said. "And you wanted my help. What sort of job?"

"Nothing too difficult, except it's in Prague."

Viktor shook his head. "That complicates things for you, doesn't it?"

Hawes nodded. He couldn't risk traveling to Czechoslovakia, not with his history, nor could Viktor, for that matter.

"I'll have to manage the operation remotely. Probably from Vienna. And the job's a bit messy. It involves the Russians."

"And the client?"

"A private client. Mideast connections."

Viktor whistled softly. "The Israelis? Feliks, are you sure you want to do this?"

"I do," Hawes said, irritated by Viktor's comment. "Why not?" Did Viktor think that he somehow wasn't up to the task? That he was past his prime? Hawes knew he was being overly sensitive, but he couldn't help his reaction.

"I don't know. I thought you tried to keep clear of politics."

"The contract is with a nonprofit, the New Exodus Project. Their director has some connections to the Israeli government."

"They used to be the tough guys," Viktor said. "The Israelis. After Munich, people thought they were invincible, that they'd go to the ends of the earth to hunt you down if you crossed them. I don't know what to think these days. The Palestinians shoot down the Israeli ambassador in the streets of London last summer. Machine pistol. The streets of bloody London."

"It's not that the Israelis didn't respond. They invaded Lebanon. Which, by the way, may be what the assassins wanted. They're radicals, followers of Abu Nidal, who hoped the PLO would be destroyed in the war."

Viktor shook his head. "They're all poison. Do you think Arafat and the PLO want peace with Israel? They want to sweep us into the sea."

"Us?"

"I'm a Jew, Feliks, as you well know. Not an Israeli, mind you, but I'm one of the tribe. The Chosen People. I have no illusions about who wants to kill us."

"You're a man of many parts. Hungarian. A one-time New Yorker. Now a British subject."

"Can't hit a moving target," Viktor said. "Let's get back to why you're here. You were vague on the phone. You need to recruit someone for this job in Prague."

"I'm looking for a Czech speaker," Hawes said. "Late twenties or early thirties. Not afraid to take some risks. British passport."

"I can ask around," Viktor said. "A bit of travel involved?"

"A bit of travel. As I said, Prague and back. It might get a bit sticky."

"A courier job?"

"Something like that. I need somebody with steady nerves at the border."

"I see. Are you willing to pay a premium, seeing as how there's some risk?"

"I have a generous client. Yes, Viktor, I'll pay a premium. You have someone in mind?"

Viktor sighed. "If I were younger and spoke Czech, I'd volunteer. But I may have someone for you. He's the nephew of one of my regulars. A smart lad. Fancy education. Parents got out after the Prague Spring in '68 and came to England. Later they moved to Canada. Rafe came back for school. He's fluent, visited relatives in Prague a few times. And he has no love for the regime or their Russian friends."

Hawes shook his head. "He can't be on their radar. He can't have a file with State Security. Tell me that he hasn't marched in any demonstrations in front of the Czechoslovak Embassy?"

"No, he's all talk when it comes to the politics. No action. He likes the ladies. Rafe's a lover, not a fighter."

"Sounds like he could fit the bill," Hawes paused. "For this job, I'm going by Townsend. Jack Townsend."

"Jack Townsend it is."

* * *

Viktor Toth was one of the few men that Hawes trusted completely. From their first encounter in Budapest in 1956, Hawes had recognized a kindred spirit. They were both direct and decisive, and they shared a hatred of the Soviets and their allies. Hawes' father, a Polish colonel and aristocrat, had been executed by his NKVD captors in the Katyn Forest massacre in 1940, along with thousands of other officers. Hawes' uncle and aunt and their three children had been loaded onto a freight train and deported to the Urals, never to be heard from again.

In more than a decade in British intelligence, Hawes had seen further examples of Soviet duplicity and ruthlessness. Nikita Khrushchev's bluster and risky moves in Berlin and Cuba were calculated to convince the Kremlin hardliners that he could stand firm against the West. It didn't work. The hardliners—Brezhnev, Gromyko, Andropov, Chernenko—never forgave Khrushchev for his Secret Speech in 1956 exposing the crimes of Josef Stalin. Nothing that happened after Khrushchev was forced out of power in 1964 came as a surprise to Hawes. Not the Soviet invasion of Czechoslovakia four years later to end the Prague Spring. Not the imposition of martial law in Poland or the intervention of Soviet troops in Afghanistan. Not the elevation of another neo-Stalinist, Yuri Andropov, the former head of the KGB, after Brezhnev's death the prior November.

Andropov's promotion to General Secretary had infuriated Viktor, for Andropov had been the Soviet ambassador to Hungary in 1956 where he earned the nickname the "Butcher of Budapest" for his role in suppressing the uprising. Viktor had experienced first-hand the brutality of the Communist regime in Hungary. He had joked that it was his father's fault. Keve Toth and his family had recognized the threat fascism posed to European Jews and had left Budapest before the war, moving to New York City. Then the Toth family made the mistake of returning. Their stay in the United States made them suspect, potential subversives, class enemies. When Viktor couldn't find meaningful work, he entered what he called his Robin Hood phase, fencing luxury items stolen from the villas of the Party elite on Rose Hill. It was a matter of time before the Hungarian police caught him. Viktor spent time in the Fo Street prison, beaten and tortured by Hungarian State Security, saved by the intervention of a family friend with connections. The Budapest uprising had found Viktor leading a group of insurgents from the city's rough-and-ready Chicago District against the Red Army.

It had taken Viktor a month to make his way to England after the uprising was crushed. Hawes had returned with the woman he had met in Budapest, Anna, the woman he would make his wife. They had socialized with Viktor and his latest girlfriend over the years, and he had taken on the role of Uncle Viktor when Nigel arrived.

* * *

Two days later, Viktor called Hawes with an update on his recruiting for the Prague operation.

"You're sure this is something you want to do?" he asked. "No second thoughts?"

"I'm committed."

"All right, then. I contacted Rafael Klima, the young man I mentioned to you. He goes by Rafe. Works as a translator and interpreter. He can handle the language, no problem. Has some relatives in Prague, an aunt on his father's side, I believe. I warned him the job might involve skirting Czech law. He didn't blink an eyelash. A cool customer."

"I'm not looking for derring-do," Hawes said. "Just steady nerves. Can he talk his way out of a jam? Is he quick witted?"

"He's a clever lad. I think he fits your bill, but I'll leave you to make your own judgment. He'll join us here at the Danube in thirty minutes."

Rafael Klima proved to be a slim young man with the confidence of the handsome. His stylish brown hair touched his collar, and he wore his sideburns long. A pair of sunglasses were propped up on his head. Judging from his expensive watch and tight-fitting clothes, Rafe was vain, or at least that was how Hawes read him.

The Danube was nearly empty. The three of them sat in a corner, well out of earshot. Viktor went over to the dusty jukebox and selected a Tom Jones song, "It's Not Unusual," and put it on repeat play. He smirked at Hawes when he returned to the table.

"Viktor made it clear that our conversation remains confidential, correct?" Hawes asked. "If you decide not to work with me, you can never reveal to anyone what I'm going to share with you."

"Viktor explained that."

"And you agree to these terms?"

"Sure," Rafe said. "Do you want me to sign a nondisclosure agreement of some sort? I've done that for one of my interpreting jobs. I'll do that if you want."

"That won't be necessary," Hawes said. "We'll take your word for it. When was the last time you were in Prague?"

"Two years ago. Spent time with my aunt and my cousin. I know the city fairly well."

"How's your Czech?"

"I'm fluent. A touch of the Bohemian dialect."

"Do you speak any German?"

"Traveler's German."

"That will do. We anticipate two trips to Prague. You'll be traveling with a woman about your age. She will be buying antiques in Prague. You'll act as her guide and interpreter."

"What's she like? This antiques dealer."

Hawes frowned. "Viktor tells me that you're quite the ladies' man. That won't do for this assignment. Your relationship with her will be strictly professional. Nothing on the side."

"Sure," he said. "I was just asking."

"She's smart and capable, and she'll keep her nerve."

"So why two trips?"

"The first trip establishes your bona fides. On the second, after you're done with business in Prague, you'll escort a different young woman by train to Vienna. She'll travel on the antique dealer's passport."

Rafe whistled. "Isn't that what they call in New York the old switcheroo?"

Hawes shook his head. "This is no schoolboy lark," he said. "The Domecek prison in Prague is a nasty place. Cold. Dirty. The Gestapo used it before the StB. That's where you'll wind up if this goes wrong."

"Well, then, we can't let it go wrong. I can handle this. I know Prague, and I could stand a little adventure in my life. And a nice fat check made out to Rafael Klima. I expect to be well compensated for taking the risk. I have a few debts to clear up, and I'd like some money left over for a rainy day."

"We'll offer you a fair price."

"I'll want half in advance. Then, the rest deposited into my account once I'm in Prague."

"Half in advance is fair. The remainder gets paid once you're back in Vienna. And a bonus if you've been a good boy."

"This isn't a job for the government, is it? MI6?"

Hawes shook his head. "Strictly private. And I'll remind you that you're not to discuss this with anyone. You keep your mouth tightly shut. Agreed?"

"Agreed."

Hawes handed him the Jack Townsend business card. "Send your banking details to this address. I'll contact you again after we've deposited the advance payment."

"Cool," Rafe said. He glanced at the card. "I look forward to doing business with you, Mr. Townsend."

They shook hands, and Rafe left the Danube with a wave of his hand to the bartender. Viktor waited a minute or so and then turned to Hawes. "What did you think?" he asked. "Will he do?"

"He'll have to. We're not going to find anyone better. Not on such short notice. And there's no question that he's a smart lad. He's a bit too cocky, though. Will he follow instructions?"

"He will," Viktor said. "You were cocky at his age, too."

"I won't be asking him to do too much. He needs to be sharp at the border. The rest is routine."

Tom Jones had stopped singing on the jukebox. Hawes looked over at Viktor. "I've been looking for someone in Prague who can host the young woman, the antiques dealer, for a night. I haven't had much luck."

"Can't she stay in a hotel?"

Hawes shook his head. "Not ideal. She won't have papers, so she has to stay off the radar."

"I'll see what I can turn up," Viktor said. "We have a stray Czech or two who wanders into the Danube. It's surprising the connections you can make when you ask around."

"I appreciate it, Viktor. I'll make it worth your while. This client has deep pockets."

"What will you do if you come up short?"

"It'll complicate matters. I'm working on a contingency plan that could pick up the slack."

"Always the contingency plans with you."

"If I'm going to put these people up on the high wire, they deserve a wide net below them and a soft landing."

* * *

After thanking Viktor for his help, Hawes took a cab to South Kensington, where he was to meet Nigel at the Britannia, his favorite pub. He settled in with a pint of ale at one of the tables and waited. He liked the Britannia for its comfortable familiarity, its dark-paneled walls and framed cartoons, and large common room. His son was always slightly late to their meetings, and Hawes had learned not to show any irritation at his tardiness. He wasn't going to let Nigel annoy him.

When he arrived, Nigel ordered a glass of white wine and stowed his leather briefcase under the table. He told Hawes that he had some good news to report.

"I've been approached by the *Guardian* to write a column about politics," he said. "I've decided to take them up on the offer."

68

"How will that be received at Balliol? Will they think it's a distraction for their star junior fellow?"

"I don't particularly care." His jaw was set. "I can't let that influence me."

"There's certainly enough to write about," Hawes said, searching for safe ground. He took a sip of his ale. "I'm glad for you, Nigel."

"Are you? It won't bother you when I take Maggie and her Neanderthals to task? And expose their slavish kowtowing to the Americans? There's something else you should know—I may be visiting Cuba and Nicaragua in December. A chance to see how workers fare with a government that puts them first. Literacy programs. Health care for the poor."

Hawes didn't reply. Nigel had always reflexively gravitated to the underdog. He was like his mother in that, Hawes thought, and in his moodiness. He didn't claim to completely understand Nigel. They didn't share many interests, and Hawes always felt he was being judged by his son and found wanting.

"What do you think?" Nigel asked.

"They keep close tabs on visitors," Hawes said mildly. "I'm not sure how much you'll get to see the way people really live."

"I didn't know you were an expert on life in Cuba."

"I'm not. But I'll wager your tour won't stop at the Villa Marista, where Castro jails the enemies of the state."

"I can find political prisoners much closer to home. What about the Irish Republicans locked up in Long Kesh?" Nigel's tone was chilly.

Hawes knew he should have kept quiet. He always managed to say the wrong thing with his son, the one phrase or offhand comment that would irritate him. He needed to choose his words with more care than normal—and it often made their conversations stilted and awkward.

He decided to make peace. "I don't like the situation in Ulster any better than you do." Hawes shrugged. "I don't expect that we'll agree on politics. Let's change the subject. I saw your Uncle Viktor earlier today."

Nigel's face brightened. "How is Viktor? I haven't seen him in ages."

"He's doing well. The Danube is looking a bit tattered, but Viktor is Viktor. We got caught up, traded some war stories. He asked about you, volunteered to set you straight on politics, but I told him it was a lost cause."

"That it is."

"Are you free for supper?" Hawes asked.

"Sorry, I've already made plans."

"I'm sure she's better looking than Dear Old Dad."

Nigel flushed. "It's not like that. She's an editor for one of the publishing houses. She's been kind enough to look over my first column, and a fancy dinner is my way of repaying her."

Hawes held his hands up, palms facing his son. "It was only a joke, Nigel."

"Sorry," he said. "We do always seem to be at odds, don't we?"

"We do. And I wish it wasn't so."

"Next time I come down to London, let's have dinner," Nigel said.

"I'd like that," Hawes said. "I'd like that very much."

* * *

The following morning, Hawes stopped by the cramped West End office of his former colleague, Freddie North. Freddie had abruptly departed from MI6 just after the New Year in 1960. It was rumored that he had been caught padding his expense account, but Hawes knew the real story—Freddie had been ushered out of the Secret Intelligence Service because of his sexual preferences. There was less room in the intelligence agencies for homosexuals—they were considered prime targets for blackmail—not after the public exposure of diplomat Guy Burgess and civil servant John Vassall, both gay, as Soviet spies.

Shortly after his exit from the Secret Intelligence Service, Freddie had set up shop as a music promoter and theatrical agent. He told Hawes once that representing singers and actors was very much like handling agents in the field.

"It's not easy, you know. You have to coddle them, buck them up when they're down, bark at them when they're lazy or sloppy. They have to believe that you've got their best interests at heart."

"Which you do, of course." Hawes had smiled, remembering their history together. While Freddie took the world as he found it, he didn't mind stretching the rules. Hawes knew he could also be trusted.

"You're a sly dog, Feliks. I have their best interests and my best interests at heart. The way the world works."

Freddie may have left SIS, but he wasn't completely done with intelligence work—he was occasionally called upon for off-the-books jobs. Word got around: Need a lock jimmied? A diplomat from a friendly nation followed? A briefcase stolen? Freddie could arrange it—he had a network of "colleagues" who could help bridge the gap between what was legal and what needed to be done. Hawes had used him several times to arrange for couriers for last-minute deliveries in France and Spain.

Now, he hoped Freddie could help him with the contingency plan for extracting Claire Markham from Czechoslovakia.

"I'd like to tap into your network of rogues and ne'er-do-wells," Hawes began. "I have a job to fill."

His former colleague and friend, a chain-smoker, wore tinted glasses, making it nearly impossible to see his eyes through the haze created by his Players cigarettes.

"Will this conversation cost me? Or cost you?"

"There's something in it for you," Hawes said. "I need a courier. A little tricky, this time. The job is in Prague."

"Oh, dear. Prague. That is a bit dodgy, old chap. Out of the ordinary. How soon would you need this person?"

"October. The first week. Anticipate they'd be there no more than four days. Best if they have a solid reason for visiting. We don't want to excite any untoward interest."

"I see. What about a travel writer? Or a salesman? I could hunt up the first. The salesman might be a tad bit harder to find."

"What about one of your singers? Or actors?"

"I'd need to wangle an invitation for that somehow. A concert or a play. Concert would be easier. What would this courier be carrying?"

"Do you want to know?"

"I do." Freddie took a drag on his cigarette.

"An extra passport and some cash. Only to be delivered in the event of an emergency."

"What are you up to, Feliks? I thought you were done with the bastards at Century House."

"This doesn't involve them, thank God. It's a private engagement." He paused. "I recognize that there's a greater element of risk, and I'm willing to pay more."

"I know someone who might prove helpful," Freddie said. "A chap named Mendelsohn. He was booking folk singers to perform in Poland and Czechoslovakia back in the days of detente, which wasn't that long ago. I can inquire if the door is still open. Artistic exchange for peace, that sort of thing. If it is, then there's a young woman, a singer, who could play the part. She's run some errands for me in the past."

"Capital. I will need to work closely with whomever you find, and

I'd ask that you help out once they're in Prague. Passing along any messages. As their agent, of course."

"Why not?" Freddie asked, blowing a smoke ring. "I could use a few thrills. Only a few, Feliks, because we've reached the age where a few will go a long way."

Six

They began their intense preparation for their first trip to Prague in a modest rented Georgian townhouse in Chelsea. Later, Claire thought of it as their crash course in applied espionage (although, at the time, she never would have breathed that word, *espionage*, aloud). After her long overnight flight from New York, she took a hired car from Heathrow Airport directly to the address she had been given a few days before. An older woman with thick glasses and white hair greeted her by name at the front door.

"My name is Dorothy, but everyone calls me Dot," the woman told her. "You must be tired from your trip. Why don't you have a lie-down?" She paused. "Mr. Singer should be here at three o'clock. You should rest until then."

She took Claire's bag and ushered her up the stairs to a small bedroom on the second floor. It had a double bed, a polished wooden floor, and walls decorated in wallpaper with a Chinoiserie pattern of weeping willows and exotic birds.

"Come see me if you need anything," Dot said, closing the door gently.

After a long nap, Claire woke to the sound of male voices downstairs. She washed her face and combed her hair, and then went downstairs. In the sitting room, she found Benjamin Singer and Jack Townsend waiting for her, along with a handsome young man dressed stylishly in a russet-colored suit and shiny black ankle boots. Townsend introduced him as Rafael Klima.

"Your guide for Prague," Townsend said. "Rafe is fluent in Czech. Makes his living as an interpreter and translator."

"I have family there," Rafe said. "But I grew up in Canada and England. Toronto and London. Best of both worlds, I always say."

Singer smiled. "Eleanor Roosevelt claimed that we were all immigrants. It's true, isn't it?"

Dorothy appeared from a side door and while she served them tea and biscuits, they sat in silence. Claire took in the room—it was tastefully furnished, with a deep red Persian rug covering the floor, Chippendale-style furniture, bookshelves in one corner, and an ornate fireplace. There were fresh flowers in a vase on the fireplace mantel.

They made small talk—about Claire's flight from New York, and Rafe's most recent interpreting job, with a toothpaste manufacturer hoping to enter the Czechoslovakian market—until Singer gently touched his spoon to the side of his teacup.

"Shall we start?" Singer asked rhetorically. "Jack, you have the floor."

Townsend began by summarizing their goal—to help Tatiana Savchenko leave Czechoslovakia so that she could live in freedom in Israel. To do so without being detected by the authorities.

76

"You could say ours is a humanitarian mission, and it undoubtedly is," Townsend said. "But there is nothing humanitarian about the system under which Miss Savchenko must live. You must remain vigilant during your time behind the Iron Curtain."

Claire thought that she caught Rafe smirking at the mention of the Iron Curtain, but she wasn't sure.

"Your first trip to Prague, in three days, will act as a dry run of the actual operation," Townsend said. "We'll spend the next two days preparing you. Your job is to familiarize yourself with the city, visit a few tourist spots, and convince the locals that you're two Britons on a business trip mixing in some casual sightseeing."

He handed them both a typed itinerary, and Claire quickly scanned it, finding it not much different from the ones travel agents had given her in the past. It listed their hotels, scheduled flights, train trips, and recommended activities. Townsend waited until they had finished reading the document, and then he talked them through the steps of their journey.

"You'll stay in Vienna for a day," he said. "Claire, while you're there, you should visit two or three antiques stores. Buy something small at one or two of them and make sure you get receipts. You can leave the items at the hotel for safeguarding, and bring them back with you after you return."

"The Austrians make fine clocks," Singer said. "I'll give you a list of the better clockmakers, and you can buy for me if you spot anything."

Townsend ignored the interruption. "You will take the train from Vienna to Prague via Gmünd, the old Franz Joseph line—it's less traveled, which is better for our purposes. First-class carriage, of course. Once you're there in Prague, the dress rehearsal starts. You check into the hotel, the Jalta, which is in Wenceslas Square. Tour the city. Visit the Old Town Hall and the Orloj, the astronomical clock. Walk from your hotel to the Charles Bridge and cross the Vltava River and wander around Mala Strana, the Lesser Town. Take photos like a tourist. Then, visit the antique stores. You buy a few pieces, find an expensive item that you tell the shop manager that you may come back for. On Day Three, you take the train back to Vienna."

"Do you think we'll be under surveillance?" Rafe asked.

"Assume that you will be. Everything you say in the hotel will be heard by the secret police. The rooms at the Jalta are bugged, full of hidden microphones. They have a listening post in the basement."

"Why would you have us stay there?" Claire asked.

"It's the fastest way to establish you as innocents abroad. We want the Surveillance Directorate of the Interior Ministry to conclude that you're not worth following around."

"I get it," Rafe said. "I don't quite get the visits to the antique stores in Vienna. Seems a waste of time."

"You're establishing a legend, a cover story. Claire needs to keep the receipts in her luggage, so if they search it at the border or when you're in the hotel, it backs up the rationale for your trip." He paused. "Don't worry about being watched or being listened to. You're in Prague for business, scouting for antiques for a wealthy client. If someone tails you, don't acknowledge their presence by altering your behavior. I'll teach you some tricks on how to evade someone tailing you, but you won't need that on this first trip. We have to establish a profile for both of you that passes muster."

* * *

The next day, Claire and Rafe presented themselves at the offices of Cedok, the state-owned travel agency, at 45 Oxford Street, made train and hotel reservations, and applied for expedited visas. Rafe did most of the talking, explaining that Claire was most interested in shopping for antiques for an important client. Townsend had insisted that they discuss their travel plans in detail with the employees at the agency, assuming that the information would be forwarded to the authorities at some point.

"We want you to be boring and predictable," he said. "Decadent Westerners with money to burn, staying at luxury hotels and buying antiques. Under no circumstances should you discuss politics of any sort. If you're asked, say you don't really pay much attention to it, you just wish everyone could get along."

"We wish everyone could get along?" Rafe said. "That's our response? I don't care to be thought of as a dolt."

Singer laughed. "Rafe, in this situation I think the better part of valor is to keep quiet. You're in Prague on business. Period. You're there to buy antiques on the cheap. Mention more than once that you're looking for bargains. That's what motivates a capitalist."

"This is not the Cambridge Union," Townsend said. "No debates. No cleverness. You're apolitical. Can you stick to that?"

"I imagine so," Rafe said.

"One other thing," Townsend said. "Be wary of new friends. Not just the locals. Be polite but distant with anyone who approaches you. The StB is quite capable of recruiting and employing foreigners as informers. And steer clear of Charles University and the student hangouts. We don't want you to stop at a coffeehouse where dissident types might congregate."

"Any other rules?" Rafe asked.

"It's not a question of setting rules. There may be situations we haven't anticipated. You'll need to adapt. On this first trip, the idea is to leave a very light footprint."

* * *

During their training, as brief as it was, Townsend spent more time in one-on-one sessions with Claire than with Rafe. He gave her a map of Prague and asked her to study it, to orient herself, and then he took it from her and quizzed her about the relative location of landmarks in the city. He had her focus on the streets around the train station and Wenceslas Square.

"Based on the street signs, you need to know where you are," he explained. "You'll find that knowing the map cold will pay dividends when you're on the ground there."

He tasked her with making sure that Rafe took three photographs of her, alone, in front of the St. John the Baptist statue on the Charles

Bridge, under the statue of Saint Wenceslas, and at the Powder Tower in Old Town. "A photo of you alone," he told her. "Please look directly at the camera."

"May I ask why?"

He smiled. "Humor me for now. I'll explain when you've returned."

They had a more awkward conversation later that day. "One rule of thumb—in operations like this, it's best to avoid personal complications," Townsend said. "You'll be alone with Rafe quite a bit. No romance, please. After it's done, you can do what you like."

She could see that he was uncomfortable. "I'm not in the market for a boyfriend, Mr. Townsend."

"That's for the best. By the way, I've had the same conversation with Rafe."

"Have you? Was that necessary?"

"Rafe fancies himself as irresistible to women. I asked him to refrain from exerting his magnetic appeal on you."

She laughed. "Thank you, but I think I can manage to resist the pull of this specific magnet."

* * *

The central train station in Prague, the Hlavni Nadrazi, was sleek and modern in design—not at all what Claire had expected. The government had invested heavily in a contemporary addition to the original nineteenth-century structure, as a way of demonstrating that Czechoslovakia could compete with the West in constructing shiny modernist buildings. That shininess stood in stark contrast to the drab clothing of many of the Czechs waiting in line to buy train tickets.

Claire and Rafe walked from the platform to the departure hall, where Rafe waited with their baggage while she went into the women's restroom. Claire quickly looked around, taking in the sink, mirror, and stalls. She touched up her makeup and brushed her hair. She imagined what it would be like when she changed places with Tatiana, the urgency, the need for secrecy. If only the bathroom remained empty when the time came, like it was now.

At the Jalta Hotel, Rafe handled the check-in, switching back and forth from Czech to English as he talked with the clerk at the registration desk. After a quick lunch in the hotel restaurant, Claire persuaded Rafe to take a walk with her—she was eager to see the Golden Prague that she had been reading about in her guidebook.

As Rafe showed her around that afternoon, and the following day, she found herself captivated by the beauty of the city. It was all charming: the narrow cobbled streets, the ancient churches with spires, the hidden alleyways, the palaces with red tiled roofs. She was drawn to the river, the Vltava, which wound its way northwards, with Castle Hill dominating the skyline, crowned by Prague Castle and the Gothic cathedral of St. Vitus.

There were signs of neglect, though; the facades of many of the buildings were dirty and stained and gray, in stark contrast to the clean, white walls of Vienna, where they had just been only days before. She wondered about the people she passed in the streets.

Several times Rafe pointed out long lines, queues mostly of women, in front of grocery stores. She studied the faces of those they encountered. Many seemed careworn, grim, especially the older men and women. The younger people seemed to smile more. What was it like for all of them, both young and old? How often did they come into contact with the machinery of the regime? From what she had read, Czechoslovakia was more like East Germany than Hungary—ruled by the hardliners in Prague Castle, the seat of government, who kept tight control over the populace, reluctantly allowing contact with the West.

She had vacationed in Franco's authoritarian Spain and saw a liveliness and energy in the people of Madrid and Barcelona that she hadn't encountered in Prague. One Spanish friend had explained that as long as you lived your private life and stayed out of politics, no one bothered you. That wasn't the case in Czechoslovakia, where the state was involved in nearly every aspect of daily life.

Much to her surprise, Claire enjoyed playing the role of tourist. She made sure to walk the entire length of Charles Bridge, posing for a photograph in front of the statue of John the Baptist as Townsend had instructed her. She had read in her guidebook that when the bridge was built, the king at the time had ordered eggs mixed into the mortar for added strength. Czechs from the countryside had sent thousands of eggs to Prague for the construction. She was delighted by the story.

Rafe was an indifferent guide, bored by their visits to the traditional tourist hot spots, impatient to return to the hotel.

"What do you really think of this?" he asked her. "This idea of traipsing all over Prague and acting like wide-eyed tourists?"

"Townsend said that it was to establish ourselves as boring and predictable. Doesn't that make sense?"

"I think it's over-egging the pudding. One morning of sightseeing should have been enough."

Claire thought he was wrong, but she kept quiet. During the first two days in the city, she wondered whether they were being followed. She caught sight of a young man wearing a fedora and a dark coat as she and Rafe were leaving the Jalta, and later she spotted him trailing them as they walked through Mala Strana. She didn't see him again—did he, or his superiors, realize that following them was a waste of time? Perhaps it was what Townsend had wanted—for their initial watchers to conclude that Claire and Rafe were what they appeared to be. Harmless business travelers who would contribute hard currency to the anemic economy.

At dinner at the Europa Hotel, in what was reputed to be one of the city's better restaurants, Claire made sure they were seated by one of the large bay windows, where it would be harder to eavesdrop on them. After a meal of garlic soup, roasted pork, Sauerkraut, and dumplings, Rafe sat back in his chair with a glass of local plum brandy in his hand. The after-dinner drink and the wine he had consumed at dinner made him talkative.

"Shall I tell you what I really want to do?" he asked. "Not being an interpreter, I can tell you that. Other people's words. Other people's stories. No, I have things to say, about the world, about the way we live."

"Are you writing a novel?" she asked, trying not to smile. The idea of Rafe as an author somehow seemed comical to her.

"Not a novel. I want to make films. I've been writing screenplays in my spare time. Have you seen any of the Czech films? The New Wave? *Closely Watched Trains? The Firemen's Ball?* Brilliant stuff. I'd like to direct, like Forman or Kubrick or Francis Ford Coppola. This little escapade of ours is quite cinematic. Think about it, Claire. A spy story. The train ride here. The backdrop of Prague, like Vienna in *The Third Man.* And then the exchange of identities. Quite symbolic, when you think about it. Identities. Who are we? The name and photo in our passport. And if that changes, who do we become?"

"Rafe," she said, in what she hoped was a warning tone. "Not now."

"All the story needs is a touch of romance."

"We shouldn't talk about this. You could be overheard."

"You're right," he said. "We need to follow Townsend's rules, although maybe not all of them. You know he told me I shouldn't get involved with you. He made that very clear, which I can't say I appreciated. I didn't like someone trying to dictate the parameters of my love life. What do you think, Claire?"

"I got the same message. It seemed reasonable to me, considering what we're here for. And as it happens, I'm not looking for romance, and certainly not under the current circumstances."

"For what it's worth, you're a very attractive woman."

"Thank you for the compliment." She paused. "I think we're best off remaining friends. Colleagues."

"I'm disappointed. I thought you were looking for thrills. Isn't that why you're doing this?"

85

"No, I'm doing this to help someone who needs help." She knew it wasn't her sole motive, but she wasn't about to reveal that to Rafe, of all people. She was tired of sitting on the sidelines of life. Why not experience what it was like to do something slightly dangerous? So far, she had been enjoying the adventure.

"How noble," Rafe said. "Not me. I like the thrill and the money. And can you blame me for trying to get you into bed? I thought we'd be good together, in all ways. A very nice way to pass the time."

"I think we should stick to Townsend's rules," she said briskly. "With that settled, then, we should plan our visit to the antique shops."

He finished his brandy in silence and was sullen on the walk to the Jalta. Claire didn't mind—it was better that he realized that she was not going to join the list of Rafael Klima's conquests, not now, not ever.

* * *

They visited three antiques stores the following morning. All of them had the same sign outside, *Starožitnosti*, and Rafe explained that since the shops were state-owned, like all of the businesses in the city, there was no need for distinctive names. The first shop, on Na Prikope, had little of interest, mostly worn furniture, ornate silverware, and a collection of ancient lamps. At their second stop, Claire purchased a simple gold bracelet, and Rafe haggled over the price with the proprietor, convincing him to give them a ten percent discount.

Their shopping expedition was rewarded with success at the third store on Narodni, which was situated next to a jeweler's shop. In the back of the store, she found a beautiful Art Nouveau jewel box in wood, mahogany, and silver, with a larger chest in the same design. Rafe calculated the combined price of both pieces would be slightly more than three thousand pounds. She took several photos of the items, chatting with the shop-keeper, Mr. Svoboda, as she did. Svoboda, an older man with a bushy mustache, spoke passable English. Claire explained that her principal would need to see the photographs before he committed to buying them and that she would return to Prague if he agreed to the purchase. Svoboda nodded.

"They are *tres cher*," he said. "A lot of money. But they are works of art. They are from Franta Anyz, a brilliant artist who incorporated Art Nouveau and Bauhaus into his designs. He had his studio and foundry in Prague."

"They're expensive," Claire said. "If my client wishes to buy them, I would want to oversee their packing for shipment to England."

"We would be happy to be of service."

Rafe cleared his throat and said something in Czech to Svoboda, who flushed with anger. "This is a fair price," he said in English. "These are unique pieces. We're not taking advantage of the lady. Never would we do that."

"Of course you wouldn't," Claire said, giving Rafe a side glance. She thanked Svoboda and asked if he would hold the jewel box and chest until she could confer with her client.

He gave her a thin smile. "I shall." He paused. "As a young man, I was in London just after the war. An amazing city. I doubt I will ever return, but I do remember the Thames and Big Ben, the Houses of Parliament."

"I will say hello to them for you," Claire said. "And we hope to see you again in a few weeks."

Once back at the Jalta, Claire placed a call to the London phone number Townsend had given her. Benjamin Singer answered, and she explained that she had found two wonderful Art Deco pieces from Franta Anyz, and she would bring photographs back for his review. She didn't have to fake her enthusiasm; the handwork on the jewel box was exquisite, and she knew two of her Gramercy Antiques clients who would pay a premium for it—if Singer didn't keep it for himself.

"I look forward to seeing you," Singer said. "Safe travels."

* * *

The return trip from Prague to Vienna was uneventful. The train had seen better days—the upholstery on the seats was worn, and some of the lights in the corridors had burned out. They sat together in a separate first-class compartment, and Claire found herself dozing off. She was not worried when a man in a gray uniform asked for their passports and studied her face, comparing it to the photograph in her passport. She was innocent, after all. Rafe joked with the man in Czech and managed to elicit a tight smile from him. Thirty minutes later, a middle-aged woman with a pinched face arrived and announced "customs and passports." She looked over the form Claire had filled out for the two antique bowls and the gold bracelet and nodded briefly.

When they reached the border town of Ceske Velenice, the train came to a dead stop. The station there seemed abandoned, with no sign of passengers on the platform. Claire noticed a lone flowerpot in the closest window of the station. She counted five soldiers in fatigues on the platform, all armed with semiautomatic rifles. Rafe translated the two billboards on the other side of the tracks. "The first one says 'Welcome to Czechoslovakia,' and the second one 'Under the Party leadership we will achieve socialism.' I guess one out of two being true isn't too bad."

They sat for twenty minutes, conversations in the carriage muted, until a large group of men in black coveralls appeared outside the train. They climbed aboard, and Claire heard them opening the lavatory doors and walking through the train corridors looking, no doubt, for signs of anyone trying to defect. Outside, several soldiers were looking under the train, making sure that no one was hiding below.

They heard shouted commands, and the soldiers left the train. A sudden jolt, and they were moving again. They passed an open grass strip, and then a wide stretch of freshly plowed soil, with watchtowers nearby. Finally, barbed wire. The train crossed a railway bridge over a small river, the Luznice. Claire noticed two sentries posted on the bridge, both smoking cigarettes. On the other side of the river, Austria.

When the train slowed at Gmünd, the first stop in Austria, Claire breathed a sigh of relief. The passport and customs check was perfunctory, and they were on their way to Vienna within minutes. Townsend had warned them not to say anything while on the train that related to their true reasons for visiting Prague, not even once they had crossed into Austria. It was likely there were StB informers who rode the train listening to the passengers.

"Back to the Free World," Rafe said.

Claire gave him a warning look. "Back to Vienna."

"Is that too political?" he asked. "Sorry. We're back to Vienna. But you really do worry too much, Claire."

Seven

Their initial debriefing took all afternoon. They gathered in a suite in the Savoy Hotel, and Claire found that she missed the comfortable surroundings of the townhouse in Chelsea. It had felt cozy there—the hotel rooms seemed cold and sterile in comparison. She was surprisingly anxious about the meeting, which she knew was ridiculous because the trip had been a success by any measure; she and Rafe had played their parts to perfection. When she arrived at the Savoy, Rafe was patiently waiting for her in the lobby. They took the lift up together to the second floor. Singer and Townsend were waiting for them, along with a dark-haired man, who Townsend introduced as Viktor. Rafe greeted him with a hug—they clearly knew each other—and Claire shook his hand, wondering what role he might play in their debriefing.

After a waiter had brought in a tray of sandwiches and coffee and tea, they settled down to work, but not before Townsend walked over to the main door to the suite, opened it, and scanned the hallway outside. He hung a "Do Not Disturb" sign on the outside handle and closed the door.

"We're very pleased with how well you've done in this first stage of the project," Singer began. "Now, Jack is going to ask you several questions, way too many questions. Please bear with us. The questions may seem strange, or not relevant, but they're vital so that when you go back to Prague for the actual mission, all will go well."

When Townsend spoke, he was all business. "This is our one chance to anticipate any challenges you may encounter on your next trip, and to explore solutions to them. While your visit is fresh in your mind, we're going to probe. We're going to test your memories. I've asked Viktor, a friend of mine, to sit in on this conversation. He's no stranger to this sort of operation, and his instincts are sound. He may have a few questions of his own. I've asked Viktor to poke holes in our plans, so that we can plug those holes."

Viktor handed sheets of blank paper and pencils to Claire and Rafe. Townsend asked them to sketch from memory the floor plan for the departure hall of the Hlavni Nadrazi. After they had finished, he compared the two drawings and sighed. "You didn't pay much attention to your surroundings," he said to Rafe. "Not much detail. Not as much as in Claire's drawing."

Rafe shrugged. "Does it matter? Isn't the plan that I wait while Claire goes to the ladies? The Russian woman meets her inside. Claire gives her the passport. I pretend that she's Claire when she comes out. We head to the platform for the train to Vienna. Our tickets and passports are in order, and off we go."

Townsend shook his head. "The details always matter. Where can you expect the police to be stationed? Where might you draw attention?"

Viktor cleared his throat. "Rafe and Claire should wait here," he said, pointing to a spot on Claire's map near the ticket window directly across from the entrance to the restrooms. "By the wall. Claire should cross over and enter the loo. Rafe keeps an eye on the departure hall, looking for signs of surveillance. He also watches the door for the moment when the Russian woman emerges."

"How will she know that it's me?" Rafe asked.

"She'll be told that a young man matching your description will be standing near the ticket window," Townsend said. "With luggage for two. Wave to her if you need to. Claire will stay in the loo for a few minutes and then leave. You and Tatiana should have reached the platform for the Vienna train by then." Townsend turned to Claire. "Don't wait too long. When you leave, you'll be wearing Tatiana's overcoat. Put a scarf over your hair."

She nodded. "Then I leave the train station, walking at a normal pace, and head to the rendezvous point with my contact."

"Why not have Claire meet the contact in the station?" Rafe asked. "Wouldn't that be simpler?" It wasn't the first time Rafe had questioned Townsend's plans. There had been growing tension between them. Claire could see that Rafe didn't like the older man, and he didn't seem to care if Townsend realized that. Were they too much alike, she asked herself? Stubborn. Confident.

"Because we want Claire as far from you and the Russian woman as soon as possible," Viktor said. "We want to break the connection. The sooner Claire leaves the station, the better. And the walk will give her a chance to check for surveillance, whether or not she's being tailed."

Rafe shrugged expressively. "While we're poking holes in the plan, I have another question. Why don't we fly back? It's two hours from

Prague to London. A lot faster than the train, and once we're in the air, we're home free."

Townsend answered him. "They pay much more attention at the airport. Tighter passport control. We can't risk the sort of scrutiny you might face. They're more likely to ask questions. Once Miss Savchenko opened her mouth, they would suspect that she's not strawberries-and-cream English. Not so with the train. After she meets with Claire, she faces no more than two or three minutes of exposure walking from the departure hall to the platform. And she may not even have to answer any questions when they check passports on the train. Your role, Rafe, should be to talk to the conductor and customs officials in Czech. Divert them from asking her anything."

"I'm only trying to be helpful with my questions," Rafe said. "Understand the how and why."

"I understand that. The plan is sound. I wouldn't let you two proceed on to the next stage if it wasn't."

"And the contact person for Claire? Who is it? Someone local?"

"The less you know about that, the better," Townsend said. "In the unlikely event that the authorities get their hands on you, you wouldn't have anything of value to tell them."

"How unlikely an event is that?" Rafe asked.

"Very unlikely if you follow instructions."

"But it could happen?"

"There's always a possibility. In my experience, cock-ups occur when people get sloppy or when they panic. If you follow my instructions, it should all go smoothly."

"And if they do bag us?"

"Demand to see the British ambassador. Say as little as possible. While they won't treat you with kid gloves, you're from the West and they'll hesitate when it comes to any rough stuff."

"What would you do then, Townsend?" Rafe asked. "If we're arrested?"

"As I said, it's very unlikely. I'll alert my friends in the Foreign Office and ask them to intervene forcefully with the Czechoslovak government on your behalf. But we've been clear about the risks, have we not?"

"You have," Claire said quickly before Rafe could reply.

Townsend didn't speak for a long moment. "Tomorrow the two of you will return to Cedoc's offices and book your next trip," he said. "You'll tell them how much you enjoyed your visit to Prague. How you're eager to return. Claire has checked with her client, and he has given her approval to buy a few antiques that she discovered on your last trip. Same train from Vienna—you loved traveling through the countryside. Same hotel. You've established a pattern. We don't deviate from that."

"We're boring," Claire said.

"That's the ticket," Townsend said, allowing himself a smile. "There's nothing out of the ordinary about you or your visit."

Townsend asked Claire to stay behind when they concluded their first session at four o'clock. He sat across from her where he could study her face, a deliberate positioning, or at least it seemed that way to Claire.

"Did Rafe behave himself?" he asked. "He can be a bit of a flash Harry. Nothing untoward?"

"He was fine," she said, deciding not to mention his clumsy advance, nor his idea of turning their experience into a screenplay. (Was he serious about that? Or was it just part of his romantic come-on to make himself more appealing—the young man as aspiring artist?) She had handled it without too much awkwardness. There was no need to involve Townsend—he might say something to Rafe. Claire had enough experience with the fragile male ego to know that Rafe would be embarrassed and angered if Townsend mentioned his failed attempt at romance. Better to leave things alone.

"You may have wondered why you have to stay the night," Townsend said. "When you go to the embassy for your emergency passport, they'll report that it's been lost to the Czech authorities, who in turn may alert the border police. We don't want that process triggered until Rafe and Miss Savchenko have left the country. Having you wait ensures no unpleasant surprises for them at the border."

"I figured there was a reason," she said.

"Now we can talk about the photos you posed for," Townsend said. "There was also a reason for them. After the exchange at the train station, a contact will meet you at the Saint Wenceslas statue and take you to a place where you'll stay that night. They'll have your photo so you know they're one of ours."

"Will it be a man? A woman?"

"I'll let you know before you go. The next morning, your contact will accompany you to the British embassy on Thunovska Street, across the Vtlata. It's quite a building, once was the Thun Palace."

"What if this contact person gets cold feet and doesn't show up?"

"There's a contingency plan. We'll give you the details later. You won't be left out in the cold, Claire."

"What about Rafe? Is there a contingency plan for him?"

"It's different for him. He won't be staying behind, like you are. He'll be back in Vienna a good day before anyone realizes Miss Savchenko is missing."

"Unless the Russians follow her to the train station."

"They would stop her long before she got there. If she's waiting in the ladies' room, then it's very likely that she's given them the slip."

"Or she's under their control, and we're being set up."

Townsend shook his head. "I don't believe so. She's shown us that she's brave enough to make a run for it. With that sort of courage, I doubt that they could bring enough pressure on her quickly enough so that she would betray you."

"But if they had time?"

"We're all human, Claire. We all break at a certain point. Tatiana Savchenko would be no exception to that rule. With any luck, we'll never have to worry about that."

* * *

After the meeting broke up, Hawes, Viktor, and Singer retired to the American Bar on the Savoy's ground floor. They waited until they had been served their drinks before anyone spoke.

"I'm not worried about Claire," Hawes said. "She's a quick study. Rafe is the problem. He's too cocky. A few trips to Prague in the past, and he thinks he's an expert."

"Can you replace him?" Singer asked.

"He's the best we could come up with on short notice," Hawes said. "He does speak the language, and he's a pretty good bullshitter. And it would be very disruptive to replace him at this late date. We lose the advantage of familiarity."

"He doesn't like you."

"The feeling is mutual. But I can work with him."

"What about the cockiness?" Singer asked. "The attitude?"

"It has to change." Hawes turned to Viktor, who had been silent, nursing his brandy. "Viktor, can you have a chat with him? Set him right?"

Viktor nodded. "I'll put the fear of the Lord into him, Feliks."

"We can't deviate from the timetable," Singer said. "There won't be another chance. Professor Savchenko has rarely been allowed to travel outside the country. Once to East Germany, and now this trip."

"It's the day of the exchange that worries me," Viktor said. "The plan doesn't work if Tatiana isn't there at the train station at the exact time. Are you sure that she understands that? And that your people have passed along the instructions, exactly what she is to do?"

"They have," Singer said. "I've been assured of that. We know that Professor Savchenko will be driven to the meeting that morning with the other scientists at the Technical University. Tatiana will become conveniently ill, stay back at the hotel. When she leaves, she can't walk through the lobby, because that's where any of her minders will be stationed. There's a rear entrance, and that's where she must exit. She walks a few blocks and catches a cab. It's about fifteen minutes to the train station."

"And what has she been told about the exchange at the train station?" It was Hawes, leaning forward and keeping his voice low.

"The bare minimum. Tatiana will go to the lavatory, where a young woman will approach her and pass her the passport. They'll trade coats. If there are other women in the restroom, they'll wait for the right moment for the exchange."

"And her English?"

"Adequate, from what I've been told, but she speaks with a pronounced accent. I don't think she can pass for English."

"We'll have Rafe do all the talking. He'll like that." Hawes finished his drink. "How much time do you think we have before her absence is noted? Before they start looking for her in earnest?"

"There's a dinner for the scientists that night. When Tatiana doesn't appear with her father, Savchenko's security people will check on her."

"Then what?" Hawes asked. "When they realize that she's gone."

"We don't know. There will be a lot of confusion."

"But with his daughter in Austria, Savchenko will already have given you the information you want. Is that how it works?"

Singer nodded.

Hawes and Viktor exchanged a glance, and then Hawes cleared his throat. "I want to be clear. Rafe and Claire will board the train to Vienna if Miss Savchenko doesn't show up. They won't wait. We'll have to assume that her father's security team has stopped her from leaving the hotel. If that happens, we can only hope that she can make some clever excuse for attempting to sneak out the back entrance. Cabin fever. Wanting to walk the streets by herself."

"I understand," Singer said.

"There's one aspect of the operation still up in the air," Hawes said. "I don't yet have a safe house in Prague for Claire, a place where she can stay the rest of the afternoon and night after the exchange. She won't have a passport, so she can't check into a hotel. I'm also developing a contingency plan. By the time Claire and Rafe return to Prague, I'll have an alternate way to get her out of the labyrinth if need be. Not a ball of thread, something a bit more modern."

Two days later, Viktor assured Hawes that his private conversation with Rafe had gone well. He didn't provide any details, but Hawes knew Viktor would have been direct and forceful.

They had met at the Danube, and Viktor had a sullen Rafe follow him into his back office, which wasn't much larger than a closet.

"I'm worried about you," Viktor told him. "You seem out of sorts. You need to listen to Townsend. He knows what he's doing. Pay attention and follow his instructions. Unless you want to play at being the Lone Ranger and you think spending time in a Czech prison would be a bit of a lark. I don't think you want that. Do you? Don't be a wanker."

"Is that what Townsend says? That I'm being a wanker?"

"Those are my words. I've been listening and watching during the debriefing. I don't blame Townsend for being worried. You're overconfident. You think you know better. You don't. And there's no margin for error."

"When was the last time Townsend was in Prague?"

"That's not what matters," Viktor said. "Townsend knows how the secret police—State Security—operate. How they think. The StB. The KGB. What Townsend knows is what will keep you from harm, whether it's Prague or Warsaw or Budapest or even Moscow. They all sing from the same hymnal."

"What do you want me to say?"

"Don't say anything. Show the man some respect."

When Rafe left the Danube—properly chastened—Viktor telephoned Hawes at his office in Knightsbridge.

"He listened to me," Viktor said. "You shouldn't have more problems with him."

"What about the safe house in Prague?"

"It won't be a house, just a flat. I found someone willing to help us. Piri Szabo, a Hungarian woman, a student at Charles University. Her place is maybe thirty minutes from Wenceslas Square, in Zizkov, District Three. At the moment, she's visiting a friend in London."

"How is she able to travel?"

"Her parents are well-connected Party members. Not out of conviction—no one buys the absurd slogans any more—but for the benefits. Better pay. Living in a villa on Rose Hill. Trips to the West. The government doesn't worry about a girl like Piri. They know she'll come home."

"Why would she help us?" Hawes asked.

"Greed. Hard currency. She's been hitting the stores in London to buy blue jeans and bring them back with her. They're worth their weight in gold in Budapest."

"So her motives would be mercenary?"

"An opportunist." Viktor made a face. "She's heading back to Hungary in two days, so you need to meet her face-to-face."

"There's no question about that," Hawes said.

"I thought that would be the case. She's coming to the Danube in forty-five minutes."

Hawes took a black cab to the Danube, where he found Viktor and the young Hungarian woman already at a corner table. There was nothing distinctive about Piri Szabo—she had a plain face with long brown hair that fell to her shoulders. Hawes would have passed her on the street without a second look. He considered that a positive, for she was less likely to attract attention.

After introductions, Viktor began the conversation in Hungarian.

"I heard a good joke the other day," he said. "Would you like to hear it?"

"I like jokes," she said.

"A factory worker named Bela is walking through Kossuth Square when he spots a pot of gold on the ground. He looks around and it appears the coast is clear. He rushes over to grab it when Istvan, a Party official, sees what is going on and follows him to the pot. 'Comrade,' Istvan says, 'let's share the gold like socialist brothers!' Bela isn't having any of that. 'No,' he says, 'let's just go halves.'"

Piri hesitated for a moment and then laughed. "That's good," she said. "Let's just go halves."

Viktor switched to English. "I've told Mr. Townsend about you, and how you might be able to help him."

"If I can," she replied in English.

"Let me explain," Hawes said. "I've been hired by a prominent family here in London to help them with an awkward situation. Their daughter—let's call her Claire—has become romantically involved with an older man that she met in Prague. He's an official with the Ministry of Culture and very influential. He's also very possessive. The girl, Claire, wants to end the relationship, and he's not handling it well. He took her passport and watches her like a hawk. We have a plan to help her. When she leaves him for good, we'd ask you to let her stay with you for a night. Then, accompany her to the British embassy on Thunovska Street where she can get an emergency passport and leave for the airport. You wait until you see that she's inside, and then you can leave."

"I'll let her stay the night, but I don't like the visit to the embassy. She can do that on her own. I'm not stupid or naïve, Mr. Townsend. I don't believe your story."

Hawes shrugged. "It's the truth. Love affairs can have messy ends."

"They can," Piri said. "I would need to be well paid for this. And I don't want to know any more than you've told me."

"It's a familiar story," Viktor said. "A young woman caught up in a romance with the wrong guy. He's the insanely jealous type."

"According to you." Piri made a face. "You could be lying to me. Get me in big trouble." She gave Hawes a skeptical look. "It's not drugs, is it? I won't have anything to do with drugs."

"It has nothing to do with drugs," Hawes said. He paused. "Let's compromise. You walk three-quarters of the way to the embassy with her. Then you're done."

"I'll want half of the money now. In pounds."

"You drive a hard bargain," Viktor said. "You had better live up to your side of it."

Hawes named a number, and Piri nodded. He took his wallet out and counted out half of the total. She took the wad of bills and stuffed it into her handbag.

"We'll pay you the second half the next time you visit London," Hawes said.

"That will be acceptable," she said. "I'll be back in three months with my parents."

"Let me explain something to you, Piri," Viktor said. "If you don't do what we've asked, if you don't follow Mr. Townsend's instructions to the letter, there will be consequences."

"Is that so?"

"It is," Viktor replied, and then, in rapid Hungarian, told her that he knew where she lived in Budapest and that she would regret it if she took their money and didn't follow her instructions.

"I said that I would do this," she said. "I will. How do I know that you won't cheat me out of the second half of the money?"

"Mr. Townsend is a proper English gentleman." Viktor turned to Hawes. "Can you give Miss Szabo your word that you'll make the payment?"

"Gladly," Hawes said. "We'll call you in a day with the details—dates and times. Viktor will bring you Claire's photograph. You'll show it to her when you first meet, so she knows you're acting on our behalf."

Piri nodded once and then got up from her chair. She left the Danube without looking back.

Hawes waited a minute or two before he turned to Viktor. "What do you think?"

"She took the money. She'll do what you ask. Nothing more."

"She's the weakest link," Hawes said. "Who knows whether she's reliable? I wish we had more time to find an alternative."

"She'll be fine," Viktor said. "She's greedy, and she'll want to earn the second payment. It's the border crossing for Rafe and the Russian woman that you should worry about. That's the most dangerous part of the operation."

"I worry about every part of the operation. You know how it is, Viktor. You review the details, try to spot the flaws, the moments when your people are exposed, vulnerable. You try to minimize those moments, but you know that you can't eliminate them."

"It will work out in the end."

Hawes shook his head. "It's the crucial minor details I worry about. 'For want of a nail, the shoe was lost.' I'll keep vetting this plan until I'm sure there's very little left to chance."

Eight

Summer Devine was bored and moody, and she had to concede, reluctantly, that the situation was of her own making. She had agreed to the Margate holiday with Duncan, knowing that it might go wrong. It should have been fun—the town was pretty in a Victorian gingerbread way—and she had been looking forward to the sand and the sea and time alone with her new boyfriend.

But her long weekend proved a disappointment. A colossal disappointment, in fact, and she had told Duncan that in no uncertain terms. He seemed more interested in smoking weed with his "mates," who had turned up unexpectedly at their rented cottage, than in spending time with her. She left him with Clive and Tony and their bong and had gone to the beach by herself in the morning, spreading a towel on the sand and sunning herself in the smallest bikini she had. She would lie on her stomach and untie her bikini top so that her back would tan evenly without any white stripes.

When she looked at herself naked in the full-length bathroom mirror, she felt both sexy and unappreciated. She was frustrated. Duncan was too stoned to appreciate how she looked or to make love to her. She ended taking care of herself while he drifted off to sleep in the bed next to her. He never stirred.

When she complained about his behavior, Duncan gave her a dazed smile. "Eliot had it right. *On Margate sands. I can connect…Nothing with nothing.* Brilliant."

"Who the hell is Eliot?" she asked.

"T. S., dear girl. T. S. Eliot. The greatest English poet of this century, but a Yank like you. Born in St. Louis, Missouri. Surely you've heard of him?"

"You're impossible." She dimly remembered something about T. S. Eliot from English class in her senior year of high school, but not very much.

She left Margate a day early and took the train back to London, resolving never to get romantically involved with a pot-head again, even if he was cute, rich, and had a posh accent. Duncan might have money and a Cambridge education, but he displayed little if any ambition. He seemed intent on squandering his inheritance on parties and drugs.

Duncan could fail, and fail again, but he had a comfortable safety net, a trust fund set up by his father, a banker and former Member of Parliament. Summer had never had the luxury of money, but she did have ambition. Her father had retired from the Parks and Recreation Department in Akron, Ohio, and her mother had worked at the hospital. Summer's future, if she stayed in her hometown, had been clear—marriage to a cop or firefighter with the prospect of popping out kids right and left. She was determined not to fall into that trap. Summer wanted to see the world, and she could sing—she won the high school talent show as a sophomore with her rendition of "Me

And Bobby McGee," and started playing a few of the local nightclubs on the weekends a year before she could legally drink.

The day she graduated from high school, she packed up her things and took a Greyhound bus headed to California. That was when she began calling herself Summer. The name her parents had given her—Audrey Rose—didn't fit who she wanted to become.

Los Angeles wasn't a welcoming place. It seemed there were hundreds of blonde singer-songwriters looking for their big break, and the truth was that Summer couldn't write songs, or at least she couldn't write songs that stood out. She had a fine voice and could more than adequately cover the hits of other singers—Janis Joplin, Patti Smith—as well as the softer folk sounds of Joan Baez and Joni Mitchell. Still, Summer knew she was never going to land a record deal without original material. She was a natural on stage—so people told her—and she found that she could piece together a living from performing and odd jobs—house-sitting, dog walking, waitressing, bartending.

She wasn't going back to Akron. Ever.

She had been lucky to land in London. On vacation there, she met Ian, a ginger-haired singer and guitar player from Aberdeen, and one night joined him on stage at a cramped Soho club. She sang one song, "Because the Night," giving it her all, and the crowd loved it. She sang two more songs that night, and the owner invited her and Ian to play the club every Thursday night. That's where Freddie North first saw her. He told her that he loved her California hippie vibe and was willing to represent her as her booking agent. That was a stroke of luck because Freddie seemed to know someone at every club in London, and she found herself with steady bookings for a while. She decided that she would stay in England, despite her dodgy immigration status.

Freddie warned her that there would be ups and downs, and sure enough, there were times when the gigs were few and far between. But she liked being the "American chick," the "Divine Summer Devine," liked being different, and however tenuous it seemed at times, she had a toehold in the London music scene, and she was damned if she was going to give it up.

* * *

She had been back from Margate only a day when things got a lot less boring.

Freddie North called her at home and asked her to stop by his office. He said he had an interesting opportunity lined up for her. With her bank account dwindling, she was eager for the details.

"A music gig? Or a side job?" she asked.

"We can talk about it when you come by."

Freddie's two-room office could be found at the top of the stairs in an aging building in the West End. On the waiting room wall, in a place of honor, was an ancient poster advertising a charity concert in Liverpool featuring the Beatles. It had been autographed by three of the four members of the group—John Lennon had been in a bad mood that day and had refused to sign—and it represented Freddie's claim to musical fame. He had been the co-promoter of the event, which had been staged before the group's meteoric rise to stardom. More than once, Freddie intimated to Summer that he had been a crucial part of the Beatles' success. "Without that concert, who knows?" he would say. "Mighty oaks from little acorns grow."

Summer had hit it off with Freddie. She enjoyed his stories about the Beatles and the Stones and the swinging London music scene of the 1960s ("Like a pendulum," Freddie would say and then cackle). Since he liked boys and not girls, she never had to fend him off, like she did many of the club owners. And not only did he try to book her concerts, but he was also constantly on the lookout for side jobs where Summer could make some cash (off the books, of course).

On her first side job, she had been paid handsomely for acting as a courier, taking a flight to Paris and delivering a briefcase to a law firm in La Défense. Freddie had told her she was carrying time-sensitive confidential documents. The briefcase was locked. Freddie's involvement was a bit strange—why was a concert promoter arranging the delivery of legal documents?—but she was content to take the cash and leave well enough alone.

Her second assignment came after she had confessed her worries about her shaky immigration status to Freddie. He had nodded and told her not to worry. A week later, he introduced her to a young man who said he worked for the government. In exchange for extending her visa, Summer agreed to deliver a package to an address in Lisbon. She placed the package, which was tightly wrapped in brown paper, in her backpack and flew to Lisbon and back to London in one day. She didn't ask any questions about what she was carrying; Summer figured that she would take the money and the visa extension and not worry about "the dirty details," to use Freddie's words.

Summer's only objection to working with Freddie was his chain-smoking. He sat at his desk in the interior office in a cloud of smoke. When she took the seat opposite Freddie, she waved her hands a few times to clear the air in front of her.

"Word has it that you turned up in the Women's Peace Camp in Greenham Common last month," Freddie began.

"I sang for them. What's wrong with that? I believe in peace. I don't think putting American cruise missiles on British soil is a good idea, do you?"

"Not particularly. But it's not a paying job."

"And whose fault is that?"

Freddie took a long drag on his cigarette. "Speaking of peace, I have a gig for you," he said. "It's different, but I think you should take it. Five glorious days in Prague, four shows. Late September, early October."

"Prague? As in Prague, Czechoslovakia?"

"The same. You've been invited by the Artists Committee for European Peace, which we can assume is backed by the government. Their director, a Mr. Sykora, is very excited about hosting you. They've reserved a small performance space—more of a coffeehouse setting. Your Women's Peace Camp appearance impressed them quite a bit. They particularly liked the idea of an American folk singer who believes in peace."

"And it's a paying job?"

"Neither of us will get rich off the concert," he said, then paused. "There's a lucrative side job involved."

"A side job? Courier work?"

"Something like that. I arranged the music gig, and a former colleague of mine has the side job. I worked with him long ago, but we've stayed in touch. This side job will pay quite handsomely."

"Handsomely? I'm more than interested. I'm excited."

"That's good," he said. "Let me make a phone call. I'd like you to meet my friend. He can fill you in on the other job."

Summer waited on the battered and stained couch in Freddie's office, leafing through old copies of *Time Out* magazine. Fifteen minutes later, the main door opened, revealing a tall, older man wearing a well-cut suit.

Freddie emerged from his office to introduce the man. "This is Mr. Jack Townsend," Freddie said. "He very much wanted to meet you."

"And who are you, Mr. Jack Townsend?" Summer asked.

"I'm a security consultant," he said, handing her a business card. Under his name—John Townsend—was his firm's name, Stonehenge Security, which had a Knightsbridge address. "Freddie and I worked together ages ago."

"Freddie told me that. Are you connected to the government?"

"Decidedly not. Strictly private sector."

"What's the job, then?"

He ignored her question. "Freddie tells me you've been part of the peace movement. Performed at the Greenham Common? Do you consider yourself political?"

"Not particularly," she said. "But I can't stand Margaret Thatcher. Or the Tories. Or those damn cruise missiles."

Townsend smiled. "My son agrees with you. I'm not concerned about any of that. In fact, it's a good thing that you're sympathetic to the peace movement. You should be well received in Prague." He turned to Freddie. "I believe the Czechs were quite happy to land the well-known folk singer and activist, Summer Devine, were they not?"

"Indeed, they were." Freddie gave Townsend a conspiratorial grin, and Summer wondered whether Jack Townsend had something to do with arranging the concerts.

"What is it that you want me to do?" she asked.

Townsend quickly described the situation for her. A young Englishwoman would be in Prague at the same time as Summer. She might need some help.

"You would be a courier, of sorts," he said. "This woman may need money and a passport, which you would pass along to her."

"Why?" Summer asked. "Why would she need a passport? Don't you need one to get into Czechoslovakia in the first place? The border police are particular about that, aren't they? Not just in Czechoslovakia. Everywhere."

"She may have lost hers."

Summer wrinkled her nose. "She *may have* lost hers. And you know that now. Weeks in advance. That's a bullshit story if I've ever heard one." She glanced over at Freddie, who wouldn't meet her eyes. "Okay, I'll play along. She's lost her passport."

"We're willing to pay a premium," Townsend said. "Considering that there's some risk involved."

"Risk? It sounds like it. Smuggling in a second passport. Tell me—what's the worst that can happen?"

"They could find the extra passport at the border. You could probably talk your way out of that. Once you're in the country, it's more complicated. In the worst case, an arrest, although I think the Czechs would think twice about that since you're an American citizen and they wouldn't want an incident. You'd be deported."

"Or they could throw me in jail."

"They might," he conceded. "Yet I doubt that highly."

She laughed. "It wouldn't be the first time."

He paused. "Will you do it? We're prepared to be quite generous."

"I'll do it," she said. "Why not? I could certainly use the money."

"Very good," Townsend said. "Freddie will handle the details. The extra payment." He took a file folder from this briefcase and opened it. He handed her several snapshots of a pretty dark-haired woman standing in front of a large Baroque statue of a saint holding a cross. The woman wore a wistful half-smile.

"This is her," Townsend said. "The woman you might give the spare passport to."

"Let me guess," Summer said. "The spare passport might have a different name than hers."

"Might it? Who knows? By the way, I'll join you for the trip to Germany, and we'll have you drive to Prague from there. I think a Volkswagen Beetle with a peace symbol would be fitting. If all goes well, you'll sing your songs and extend the hand of friendship to the people of Czechoslovakia and return none the worse for wear."

"And if it doesn't go well?"

"Then you'll become friends with the young lady in question. An instant friend." He smiled. "One other matter. I'll need your guitar for a day or two."

"My guitar?"

"We're going to affix the spare passport inside. Once you get to Prague, you can unstring the guitar and reach inside and retrieve the passport. Restring it, and you're on your way. No one the wiser."

"Why don't I just keep this spare in the back pocket of my jeans?"

"That would complicate matters if they decide to search you at the border. It's why you couldn't carry it in your luggage, either."

"What if they search my guitar at the border and find it?"

"If it happens, you'll tell them that you borrowed the guitar from your friend, Carol Jordan. That's the name on the passport. She's a fellow singer. Carol must have taped it there for safety and forgotten to retrieve it."

Summer grinned. "That's another bullshit story."

"Who is going to prove you wrong? Carol Jordan lives in Portsmouth. It says so on her passport."

"They're not stupid. They'll know something is up."

"But what? There's no connection they can make. You just have to stick to your story. I think you're more than capable of that."

"You mean that I can bullshit with the best of them?" she asked.

"I think you can think on your feet."

"And what is it I have to do?"

"You will need to visit the Charles Bridge at one o'clock on Monday. The young Englishwoman may be waiting for you there in front of the St. John the Baptist statue. If she's not, you go back the following day at one. There should be no need for you to go there on Wednesday unless you hear differently from Freddie. You'll make a collect call to him every morning from the Main Post Office." Townsend handed her a business card. "Memorize the number. You'll ask Freddie whether he's made any progress in setting up more shows for you. Anyone listening won't hear anything of importance."

"Who will be listening?"

"It's a Communist country. The police listen in on every long distance call."

"So what's the actual purpose of the call?"

It's a way to pass a message to you. 'Brighton' is the magic word. If Freddie uses it on Wednesday, then you need to go back to the Charles Bridge that afternoon at one o'clock, because the young woman will be there. If he doesn't, you should destroy the passport. Find a fireplace and burn it up. You finish your last show in Prague, and drive back."

"It seems too easy."

"There's a remote possibility we might ask you to do more."

"How remote?"

"Who can ever say? This is the last resort plan. She may need a lift back to Germany, in the Beetle."

"Why wouldn't she take a plane or a train?" Summer asked.

"It's best if she avoids the sort of scrutiny you get at the airport and at border control for the train."

"No scrutiny. I see. Is this woman a spook? A spy?"

"No, she's an antiques dealer. There's no connection to the government or the security agencies."

"That's the truth?"

"The truth. She's involved in a private operation. It may prove awkward for her to leave Czechoslovakia the way she came in. And it's best that you know nothing more about it. You just met at your show, and you offered her a ride to save her some money. If this should come to pass, you'll be generously rewarded. A thousand pounds." Hawes looked at Freddie. "Tax free."

* * *

Freddie confronted Hawes after Summer had left the office. He paced around, waving his hands, pausing only to puff on his cigarette, clearly upset.

"I'm going to ask you again," he said. "Are you acting on behalf of those heartless bastards at Century House?"

"I am not."

Freddie shook his head. "For the life of me, this smells like one of their operations. Have they subcontracted something unpleasant to you, Feliks?"

"I won't take offense at your suggesting that I'm a liar," Hawes said. "As I told you before, there's no connection to our former employer. Cross my heart."

"Your black heart." Freddie squinted at him through his tinted glasses. "She's a nice girl, Summer. The Divine Summer Devine. I wouldn't want her to get caught up in anything nasty. That wouldn't be fair to her, or to me. She's hustling to make ends meet to stay in Old Blighty."

"Summer's role in this is minor. Your role is minor."

"Answering the phone when she calls."

119

"Answering the phone. She'll ask if you've booked any shows for her. You tell her 'no,' you ask how she's enjoying herself, and get off the line. At some point I may ask you to tell her that you've arranged a concert in Brighton. That means the contingency plan has gone into effect."

"Where will you be during all this?"

"In Vienna. I'll call you from my hotel."

"I'll be very cross with you if Summer runs into any trouble." Freddie stubbed out his cigarette in his ashtray. "As I said, she's a nice girl."

"I can tell. Don't worry, I'll make sure she's prepared for anything that happens."

* * *

They met at the Naval and Military Club in Mayfair. Hawes and Tobias Kent had played squash racquets there for many years—Tobias, the former naval officer, held the membership and Hawes had been his frequent guest. Kent was a better player, and Hawes had struggled to win one game out of five. Their matches had ended when Hawes' heart issues had surfaced, and he had reluctantly obeyed his doctor's order to stop. While they didn't see each other as much, they had remained friends. Hawes liked Tobias, who, despite his stately country house and aristocratic background, didn't put on airs.

Hawes could imagine what Nigel would think of the Naval and

Military Club, known informally as the In and Out Club, with its leather chairs, oil paintings of military leaders, and a membership drawn from the upper ranks of the British establishment. The last gasp of Empire? Hardly, since there was no Empire left.

During one of their more heated political arguments, Nigel had attacked Hawes for what he had scornfully called his John Bull patriotism. "The bloody irony is that we're not truly English," Nigel said. "You're half Polish and I'm that and a bit more. We're never going to be fully accepted by the elites."

"Don't be absurd," Hawes had said. "We belong."

"I don't know why you would want to," Nigel said. "The class system is what's wrong with this country."

Hawes and Tobias took their drinks to the sitting room and found a quiet corner.

"I've taken on an assignment that involves one of my colleagues visiting Prague," Hawes said. "I wanted to get your thoughts on the situation there, from the Foreign Office perspective. What do you hear about the atmosphere there?"

"It's not Poland or Hungary," Tobias said. "We haven't seen any cracks in the ice. No Solidarity or goulash Communism. Husak is cut from the same cloth as Herr Honecker in the Deutsche Demokratische Republik. I'm sure they have statues of Stalin in storage, just in the hopes that somehow, some day, the old Georgian bastard will be rehabilitated."

"It's eased up some, though. Hasn't it?"

"I suppose for the average Czech it has, if he steers clear of politics. Stays quiet, keep your head down, mouth the proper pieties, and you're left alone. The government continues to harass anyone who signed Charter 77—the artists, writers, and assorted intellectuals. A fair number of them were encouraged to leave Czechoslovakia. It's been a lifetime since the Prague Spring."

"Hardly socialism with a human face."

Tobias grunted. "It was always a contradiction in terms."

"So Prague's not the most inviting place to do business."

"It depends on the business. They're starved for hard currency. You're not looking to go into the import/export business, are you? The Czechs are quite good at machinery, they say."

"No, we're providing security services for a new client. Been asking around, wanted to get the lay of the land."

"I hope you're being well paid for this," Tobias said.

"We are. Haven't worked in Prague before. The client is sensitive. Doesn't want to draw any attention from the local authorities."

"I can imagine," Tobias said. "Do let me know if there's anything we can do. The ambassador in Prague is a friend."

Hawes thanked him. "Appreciate the offer. Doubt we'll need the help, but you never know."

Nine

The night before her return to Vienna, Claire's sleep was interrupted by troubling dreams.

In one particularly vivid dream, soldiers in dark uniforms and snarling dogs pursued her through the narrow streets of Prague. The dogs, German shepherds, strained at their leashes as they barked and snapped at her, and she ran and ran, desperate to reach the rendezvous point in Wenceslas Square. To her horror, Claire couldn't remember how she was supposed to get there and she couldn't dare stop to read her map. She ran down a narrow, cobblestoned side street where she thought she might find Rafe. She knocked on door after door to no avail. More and more frantic, she hurried toward the end of the street, which to her horror she found to be a cul-de-sac with no exit. Suddenly a harsh spotlight caught her in its beam, blinding her. She tried to cover her eyes, gasping from the pain of the harsh light. Then, Claire woke with a start, her heart pounding. She scrambled out of bed and unable to go back to sleep, tried to calm herself with a cup of tea.

She knew perfectly well why her subconscious was acting up—she was anxious about the trip to Prague. It wasn't hard to imagine how things might go awry, and despite Townsend's assurances, she worried that something would go terribly wrong.

She told herself that it was natural to have the jitters. She had to trust Townsend—he was careful and experienced, and he seemed to have everything under control. She sat cross-legged on her hotel bed and reviewed the notes she had made in her last session with Townsend. Her role was very straightforward and she had to admire the simplicity of the plan. She was reminded of a phrase from a magazine article about Chinese antique furniture she once read: "simplicity is the ultimate sophistication." Townsend's simple plan had a certain sophistication about it; it recognized that the border officials were trained to compare passport photographs against passenger faces. When the face matched the photo, they were satisfied.

She believed that she was ready for the mission, as ready as she would ever be. (It was a mission, she had decided, because of their goal—helping a young woman gain her freedom.) Townsend had finally shared with her the first names of her contacts in Prague. In Wenceslas Square, she was to meet a young Hungarian woman named Piri, a student attending Charles University. If for any reason that rendezvous didn't happen, Claire was to make contact at one o'clock that afternoon at the Charles Bridge with a young American woman whose name was Summer. "No last names," Townsend said. "I'd rather than you not make Summer's acquaintance, but she'll be there Monday and Tuesday at the rendezvous spot."

"At the St. John the Baptist statue."

Townsend nodded. He explained that Summer would give Claire a doctored passport in the name of Carol Jordan and some additional cash. Claire could rent a hotel room for the night under her new identity. The next day, she could go to the embassy for her emergency passport. She should destroy the forged passport and head directly to the airport for her flight to London.

"We can send Summer to the bridge rendezvous on Wednesday if for some reason you can't get to the embassy," Townsend said. "And you can use the Carol Jordan passport to get out of the country." If it came to that, he continued, he had briefed Summer on what to do; she would be driving back to Germany and Claire could join her.

"It seems that you have thought of everything, Mr. Townsend," Claire said.

He shook his head. "I've learned from bitter experience that I haven't. Sadly, that's not possible. I could have overlooked something. With any luck, it won't matter. If it is consequential, you'll need to improvise. You strike me as having sound instincts. Follow them. Trust your instincts."

* * *

They retraced their steps from the first trip. The same train from Vienna to Prague. They sat facing forward, with Claire sitting by the window. She watched the countryside pass by, the fields of wheat and potatoes, small villages with their onion-domed churches, the occasional pond. Then, once in the city, the same hotel, the Jalta, situated in Wenceslas Square. The front desk clerk remembered them, as did the concierge. Rafe went out of his way to chat up the hotel staff, and Claire had to admire his cool. He gave no outward signs of nervousness.

They had two days to kill before D-Day, which is what Rafe had jokingly dubbed it, when she would hand her passport over to Tatiana Savchenko. She didn't think calling it D-Day was funny, and she told him that directly. He sulked for a few minutes after her rebuke. There was a disconcerting immaturity to Rafe, she had decided, a callowness that surfaced every so often. He was smooth and charming, but he was also flippant and impulsive. She tried not to show her annoyance with his childishness.

At least, it didn't seem the police were watching them this time. Claire saw no telltale signs of surveillance, no young men trailing them when they left the hotel. If they were being shadowed, she couldn't detect their followers. Did that mean they had played their parts well enough during their first trip to allay any suspicions?

She had one strange encounter at the hotel. A young Italian woman had approached Claire in the lobby as she was waiting for Rafe to join her. After introducing herself, she asked if Claire and Rafe would care to join her and her husband for dinner that night. "Seeing as we are both foreigners," she said in her heavily accented English. Claire thanked her but explained they had other plans. The woman, Flavia, persisted, wondering if they could meet for lunch. Claire remembered Townsend's warning and politely declined.

"I'm sorry," Claire told her. "Our schedule is so very tight. We're here on business, and we're booked solid all day long." She was thankful when Rafe appeared, and quickly excused herself, leading the way out of the Jalta.

Was she being overly suspicious? It seemed unlikely that the Italian woman was an informant for the Czech police, but how could you be sure? She and Rafe weren't there to make friends, and Townsend had warned them not to take anything, or anyone, at face value. It was better to be slightly paranoid under the circumstances.

That afternoon, they made the rounds of the antiques stores, buying an Art Deco vase from the shop on Na Prikope that Rafe would bring in his luggage and declare at customs. Townsend had insisted that Rafe carry back at least one purchase to validate the story that they were in Prague shopping for antiques.

"We want no loose ends," Townsend said. "You need to play your part as buyers looking for antiques."

"Why should it matter?" Rafe asked. "If your plan works, we'll be long gone."

"I'd rather that the Czechs and Russians stay in the dark," Townsend. "These are people with very long memories. You don't want Moscow Central to have a file with either of your names on it."

"As they do with you?"

Townsend didn't answer the question.

They returned to the store on Narodni Street to buy the jewel box and chest, and to arrange their shipment to a London address Singer gave them. Mr. Svoboda beamed with delight when Claire entered the store. She gave the envelope with the crowns for her purchase, and he quickly counted the bills. Rafe pocketed the receipt—more proof for his cover story.

Svoboda hummed as he began packing the jewel box and the chest, surrounding them with crumpled newspaper, in a large cardboard box. Claire watched as he worked, and he looked up and smiled at her. "These are beautiful pieces," he said and sighed. "The craftsmanship today is not as good. We have no one today like Franta Anyz."

"I said hello to Big Ben for you, Mr. Svoboda," she said.

"You are very kind to remember."

She realized Rafe wasn't standing there next to her. He had wandered to the front of the store, and she heard the sound of a conversation—Rafe talking with someone with a lowered voice. She wondered what he was doing—had he struck up a conversation with another customer?

She left Mr. Svoboda and went to the front of the store. A dark-haired man with a narrow face, quite handsome, was shaking hands with Rafe. He flashed her a glance and then left the shop and walked up Narodni Street without looking back. Rafe didn't say anything.

She waited until they were on the way back to the Jalta before she asked Rafe about the man in the store.

"Who was that?" she asked. "We're not supposed to do that."

"Do what?"

"Talk to strangers."

"Ah, but he's not a stranger. It was my cousin, Jan. I asked him to meet me at the store."

"Was that wise?"

"Wise? No one saw us." Rafe shrugged. "If anything goes wrong tomorrow, we may need Jan. You may need him." He handed her a piece of paper with an address on it.

"What am I to do with this?"

"It's Jan's address, my love. If you run into trouble after I'm gone, he'll do what he can. Find you a place to hide until you can get to the embassy. He's willing to help."

"Does Mr. Townsend know about this?"

"This has nothing to do with Townsend. I arranged this on my own. I've explained the situation to Jan. You can trust him."

"And you don't think I can trust the contacts Mr. Townsend arranged?"

Rafe shrugged. "Who knows? Whoever they are, they'll be doing it for the money. That won't be the case with Jan. He's family. And he hates the regime. He has good reason to. They've made his life difficult." He paused. "Townsend isn't omniscient, after all. He doesn't know what's going on here. It's been more than thirty years since he was last in Prague. That doesn't raise my confidence level about any arrangements he may have made."

"He seems to know what he's doing," she said. Claire didn't want to quarrel with Rafe. She had confidence in Townsend. He was a stickler for detail, with every step of the operation choreographed. Rafe bridled at being told what to do and arranging to meet with his cousin was a way of asserting his independence.

"He's a confident old bastard, I'll give him that. But keep Jan's name and address, just in case. He lives in Smichov, on the other side of the river. The neighborhood is a bit gritty. It's best known for the brewery there, where they make Staropramen beer. Not a bad place to hide out—it's not exactly a tourist hotspot. It's your call as to whether you contact him. He's seen you, so if you show up at his doorstep he'll recognize you immediately. I told him that you'd be staying behind for a day and that you might need his help."

"Was that wise?"

"I thought so, or I wouldn't have involved him. You're the one staying behind. I didn't want you left high and dry."

"Thank you," she said.

"Think nothing of it," Rafe said. "If all goes well, you'll miss your blind date with Jan. But if you need help, he's a clever lad. He has lots of friends and connections in the city." He paused. "Have you played Monopoly? Think of Jan as your 'Get Out of Jail Free' card."

"That's hardly a comforting thought." She paused. "If the worst comes to pass, and I need his help, wouldn't that compromise him terribly? Cause him great trouble? That is, if the police find out?"

"Don't worry about that. Jan will make sure they don't find out. He'll keep you off the radar. Remember, he's a Czech. He's no hopeless romantic." Rafe looked at his watch. "This adventure of ours will be over and done twelve hours from now. My part, at least. I've never liked the idea of you staying behind. I wish that Townsend had a way to bring you out at the same time as me."

She shook her head. "I'll be fine. You're the one with the difficult task. You have to get past the gatekeepers, the customs officials and the border guards."

"I'll be careful," he said. "My friends claim I have a silver tongue, that I can talk my way out of any tight spot. But I have a good feeling about this. I think your double and I will sail through border control. They'll never know what hit them."

Ten

They took an early morning British Airways flight to Munich. Summer kept her guitar by her side, refusing to check it in as baggage when they reached the gate at Heathrow. "I'm on my way to play in a concert or two, and I'm superstitious," she explained to the woman taking her ticket at the counter. "It's my lucky guitar, and if you don't mind, I don't want to let it out of my sight."

As they waited to board the plane, Hawes spotted smirks on the faces of several of the male passengers sitting near them—they mistook them for a couple, a randy old man and his hippie girlfriend on a getaway to Germany. They were wrong, of course, and not for the first time Hawes considered the natural human tendency to make assumptions, to jump to conclusions, on the flimsiest of evidence. He did it himself, and he knew how easy it was to get things wrong.

Summer must have sensed the same thing, and she had fun with it, flirting with Hawes, looping her arm in his as they walked on the tarmac to the plane.

"I hope they're properly jealous of you," she told Hawes. "Young girlfriend. They're going to torture themselves wondering what we get up to in the bedroom."

"I'm flattered that you'd even include me in that fantasy," he told her. "I'm a bit worn around the edges, wouldn't you say? Thirty years too old for a young 'un like you."

"You can pass for fifty, Mr. Jack Townsend," she said. "If that is actually your name."

"It's the name on my ticket."

She laughed. "I should know better than to expect a direct answer."

"That was a direct answer. As direct as you're going to get."

They checked into the Eden Hotel Wolff on Arnulfstrasse near Munich's central train station, and Hawes encouraged Summer to relax in her room while he ran some errands. He had a busy afternoon in front of him. It took him visits to three used car dealers before he found what he was looking for—a 1976 Volkswagen Beetle. He paid in cash and drove the vehicle to a parking lot near the hotel. He painted a peace symbol on the side of the Beetle. Then, he had Summer spend the rest of the afternoon practicing driving the car. She proved to be a quick study, explaining that a high school boyfriend had taught her how to drive a stick shift, "among other things," a line she delivered with a mischievous grin.

"You've done well," he said. "Your reward will be a fancy dinner."

He waited for her in the lobby and was surprised when she turned up in a demure blue dress with her hair tied back. She gave him a mock curtsy and laughed when he bowed in return.

They took a cab to the Halali restaurant, near the Englischer Garten, a more formal place with dark paneling and antlers on the walls.

Summer wanted traditional Bavarian food, so they had Leberknödelsuppe, liver dumpling soup; Weisswürste, boiled, white veal sausage; sauerkraut; and mugs of Helles, a pale lager.

Over dinner, she peppered Hawes with questions in between bites of her meal and sips of her beer.

"Do you like what you do?" she asked. "Your job? The security work?"

"I imagine it's like any job," he said. "There are satisfying moments and frustrating ones."

"And do you think you make a difference? A positive difference?"

"I do. These days, one aspect of my job is to keep people safe from harm."

"Rich people."

He nodded. "For the most part, yes. They have something to lose, after all, and there are others who want to take from them. Violently. We live in a fallen world, after all."

"I wish that we didn't. It doesn't have to be so."

"Wouldn't that be lovely? That would be Utopia, and Utopia is the Greek word for 'nowhere.' We haven't advanced far enough along that evolutionary ladder to eliminate our violent natures."

She shook her head. "That's too gloomy a view of the world for me. I'd like to think we can do better. Peace. Justice. Harmony."

"In my experience, many of those who call most loudly for peace and justice are more interested in power. They think they can construct a better world, a world of their liking, but they discover their fellow humans can be intractable. Then, the Utopians turn to force and God save you if you don't fall into line."

"That's too cynical for me," she said. "I think most people are drawn to the light. Want the light."

Hawes remained silent. He took a long drink from his mug. There was no point in arguing with her. He didn't consider himself a cynic; he saw much that was good in the world, but he also knew how quickly that world could slide into violence and barbarism, into a place with torture chambers and concentration camps. He admired the civility and ordered peace of his life in England, and he knew "this precious stone set in the silver sea" was worth fighting for—and for most of his adult life, he had. As he grew older, it had become a matter of pride for him.

"How did you become Mr. Jack Townsend, security consultant?" she asked.

"I began by serving King and country ages ago in His Majesty's Commandos. After the war, I was recruited for government intelligence work. Then, about twenty years ago, I left to work for a private company. Better pay, better hours, a happier wife. And we had Nigel, my son. Put up my own shingle ten years later, and I haven't looked back since." He looked over at her. "And you? How does one become a folk singer?"

"You have to love to sing," Summer said. "And to perform. It's a hard way to make a living, but I can't imagine doing anything else. I don't think I would be happy."

"Freddie tells me you're no prima donna. You're willing to take gigs some of his other singers won't. Off the beaten path."

"Like Greenham Common, where I didn't even get paid. What do you think of the protests?"

Hawes shook his head. "I think they should be demonstrating in front of the Russian embassy in London, not at an American airbase. If the Soviets hadn't placed SS-20s in East Germany and Poland, there'd be no need for the Pershings in the West."

"So they're always the bad guys? Won't you concede that we share some of the blame?"

"You sound like my son."

"He agrees with me on this?" Summer asked, surprised.

"Nigel has bought the Labor Party manifesto, lock, stock, and barrel. We try not to talk about it because we're so far apart on the issues." Hawes drank some more of his lager. "He doesn't believe me when I tell him that the KGB is financing the peace movement, just as they're bankrolling these terrorist groups like the Red Brigades. The people who are attracted to the demonstrations sincerely want peace, but they're being manipulated."

"I'll bet your son doesn't take well to this lecture."

"Am I lecturing?"

"Yes, Jack Townsend, you are."

"I'm sure Nigel would agree with you. Not that we've had that discussion. We're not close."

"Are you estranged?" she asked.

"We're polite. Nigel always had a rebellious streak. And our politics are miles apart."

"What about his mother? Your wife?"

"We lost Anna when he was seventeen. I didn't handle it well, and that seemed to push him farther away. I'm to blame. I was rough on him, didn't let him grieve the way he wanted to."

"I'm sorry about your loss."

Hawes nodded. "Thank you. It's something you have to adjust to, although it never feels quite right. Anna and I had a good life together." He stopped, lost in memories. She remained silent until he glanced over at her.

"That's something," she said. "Something good."

"What about your parents?" he asked.

"They're happy as clams living in Akron, Ohio. My father is retired, and my mother works at the local hospital. We're not close. They don't understand me. Never have. I think differently than they do. I didn't take the path all my friends did, getting married and popping out kids right and left. Instead, I ran for it. No regrets about that. I picked a different life, and I thank my lucky stars that I did. What do they say—better to burn than rust?"

"I would think it would be better to do neither."

* * *

On the drive to Nuremberg the next day, Hawes reviewed in detail what he needed Summer to do. He warned her that she would be watched by informants during her stay in Prague and that she should be especially wary of any young Czechs who offered to get high with her—it might very well be an attempt by the secret police to compromise her. Smoking marijuana was a crime in Czechoslovakia, as many Western backpackers had discovered to their dismay.

"From the start, let your hosts know how much you love wandering around a new city," he said. "Walking around by yourself, without a guide. You may be trailed the first few times, but you should be able to spot your followers."

She was to pass by the rendezvous point on Charles Bridge, the statue of St. John the Baptist, at one o'clock on Monday and Tuesday, in the event that Claire, the young Englishwoman, needed help. "It's on the north side of the bridge," he explained. "The good saint is holding a cross and pointing toward Castle Hill. You can't miss him. Hold your pocketbook or bag in your right hand to indicate that you're not being followed. When the young woman arrives, you should find a place to pass along the money and the passport. You'll be able to recognize her from the photo I'm going to give you."

In the mornings, Summer was to stop at the Main Post Office and call Freddie for possible instructions. If he mentioned a gig in Brighton, it meant that Summer had to visit the bridge on Wednesday. "Brighton is the magic word," Hawes told her. "Stay alert if you hear it."

"How do I know that the police won't be there waiting for the two of us?"

"There's no way to eliminate all risk from this. If you're detained, scream bloody murder and insist on your rights as an American. A peace-loving American."

"I can do that."

"There's the possibility that Claire may need to come with you on your drive to Germany."

"No problem," Summer said. "I'm cool with that. It's a boring drive, and I could use some company."

"The odds are that will never happen," Hawes said. "What's likely? You'll make two trips to the bridge, but Claire won't need your help. She'll have already left Prague. If that's the case, destroy the passport. Lock yourself in a bathroom and tear it up, or burn it. There's no need for you to bring it back with you."

"And the money?"

"You can keep it, an advance on your payment."

"Cool," she said. "This is all cool. I feel like one of the Bond girls."

He smiled. Hawes had grown to like Summer, her off-beat sense of humor, her openness, and her distinctly American confidence and fearlessness. There was a toughness to her that he admired, and yet a vulnerability that softened her edge. He could see why Freddie was so protective of her.

Hawes glanced up at the road sign. They were only ten kilometers from Nuremberg.

"Have you ever killed anyone?" she asked suddenly, not taking her eyes off the highway in front of her.

"I suspect that only an American would ask a stranger a question like that."

"We're not strangers. Not really."

He didn't respond, and she didn't repeat the question. A few minutes later, he spoke. "The answer is yes. During the war, when I was a young man, in the Commandos. Then, later, again when I was in the field and I was left with no choice. I did what I had to do." He paused. "I don't care to talk about it."

"Does it bother you?"

He frowned. "I had to choose. Them or me. I don't apologize for choosing as I did. I don't dwell on it. What's the point?"

She didn't say anything for a long time. Then, as they reached the city outskirts, she spoke.

"You should call him," she said. "Your son. Tell him that you love him. I know that isn't very British, but you should tell him."

"It isn't very British, you're right."

"You should try it. That stiff upper lip thing isn't healthy. I'll bet your son would welcome hearing that you care for him. However you want to phrase it. And don't lecture him about anything."

He was amused by her certainty, that this young woman would offer advice about his personal life—as if she could have any insight into his relationship with his son. She didn't know the history, but that didn't matter. She was very American in that, convinced that "love" and "openness" could heal any rift.

"I'll consider it," he said.

"Please do," she said.

He had her drop him off in front of the Grand Hotel, in the center of the city, where he would take a taxi to the airport and catch a flight to Vienna. Before he left the car, she surprised him by kissing him quickly on the cheek. Hawes got out of the Volkswagen and stood by the rolled-down passenger window. "You should have enough petrol to make it all the way to Prague," he told her. "Keep an eye on the oil gauge."

"Wish me luck, Jack Townsend," she said and gave him a wave before she pulled out abruptly into the street, nearly colliding with a passing Mercedes sedan and eliciting an angry double beep from its driver.

* * *

Near Waidhaus on the German side, Summer passed through border control without incident. She joined the line of vehicles crossing into Czechoslovakia. She smiled at the guards and strummed her guitar, playing a bit of the Beatles' "We Can Work it Out," singing the chorus softly. She could see them staring at her in what she imagined was a mixture of desire and caution. Here was this long-haired blonde American hippie chick in blue jeans and a peasant blouse—the antithesis of the modest socialist female, and yet so alluring. Or so Summer thought.

She showed the border official the letter of invitation from the Artists Committee for European Peace, signed by its artistic director, one Anton Sykora, and he nodded while examining her passport and visa. She breathed a sigh of relief once he had waved her through.

She passed through the village of Rozvadov and found her way to E50, the highway to Prague. It was a lovely day, with no clouds in an azure sky, and she sang to herself as she enjoyed the rural landscape on either side of the road. Some ten kilometers from the border, she slowed for a checkpoint on the highway. The border guards were searching several cars that were headed in the other direction toward West Germany. It took only a few minutes for them to glance over Summer's passport and send her on her way.

Ugly, Soviet-style concrete apartment buildings began to appear as she reached the outskirts of Prague. She was pleased when she reached the historic center city, with its mix of Gothic and Baroque architectural styles, and spired churches. It took twenty minutes for her to find a parking space near the address she had been given. She decided it would be safe to leave the Volkswagen there.

Anton Sykora, her contact with the Artists Committee for European Peace, proved to be a middle-aged man with slumping shoulders, thinning brown hair, and a smile marred by discolored teeth. His office was plastered with posters announcing concerts, with doves and peace signs on many of them.

He greeted her warmly, giving her a hug and kisses on both cheeks, as if they were French. He smiled and told her how happy the Committee was to host her shows. "You will get a good crowd," he said. "We have a very nice performance space near the University."

There was a knock at the door. Anton opened it to a young woman with curly brown hair and wire-rimmed glasses. His demeanor immediately changed—he introduced the woman as Marjeta Nosek, who had volunteered to act as Summer's guide during her visit.

Summer didn't like the look of Marjeta, who was all smiles, praising Summer in accented English for her efforts on behalf of peace. Anton had said that while he was employed by the Ministry of Culture, Miss Nosek had been assigned by the Interior Ministry to act as Summer's guide. Summer assumed that meant Nosek answered to the secret police.

Marjeta dug into a brown briefcase and presented Summer with a detailed schedule for her visit. Summer laughed and handed it back to her, explaining that she was too much of a free spirit for schedules and agendas.

"It's a lot cooler if I hang around with your young people," Summer said. "People-to-people. That's why I'm here, isn't it? That's the idea behind detente, right? It's cooler that way."

"Cooler?" Marjeta asked, confused.

"Better. It would be a lot better if I got to know your peace activists. That's how we're going to achieve peace, isn't it? Keep the American cruise missiles out of Western Europe. Get all the missiles and bombs out."

"You're an American, aren't you?"

"We're not all cowboys like Reagan," Summer said. "Or cowgirls. Many of us want peaceful coexistence."

"Miss Nosek has a full schedule planned for you," Anton said. "A chance to see Prague. All the sights."

"Thank you," Summer replied. "But I'll skip the tour for now. I like walking around, learning a new city, by myself."

"That may disappoint Miss Nosek," Anton said, and Summer couldn't help but wonder if he secretly enjoyed the thought of her disappointment. It seemed he had been on guard ever since she appeared.

"Let me get to know the city, first. Then Marjeta can show me the special places that tourists don't know about."

"If you wish," Marjeta said.

"I promise not to get into too much trouble," Summer said. "I won't end up in jail or skinny dipping in the Vltava." She smiled, but neither Anton nor Marjeta smiled back.

"What does skinny dipping mean?" Marjeta asked.

"Swimming in the nude," Summer said, trying not to laugh out loud. "But don't worry, I won't."

She decided she would go for a long walk through the city, by herself, before dinner and her first performance that night. Then, she would call Freddie in the morning, and do some more wandering around Prague, making sure to cross over the Charles Bridge at one o'clock. She would take her guitar with her, slung over her shoulder on her cotton and leather guitar strap, so she would have the passport for Claire, ready to hand over, although she had her doubts—based on what Jack Townsend had told her—that the rendezvous would ever happen.

Eleven

On the morning of the exchange, Claire could barely stomach her breakfast. She made the mistake of drinking two cups of black coffee, which made her even more jittery and anxious. Rafe didn't seem worried at all; he attacked his food with gusto, wolfing down two plates of scrambled eggs and eating all of the buttered toast brought to their table. Like the last meal of a condemned man, Claire thought. She quickly retreated to her hotel room and found herself on her knees in front of the toilet, vomiting up the little she had eaten. After washing her hands and face, she packed her bag.

When she knocked on Rafe's door down the corridor, she found him ready to leave. They took the lift down to the lobby. Rafe was particularly charming at the front desk as they checked out, joking and flirting with the young clerk, and he made small talk on the brief cab ride from the Jalta to the central train station. Claire didn't know how he could be so nonchalant. Her mouth had gone dry and she could feel her heart pounding. It was too late to turn back, now. They had to see it through; they had arrived at the turning point of their mission, but she had a sudden moment of doubt. What if something went wrong? Wouldn't it better if the Russian woman didn't turn up, and she and Rafe boarded the train to return to Vienna? Then

147

it wouldn't be their fault. She felt vaguely ashamed by her train of thought. Where was her courage?

She closed her eyes, trying to calm herself. It was so simple, what she had to do. Claire clutched her handbag, the handbag with her passport tucked inside, a passport she was about to hand to a complete stranger. How long would that, and exchanging coats, take? Two minutes? She could get through that, couldn't she?

They arrived at the central station thirty minutes before the departure time for the train to Vienna. Once inside the station, they waited by the ticket window in the departure hall. Claire checked her watch twice. Townsend had instructed her to go to the women's lavatory with fifteen minutes to spare before the posted time for the Vienna train. That would shorten the time that Rafe and Tatiana would spend in the open.

Rafe touched her arm. "It's time," he said. "Good luck, Claire. Quickly, now."

She took a deep breath and made her way toward the women's restroom, her heart racing again. She opened the door slowly and stepped inside. A slim woman in a dark coat, her hair covered by a scarf, stood by the sink, gazing into the mirror. Claire walked over to check the three stalls—they were empty. A bit of luck. They wouldn't have to execute the exchange with the complication of potential witnesses.

Claire turned and went to the sink and stood next to the woman. It was strange to see Tatiana's face in the mirror next to her, the eerie resemblance. Singer and Townsend had been right—this stranger would be able to pass for Claire. Her face was slightly narrower, and she had more lines around her eyes, but she could have been Claire's sister. Most importantly, her looks matched Claire's passport photo.

They stood at the sink, frozen, for a long moment, and then the woman sighed. Claire wondered what she was thinking? Had she been startled by the likeness between them? Claire couldn't tell.

"We must do this quickly," Claire said to her. She reached into her pocketbook, found her passport, and passed it to the woman. "Your new name is Claire," she said. "Claire Markham. That's the name in the passport. That's me."

The woman nodded. "Claire Markham," she repeated. "May God bless you for doing this."

"Your coat and scarf," Claire said. "We must switch." She worried that any moment someone might barge in on them. Claire shrugged off her coat, and Tatiana followed her lead.

"Rafe is waiting for you," Claire said. "He's in a brown coat, near the ticket window."

"Thank you," she said, squeezing Claire's hand, and then she was gone.

Claire fiddled with Tatiana's scarf, arranging it so it covered her hair in the way the Russian woman had worn it. She checked herself twice in the mirror and then took a deep breath. When she walked back into the departure hall, who would be waiting for her? The Czech secret police? Would they have already arrested Rafe and Tatiana? Or would she be free to go, to make her way to Wenceslas Square where she was to meet her contact?

The door to the lavatory swung open, startling Claire, and an elderly woman crossed over to the bathroom stall, went inside, and locked the door. Claire waited a minute before she moved to leave, stepping out into the station. She felt herself tensing—she looked around quickly. If she was going to be arrested, this was the moment when the police would detain her—at least that was the scene she had imagined numerous times over the past few days. Her hands were shaking slightly, and she jammed them in her coat pockets. The men and women hurrying across the hall to catch their trains ignored her. She exhaled. Now, she was supposed to walk to the far exit, taking her time. She wondered if anyone had watched Tatiana enter the bathroom.

Claire crossed the departure hall and reached the exit. No police whistles, no calls for her to stop, as she had imagined and dreaded. Once outside the station, she walked through the park, veering to the left to head toward Wenceslas Square. She told herself not to walk too quickly, to keep to the pace of the people near her. She could feel her heart pounding rapidly again. She stopped halfway to the square and ducked into a doorway and waited to see if anyone was following her. An elderly lady in dark clothing passed by, but no one else. She resumed her walk, her heartbeat and breathing closer to normal.

She felt a sense of exhilaration. Her part of the plan had come off so smoothly. Why had she worried so much? Claire wished she had been able to stay and watch the train for Vienna leave with Rafe and Tatiana Savchenko aboard. She looked around, enjoying the sunshine, the sight of the buildings bathed in the afternoon light. Now all she had to do was to meet her contact, the woman named Piri. She approached the end of Washingtonova Street, the National

Museum to her left, the statue of Saint Wenceslas on his massive horse ahead of her.

She checked her watch—she was right on time. Would Piri be as punctual? Townsend had told Claire that she could wait by the statue for more than fifteen minutes without drawing attention because it was a popular meeting place—he explained when the locals said "Let's meet by the horse," everyone understood it meant the Wenceslas statue. After the initial fifteen minutes, she was to walk away and then return in thirty minutes. If Piri didn't show up, Claire was to make her way to Charles Bridge for the one o'clock rendezvous. She walked over to the base of the statue, suddenly feeling vulnerable and exposed. Claire looked up at the face of the famed warrior with his upright lance, the stone pedestal surrounded by the statues of four Czech patron saints. She remembered singing the Christmas carol "Good King Wenceslas" when she was a child. What a strange time to have that memory triggered, she thought. She heard a rumbling sound and turned to find two red trams with cream-colored roofs rolling down the sloping tracks of the Square. A moment later, a well-dressed young woman approached her, a snapshot in her gloved hand. She excused herself in English.

"Claire?" she asked. "Is that you? I'm Piri. Your new friend."

Claire nodded, and the woman handed her the photo—it was of Claire by the statue. She let the woman guide her away from the Square, toward the north. "All is well," the woman said in her accented English. "I'll take your arm." She paused and looked Claire up and down for a long moment. "Nice shoes, nice bag," she said. "The coat is something else. Doesn't match. Where did you get it?"

151

Her comments were so unexpected that Claire burst out laughing. "I borrowed the coat," she managed.

"I would hope so."

Piri kept talking, going on about her last trip to London and the nice clothes she had bought, and Claire smiled at the incongruity of the conversation. She saw a police officer in uniform walking toward them, and she told herself to relax. He ignored them as they passed by, and Claire felt a sense of relief.

"Where are we going?" she asked.

"My place. This man Townsend said you would stay with me for one night. We'll go to my flat in Zizkov. It's out of the way. Very small, but you won't be there for long."

Claire wondered what the woman thought of the story Townsend had told her. Did she suspect something else might be going on? Did Piri care, or was she only concerned whether she would get paid? Townsend had coached Claire to be polite and vague about her situation, offering few details, and turning the conversation to other topics.

"I'm a student at the University," Piri said. "Just back from a brief trip to London."

"You're allowed to travel?"

"I'm Hungarian, not Czech or Slovak. We're able to travel to the West. I've been to Paris and London." She paused. "It's been easier to get a visa from the government of late."

"What else did Mr. Townsend tell you?"

"Tomorrow I'm to walk with you halfway to the British embassy. It's on the other side of the river. I don't need to know any more. It's best that way. It's an easy way to make some money."

"How do you know Mr. Townsend?"

Piri frowned. "Through a Hungarian man in London, who introduced me to him. Townsend asked me for this favor, and he offered to pay me." She shrugged. "That's the story."

They walked for twenty minutes, winding their way through narrow streets, encountering fewer and fewer pedestrians. Piri's neighborhood in Zizkov was run-down, filled with cracked sidewalks and aging buildings with paint peeling from their facades. Her building was in the middle of the block. The glass on one of the windows on the ground floor had been replaced with plywood.

With Piri leading the way, they climbed three flights of stairs to reach her flat. She fiddled with her key in the lock, cursing until it opened. "The damn thing sticks," she said.

Inside, there was a cramped kitchen, a table and chairs, and a small open area with a couch. Through a door left ajar, Claire could see an unmade bed and, on the wall, a poster of Budapest.

"You can sleep on the couch," Piri said. "The bathroom is down the hall. Make sure you lock the door. My neighbor, Pavel, is a bit of a pig and may barge in. Townsend said you should stay inside. We'll have our dinner here. I must go to class tomorrow morning, so you will be alone until lunchtime. After lunch, we'll start the walk to the embassy."

"I understand," Claire said.

"You're very pretty," Piri said. "I can believe that a man might be very jealous about you."

"I don't want to talk about that. I want to put it behind me. The sooner I can leave, the better." Townsend had warned Claire about discussing her cover story at any length. She should stick to the broad outline—she was escaping from a possessive, controlling boyfriend with powerful friends in official circles.

"I had a boyfriend like that once. Very jealous. He wanted to run my life, to know where I was going, who I was talking to. All the time. He was convinced I was cheating on him. I wasn't. When I broke it off, I was worried. My father contacted the police, and they went and talked to him, made sure my ex-boyfriend didn't ever bother me again."

"I'm sorry you had to go through that."

"What can I say?" Piri made a wry face. "I had bad luck with that one. I didn't know any better. Now, I know what to look for in a man. But don't worry. Your boyfriend won't find you here. You can depend upon that." She looked around the flat. "Who would look for you in this dump? If anyone asks, you're my distant cousin visiting from London. Pavel the Pig speaks some English and if he sees you, he will try to chat you up. He's the only one who might bother you."

"I want to thank you for what you are doing," Claire said. "I appreciate it."

"I hope your Mr. Townsend appreciates it," she said and smiled. "He's the one paying for it, after all."

Twelve

Hawes had never been in the Franz Joseph Station before, but he didn't care for its sterile modern design. The original Ringstrasse-style station had been knocked down and rebuilt eight years before, and there was nothing distinctive or attractive about its replacement. Having Claire and Rafe travel via the older, less direct route from Vienna to Prague had been a deliberate choice on Hawes' part. He figured there would be less scrutiny along the way. The alternative, traveling through Breclav, which was an important railway junction as well as a border control point, seemed riskier even if the winding Franz Joseph route added an hour or so of travel time.

He tried to control his anxiety, pacing back and forth on the platform where the Prague train would arrive, a cup of coffee in a paper cup in his hand. Hawes had one operation end in failure in Vienna, many years before, and he worried that history would repeat itself, even if he knew that his fear was irrational.

He checked his watch. The train from Prague was due in five minutes. He looked over and spotted Benjamin Singer, accompanied by two dark-haired younger men, athletic and alert. Hawes recognized the type: they had to be Mossad, or former Mossad, there to guard Miss Savchenko when she arrived.

Singer nodded to him and came over. "They should be here soon," he said. "Not to jinx it, but I fully expect them to be on this train. Your plan was sound."

Hawes didn't respond. He knew better than to assume anything. Rafe and the Russian woman might very well be cooling their heels under guard in Prague. Or they could have been detained in Ceske Velenice. Or everything could have gone smoothly. He had learned to wait and see.

In the distance, he caught the sight of the headlamps on the train, still quite far from the station. He felt his chest tighten. He tried to breathe slowly, to relieve the sudden pressure he was feeling in his chest. Hawes reached into his pocket to find his pill box; he decided to wait on taking his medication.

He reflexively stepped back as the train came to a stop, brakes squealing. When the doors opened, Hawes scanned the first passengers coming off, watching for Rafe. He spotted him disembarking from the fourth carriage, followed by a slim young woman. Rafe had a suitcase in each hand.

"There they are," Singer said. "We're home free."

He followed Hawes as they moved to greet Rafe, who gave them a smile and a nod. He dropped the suitcases and shook Hawes' hand and then Singer's. Tatiana Savchenko stood behind him.

Hawes stepped forward so she could see him. "I'm pleased to meet you," he said in Russian and introduced himself. "We've been waiting anxiously."

"Thank you," she said in heavily accented English. "I am happy to be here." She looked over at Rafe. "Thank you for what you have done."

"Mr. Singer is most responsible for us being here," Rafe said, motioning toward Singer. "He has arranged for your trip to Israel."

"We have a private plane waiting for you," Singer said, smiling.

"So soon?" she asked, surprised.

"No reason to wait. You'll be in Tel Aviv within a few hours."

Hawes was pleased with the news—the sooner Tatiana Savchenko left Vienna, the better.

"I believe Mr. Singer and his friends will take over from here," Rafe said to her, and she nodded.

She thanked Rafe and Hawes again, and Singer took her by the arm and led her toward the exit from the platform. The two young dark-haired men took up flanking positions. Hawes could see that they had been well-trained, and he felt a sense of relief. One less thing to worry about.

"Any problems at Ceske Velenice?" Hawes asked Rafe.

"They waved us through," Rafe replied. "Tatiana kept a handkerchief to her nose and mouth and coughed a lot. I handed the border control official Claire's passport, and he gave the photo a quick glance. No questions. I think perhaps he recognized us from when we passed through the last time. Of course, it wasn't the same bird, but he didn't know that."

"You left Claire at the train station in Prague?"

"She went into the loo. Last I saw her. Tatiana came out in her place, wearing Claire's coat. I couldn't tell the difference between them at first glance. It worked like a charm, the substitution. Quite clever."

"It won't be that clever until we have Claire on this side of the border."

"When will that be?"

"Tomorrow night. She has a seat reserved on the last British Airways flight to London."

"She never hesitated, not for a moment. I wasn't sure she was up to it, but she came through with flying colors."

"I never doubted her."

"No," Rafe said with a slight smile. "You doubted me."

"I did, somewhat," Hawes said. "Viktor was sure you would be fine. And you've handled yourself well. Quite well."

"I did some acting at university. If you can imagine yourself as this other character, you can convince others that you're who you say you are. So I imagined myself as Rafael Klima, worldly guide and veteran translator. Nothing to hide. Bored by the inspection of papers."

"How about Miss Savchenko?"

"I don't think we exchanged twenty words. We only talked when we were alone because I didn't want anyone to hear her accent. She seemed very withdrawn, but you'd expect that. I'll give her credit—it takes courage to make a bolt for it, the way she did."

"Let's head back to the hotel," Hawes said. "I'll buy you a drink."

"I could use one. Perhaps more than one."

* * *

After a quick beer in the bar of the Hotel Imperial, Hawes went to his room to make some phone calls. With Tatiana delivered to Singer, the most difficult part of his plan had been completed. He had worried that she might have been followed to the Prague train station and that she and Claire and Rafe would have been taken into custody right then and there. That hadn't happened. And the border crossing, where Tatiana could have been questioned and exposed, had been successfully navigated.

Now, all that was left was Claire collecting her passport at the embassy and then taking the night flight to London along with the other Western tourists and businessmen.

Sometimes your luck held up—this might be one of those times. The Russians and the StB might not figure out what had happened for some time, or might never connect Rafe and Claire to the disappearance of Tatiana Savchenko. Perhaps some functionary in the Interior Ministry might note that a woman named Markham—a common English surname—had left Czechoslovakia from two different places within two days. That was assuming they were comparing the records—the Czechs weren't Germans, after all, and they weren't particularly compulsive about paperwork. He had heard the stories about how the Stasi handled passport checks, employing a yardstick to measure those few East Germans allowed to leave the country to make sure that it matched the height listed in their passports.

Hawes was ready to shut down the contingency plan. He would call Freddie early tomorrow—Freddie could tell Summer not to visit the Charles Bridge that afternoon. She could finish her shows in Prague as folk singer, peace activist, and goodwill ambassador, and return to West Germany with no one the wiser. He would meet her in Nuremberg, sell the Volkswagen Beetle, and they would fly back to London together.

He had one other task to complete. He placed a long distance call to Tobias Kent's direct line in the Foreign Office and waited until his friend picked up. Hawes got straight to the point. "I was hoping you could help me, Toby," he began. "I have a colleague of mine in Prague who has lost her passport. Stolen handbag. She'll need temporary papers. She knows to go to the embassy, but I think I'd rest easier if I knew she had someone there who would expedite the process."

"Prague? You took the assignment, then?"

"I'm a businessman, now, Toby. If that's where the client needs us, there's where we go. My associates, that is."

"What's her name?"

"Claire Markham. She'll drop by the embassy tomorrow, in the afternoon. Would that give you time to arrange things?"

"I'll alert them pronto," he said. "She'll be welcomed with open arms."

Hawes thanked him. "I owe you dinner," he said. "When I'm back in London."

"Where are you?"

"Vienna."

"Have a cup of coffee and a Sachertorte for me. I'll take care of this post-haste."

* * *

Singer had summoned Esther to Vienna from the New Exodus Project offices in Tel Aviv two days before, so she could fly back to Israel with Tatiana Savchenko. Esther had emigrated from Moscow four years earlier, and Singer thought she would be a sympathetic presence for Tatiana, a Russian-speaker who could put her at ease.

When he reached the Israeli embassy, Singer found Dov waiting for him, and he greeted Singer with a bear hug. "Great news," Dov said. "The plan worked perfectly."

"Our end of it did," Singer said. "She'll arrive tonight. Private jet to Ben Gurion."

"What is she going to do for papers?"

"One of our passports. After all, that's the point of the whole thing, isn't it?" Singer studied Dov for a long moment. "And your end of this, the exchange of information?"

"Her father agreed to give us what we requested once we informed him of her arrival in Vienna. We've done that, as per the agreement with him. We're taking photographs of his documents and we'll have the microfilm here within hours. Once it's in Tel Aviv, our scientific people can review the technical details. Military intelligence will vet the strategic information."

"A shame we couldn't bring him out, too."

"Savchenko understood the situation. He's watched too closely. Getting the girl out was the key. With his daughter in Israel, she can't be persecuted for what he's done."

"But he can be persecuted."

Dov shrugged. "That's assuming that they figure out that he traded information for his daughter's freedom."

"If we're lucky, the Russians won't realize that she's with us, not for some time." Singer said. "Tuck her away in the Upper Galilee for a time, give her a new identity. Wait until the dust settles. Then you can bring her to Tel Aviv or Jerusalem."

"Even if the KGB puts the puzzle together, there's not much they can do," Dov said. "Savchenko understood the risks. Then, there's the cancer. He has a year, maybe less. There's not much you can threaten a man with when his time on earth is quite limited."

"There's only one loose end," Singer said. "The Englishwoman. She flies to London tomorrow night. Once she's safe and sound, we can declare victory."

Dov shook his head. "That's incidental. The victory comes when the microfilm arrives."

* * *

A golden light suffused the streets of Vienna in the early morning. After a light breakfast, Hawes took a long walk through the Stadtpark, which was near the Hotel Imperial, stopping to admire the Italian Renaissance exterior of the Kursalon, the famous music hall. He had one more day in the city, and then it was off to Nuremberg to wait for Summer's return.

He was reading the morning papers in his hotel room, struggling with some of the German words, when the phone rang. It was an out-of-breath Rafe.

"Turn on the television," he said. "There's something you need to see. I can't believe it. Tatiana Savchenko is on the news."

"What?"

Hawes hung up and flipped through the channels on his television until, aghast, he found the image of Tatiana Savchenko on the screen. She stood at a lectern next to a handsome man in a blue suit. An American flag pin adorned the lapel of the man's suit. Journalists called out questions, and she appeared to be confused by the noise and commotion.

The man in the blue suit looked directly at the camera, raising his hand to stop the questioning, and spoke into the microphone. "I challenge the Soviet Union to release all of the other Jews who want to emigrate to Israel," he said. "Set them all free. There is a home waiting for them here, where they can live in freedom and worship openly. Prove that you will abide by the Helsinki Convention and international law. Prove you believe in human rights and deserve a place among civilized nations."

One of the journalists interrupted. "Congressman Stephens, we've learned that Miss Savchenko escaped through Vienna, using a false identity. A passport in a different name. Is that so? Was there American involvement in her defection?"

The man in the blue suit turned to Tatiana, but she shook her head, unwilling to reply. "My government was not involved," he said. "The New Exodus Project, a private foundation, organized it, arranged for her to escape Prague on a train to Vienna. As to the passport, let's just say she didn't use her Russian one. Everyone involved should be applauded for this daring rescue."

A younger woman stepped forward to the microphone. "Thank you, Congressman," she said in accented English and then paused. "Miss Savchenko is very happy to have reached Israel. She asks that you respect her privacy, and she will not be answering any further questions at this time."

The screen was filled with the bland face of the news anchor, who promised more details about the defection when they were forthcoming. Hawes shook his head in disbelief. Why would Benjamin Singer and the New Exodus Project have allowed the news conference? The Soviets would never forgive or forget. Hawes was perplexed—Tatiana Savchenko wasn't a public figure, a well-known dissident. What could the Israelis hope to gain by publicizing her defection?

Then the phone rang, and Hawes was surprised to hear Singer's voice on the line, asking to meet him in the lobby. Hawes took the elevator to the lobby floor, ready to confront Singer over what he had just seen.

"What the bloody hell is going on?" he asked an embarrassed Singer.

Singer shook his head slowly. "I'm sorry," he said.

"How could you let that politician reveal details about the operation? Claire is still in Prague. It won't take the Russians long to figure out how we did it."

"I didn't have a say in the matter. Once they reached Tel Aviv, it was out of my hands. The Congressman spoke out of turn about the passport. He never should have been given any details. He acted on his own."

"On his own? He had the girl by his side at the news conference. Your people let him stand her there and be photographed. A daring escape by train to Vienna. An assumed identity. A flight to freedom. That's rubbing their nose in it."

"They were supposed to wait," Singer said. "The announcement was scheduled for next week, but Congressman Stephens leaves for the States tomorrow. Having him present at the news conference ensured that the American networks would cover the story."

"Why him?" Hawes asked.

"He's well-connected. Well-liked."

"Does he just happen to be on the committee that approves military aid for Israel? You make him look good, and the payback is funding?"

"He's a friend. And he does care about religious freedom."

"And that justifies leaving Claire to twist in the wind?"

"I was blindsided on this. They didn't tell me."

"How convenient." Hawes cursed. "What an utter mess. Prague will be crawling with angry KGB officers. They're not stupid. They'll be looking to make arrests. This not only puts Claire in danger but also may compromise the people in Prague helping her."

"How soon can you get her out?"

"I don't know. She was supposed to get her passport this afternoon, then fly out tonight. Now I don't know if it's safe for her traveling under her own name, thanks to your pet Congressman. They know Tatiana came out by train. It'll be child's play to review the paperwork and surface Claire's name."

"What can I do to help? Do you need funds?"

"You could hand me a million pounds sterling and it wouldn't matter. There is a contingency plan, another way for her to leave the country, but it doesn't matter if State Security finds her first. I'll make some calls, see what I can find out."

"I'm sorry."

"You should be. If it goes wrong now, you're to blame. You and the arrogant bastards in Tel Aviv."

Thirteen

Claire woke to sunlight streaming through the one small window of Piri's flat and illuminating the wooden floor by the couch. She rose and washed her hands and face in the sink, combed the tangles out of her hair, and dried off with a bedraggled towel. A glance at her watch told her that she had slept later than usual.

The flat was empty—Piri must have left for school. Claire sat at the kitchen table, suddenly hungry. She had been too nervous to eat much of the goulash Piri had served for dinner, and her stomach growled softly in protest. She hoped Piri would return soon with lunch.

She had been elated yesterday by the success of the exchange, but now she only felt tired. She was eager to get her emergency passport and fly back to London.

She heard the key turning in the lock and stood up. The door opened to reveal Piri, who walked into the flat and placed a bag of groceries by the kitchen. She rummaged in the pockets of her coat and found a package of cigarettes. She lit one and took a long drag, and turned to Claire.

"There is very strange news this morning," she said. "A friend of mine, another student, heard on the BBC that a Russian woman, a dissident, had escaped from Prague by train and is now in Israel. There was a news conference in Tel Aviv and this defector was introduced by an American congressman who said she fooled the border police by traveling under an assumed identity. A false passport." She paused. "The woman's name is Tatiana Savchenko."

Claire didn't respond, but she could feel her hands begin to tremble. She quickly jammed them into the pockets of her pants. For a long moment, they stared at each other.

"The police came to the University today," Piri said. "They took some of the students for questioning, the Jewish students that are known to be political. My friend said they are suspected of helping this Russian woman, but I don't believe that. It had to be the CIA. And the Zionists."

"I wouldn't know. I'm definitely *not* political."

"You're an American," Piri said, her tone hostile. "Like this Congressman. Like the CIA."

"I'm British."

"But you said that you live in New York." She took a long drag on her cigarette. "I don't believe in coincidences. I'm asked to hide you for a night on the very day that this woman defects. Is it just by chance? What should I think?"

"I have nothing to do with any of this. Nothing. It's absurd for you to think so."

"Why are you so anxious?" Piri asked, blowing out a cloud of cigarette smoke. "What do you know about this?"

"Nothing," Claire said. "It has nothing to do with me."

"I don't believe you. I thought from the start that there was something wrong about this. This man Townsend lied to me. I should never have let you stay here. Do you know what they will do to you if you're involved? What they will do to me?"

"I'm not involved," she said weakly.

Piri snorted in derision. "You would say that even if you were mixed up in it."

Claire stood up. "I can't prove a negative, but I'm not a spy. I don't work for the CIA. This is absurd. I'm here because of an insanely jealous man."

"What is his name? This lover of yours."

"Georg. Mr. Townsend was hired by my parents to help me get away from him. Georg took my passport when we began living together. That's why I need to get to the British embassy for an emergency passport so I can leave."

"Why didn't you just go directly to your embassy? Why stay here with me? Your story makes no sense."

"Georg has powerful friends in the government. Mr. Townsend wanted me someplace where he couldn't find me." Her explanation was flimsy and unconvincing, Claire knew, but she hadn't expected to have to mount a prolonged defense of her cover story.

Piri studied her. "This is not what they told me was the job."

"But it is. You agreed to help. You were paid. I'll leave now, if you like."

"Not until I have a conversation with this man Townsend," she said. "I have his phone number in London. I'll need to be paid more. Stay here. Don't go out. I'll be back in an hour or so."

"Where are you going?"

"I have a friend with a phone in her house. I can call Townsend from there."

"I'm feeling cooped up," Claire said. "I want to go out."

"You can, once I've talked to Townsend." Piri reached into the bag and placed a loaf of bread and some cheese on the kitchen table. "Here is lunch." She waved at the stove. "Make yourself tea. I will return."

After she had left the flat, slamming the door behind her, Claire made herself a cup of tea and nibbled some of the bread and cheese. She was worried and confused. She had assumed the entire operation would be kept secret, and Townsend had never said anything about publicizing Tatiana's escape. When Piri had confronted her with the news of the defection, had Claire's reaction, her hands trembling, betrayed her?

What had she gotten herself into? What had been so thrilling yesterday, almost a lark, had become something dark and frightening. Would the police connect her with Tatiana's defection? At some point, she thought that they might. Could they be looking for her already? Would Townsend give Piri instructions on what to do when she called him? Would he ask Claire to connect with her other contact, the woman who would rendezvous with her on the Charles Bridge?

She could feel herself becoming more and more anxious. Her mouth had gone dry, and she felt an urge to urinate—she went to the bathroom down the hall and relieved herself. She looked in the streaked mirror, finding a pale face staring back at her. She rubbed some rouge into her cheeks and smoothed her hair with her hands.

Back in Piri's modest flat, she felt an overwhelming urge to leave, to get outside, to walk around in the fresh air. She wouldn't go far; she would stay in the neighborhood, keep the scarf over her hair, and avoid other people. She took her handbag with her, and closed the door to the flat, leaving it unlocked, realizing that Piri hadn't left her with a key. Claire didn't expect to be gone for long, and she doubted anyone would make the long climb to the top floor while she was out.

* * *

Claire felt better once she was on the street. She adjusted the scarf to fully cover her hair, and she hid her eyes behind her sunglasses. Wearing Tatiana's shapeless gray coat would help her fit in. She walked slowly around the block, breathing deeply. It helped her to calm down. All was not lost, she told herself. There was nothing concrete to connect her to Tatiana's defection. Piri had her suspicions, but no proof. Claire could still go to the British embassy later that afternoon as planned and get her emergency passport. Then, as planned, she would purchase a small suitcase and some clothing—slacks and a few blouses—before she took a taxicab to the airport. If she was going to play the part of the innocent tourist returning to Britain, it would help to arrive at the gate with some luggage.

It was quiet in the neighborhood; most of its working class residents were away at their jobs. Was it Rafe or Townsend who had told her that even Praguers of retirement age continued to work? As she started walking back up the street, a dark sedan drove past her at a high speed and pulled up in front of Piri's apartment building. Two men jumped out of the vehicle, followed by a brown-haired woman. The woman waved toward the front door of the building, and one of the men, quite fit in his dark clothing, nodded his head. He called out to the other man, and they entered the building. Claire stopped, shocked, when she realized that the woman was Piri.

She removed her sunglasses, wondering for a brief moment whether she was mistaken. But when she looked again, she could see that it was indeed Piri. Claire realized that she had been betrayed—Piri had lied about going to telephone Townsend and instead had gone to the police. Claire was dismayed at how quickly Piri had decided to turn on her.

She turned on her heel and walked down the street in the opposite direction, careful not to draw attention to herself by picking up her pace. She needed to put as much distance as she possibly could before the police discovered she was not upstairs in the flat. Within minutes, they would be searching the nearby streets.

She took a sharp left and began to walk faster, fighting the urge to run. At the end of the street, she saw there was a small church facing a park with several benches and overhanging trees. Could either offer her a hiding place? She knew she had to make a choice, and found herself pulling the front door to the church and entering. It was dark inside, with a lingering smell of incense. She glanced around: a baptismal font at the back of the church, an altar with a crucifix at the front, a statue of the Virgin Mary to the far right. The pews were empty. She was alone.

She made her way to the far left side of the church and found a place behind a pillar that couldn't be seen from the front door. She sat there, hunched over, and waited. She heard the sounds of a car engine and then the squeal of brakes. A minute later, the sound of the church's door being opened. She crouched down behind the pillar, holding her breath, feeling the sweat run down her back.

She heard male voices, followed by the sound of boots on the floor. Someone was walking up the center aisle. She slumped to the floor, convinced that she was moments away from being found and arrested. From the front of the church, voices now in conversation, followed by deep laughter, and the entrance door opening and closing. Then, silence.

She sat on the floor for thirty minutes, not moving. Was it safe to leave? What if the police were waiting for her outside? Had she waited long enough? She couldn't stay there for too much longer, she told herself. Someone might come into the church and find her. She made her way to the church entrance, where she stood in front of the door, not yet willing to leave. She finally summoned up enough courage to push it open and step into the street.

She kept moving, her anxiety rising, heading south from Zizkov.

Should she go to the British embassy? Throw herself on the mercy of the diplomats there? But Piri knew Claire planned to go there, and what if she had told the police? They would be waiting for her. Claire checked her watch; it was ten minutes after four. She had missed the rendezvous at Charles Bridge by three hours, so she would have to wait until tomorrow. But how?

She walked through the narrow, cobblestone streets of Old Town in a daze. What was she to do? How could this have happened? In her worst nightmare, she could not have imagined the events of the last few hours. The announcement of Tatiana's defection. Her betrayal by Piri. Claire had been lucky to avoid arrest. If she hadn't gone outside for a walk, she would have been caught when Piri returned with the police.

She wondered why the news of Tatiana's escape had been broadcast to the world. Would Benjamin Singer or Jack Townsend have agreed to the news conference in Tel Aviv before Claire was safely out of the country? She couldn't believe that. Was it possible that they had been manipulated? That neither man knew what had been planned for Tatiana after she reached Israel? And who did Singer answer to? She had found Townsend to be sincere, thoughtful, but how much leverage did he have? She had too many questions without answers.

Townsend had told her to trust her instincts—and her instincts told her that she needed to find an out-of-the-way place to hide, a place to stay that night. There would be no help until the following afternoon when she could go to the Charles Bridge for the next scheduled rendezvous.

Without papers, she couldn't check into a hotel. That left Rafe's cousin. She rummaged through her handbag and found the piece of paper with his address. She consulted her fold-up map. Smichov was south of Mala Strana, the Lesser Town, on the other side of the river. She wouldn't risk taking a bus or tram, nor finding a cab. She had a long walk in front of her.

Fourteen

Hawes had learned some hard lessons in the past about dealing with a sudden crisis in the field. What mattered was how quickly you figured out what was happening on the ground. Fashioning a response depended on what you knew, on the quantity and quality of your information, and Hawes desperately needed to collect whatever intelligence he could about Claire Markham and the situation in Prague.

He was hampered because he couldn't tap into the resources of a larger organization like the SIS. He had designed the operation to keep communication to and from Rafe and Claire to a minimum, recognizing that international telephone calls and telegrams were closely monitored by the Czechs.

He felt a twinge of pain in the center of his chest. He took a nitro tablet from his bottle and washed the medicine down with a full glass of cold water from the hotel bathroom sink. He would be under stress for the next few days, and he couldn't afford to be distracted by chest pain.

He checked his watch—it was four o'clock. There was no avoiding what he had to do. He decided he would start with Tobias Kent. He dialed his number and his friend answered on the third ring. Hawes apologized for calling on what was a minor matter and then asked Tobias if he had heard whether Claire Markham had turned up at the embassy in Prague.

"Not a word," Tobias said. "I made it clear to the chaps there that they were to call me immediately when she did, and then I had planned to call your secretary. Charlotte, isn't it?"

"Yes, it's Charlotte. Would you mind giving them a ring? Just to double-check?"

"Haven't you heard from her, Feliks?"

"She's been out of touch."

There was a long silence. "Is there anything that I should know about?"

"Not at this juncture." Hawes found he was gripping the phone receiver so tightly that his knuckles had turned white. "Doing business there has proven to be a bit more challenging than I had anticipated."

"I don't want to be surprised, Feliks."

"No surprises."

"I would imagine that it's a bit tense there at the moment. In Prague. The defection of that Russian woman, the one they paraded out in Tel Aviv before the cameras with that American politician must have certainly ruffled some feathers. She came through Vienna, didn't she? This hasn't affected your associate, has it?"

Hawes wasn't going to lie to Tobias, but he had to be careful in what he said. "You're spot on. It's possible Miss Markham has been caught up in an overreaction by the Czechs. The authorities will be looking for someone to blame. But I don't know what's happening there."

"I don't suppose you're going to tell me what she's been up to."

"I'd rather not. The client is a bit sensitive about his business dealings."

"I see. A sensitive client. Aren't they all?"

"If you could call me if you hear anything," Hawes said.

"Will do. I must say, however, I hope that you have matters under control. The Czechs aren't the most friendly chaps when it comes to us. A fair number of them remember how Neville sold them out to Adolf. Can't blame them for that."

Hawes waited a long moment before thanking Tobias and ending the call.

He didn't like having to evade Tobias' questions, but if he told him the truth, he would lose control of the situation. Tobias would have no choice but to alert others in the Foreign Office, and the proper course of action would be to bring in MI6. Hawes didn't want that, nor, he believed, did Tobias.

What had happened? Why hadn't Claire made it to the embassy? Had the Czechs taken Piri and Claire into custody? Claire would have no way to get out of the country until she made contact with Summer Devine.

His next steps weren't clear. Should he pull Summer out of Prague? In the worst case, the Czechs had arrested Claire, and they might have pressured her into telling them about the rendezvous on the Charles Bridge. They would be waiting for Summer by the statue of St. John the Baptist, and things would go from bad to worse. But there could be other explanations for why Claire hadn't shown up at the embassy. For all he knew, she had already connected with Summer, collected the Carol Jordan passport, and was on her way out of the country. The passport would pass muster at the border—Hawes had purchased it from Abraham Beckleman, a man considered the best in the business when it came to forging documents. Beckleman had charged a premium because Hawes had insisted on an original British passport altered with Claire's photograph.

Hawes reached Freddie North an hour later, after phoning his office twice and his home once. "Looks like we're going to need Summer's help," Hawes told him. "When she calls tomorrow morning, you need to ask her if she is available for a folk show in Brighton. It's vital that you say the word 'Brighton.' Do you understand?"

"I do. As long as you're not getting my girl in over her head. You aren't, are you? That wouldn't be cricket."

"She took the money with her eyes wide open. I prepared her for several different scenarios. One has come up. It's what happens, Freddie. For Christ's sake, you know the game."

"I don't like this, at all. She's not properly trained for whatever you're asking her to do."

"She's a natural. She can think on her feet. I gave her a full briefing before she crossed into Czechoslovakia. She knows what to do."

"I don't like it," Freddie replied.

"It's important what she's doing, Freddie. There's someone else involved, who needs help. Summer is her best bet at this point. It may be nothing more than a simple hand-off. She'll be fine." He understood Freddie's concern—anytime you operated behind the Iron Curtain, there was danger. The security forces in the satellite nations weren't any less vicious than they had been in the late 1950s and 1960s. Some of the regimes had relaxed their hold on average citizens, but when it came to the twilight world of espionage, there was no forgiveness.

"I'll pass along your message. I must say, I hope you have this under control."

"I wouldn't turn to her if I didn't have to. I'm out of alternatives. Call me here at the hotel as soon as you've delivered the message." He gave Freddie his room number.

"This better be worth it," Freddie said. "Because it seems to me that you're asking a lot of her. More than you should."

* * *

Hawes ate dinner by himself in the hotel dining room. He decided not to invite Rafe to join him because Hawes didn't want to answer the questions he knew he'd be asked. So he sat by himself, drinking beer and picking at his Tafelspitz and fried potatoes, and brooding over the turn of events.

He had made what appeared, in retrospect, to be a troubling mistake. He should have found a way to get Claire out of Czechoslovakia on the same day that Rafe crossed the border with Tatiana. Hindsight was twenty/twenty, he told himself, but he also knew it was easy to come up with excuses for his failure.

His initial plan had been sound, with none of the stupid mistakes that he had seen doom operations in the past. Everyone had played their part to perfection. But he had been completely surprised by the news conference in Israel.

When Hawes returned to his room, he poured himself a scotch from the honor bar and sipped it slowly, thinking about his next moves.

He called the Danube and asked for Viktor. He heard the jukebox in the background playing a Frank Sinatra song, and then his friend came on the phone.

"Good news?" Viktor asked.

"Some. A largely successful job."

"How did Rafe do?"

"He came through with flying colors."

"I'm glad to hear that."

"There have been some complications. Have you watched the news?"

"Not the last few days."

"There's been a bit of excitement. A news conference in Tel Aviv announcing a clever defection of one Tatiana Savchenko. A daring escape by train from Prague."

"My God." The line went silent for a long moment. "What were the stupid buggers thinking?"

"According to Singer, they decided there was a great benefit in having an American politician pose for pictures with Tatiana, despite the potential for damage."

"Has there been damage?" Viktor asked.

"Our friend from New York hasn't checked in."

"I see. A cause for worry."

"Yes, a cause for worry. Perhaps you'd like to join me here. Two hands are always better than one. Charlotte can arrange for a ticket on a flight tomorrow morning."

"Whatever I can do, Feliks. I'll get there as fast as I can."

Hawes thanked him and hung up the phone. He had no idea what he might encounter in the next few days, or what he might need to do. He knew that he could trust Viktor. His friend was tough and clever. If Claire had avoided arrest, their task was simple. How could they give her a fighting chance to make it out of Czechoslovakia before the security apparatus closed in on her? Every minute counted, and it was up to Hawes and his friend to find a solution, however makeshift, before time ran out.

Part Two

Fifteen

Sergei Mikhailovich Baranov's day began without complication. He drove his freshly washed two-door Zhiguli sedan carefully through light traffic out past the Moscow ring road to the Village. With the driver's window down, he enjoyed the balmy autumn weather and the sunlight cascading onto the pine and birch trees of the nearby woods. Once past the gate, he glanced over at the shining glass headquarters of the First Chief Directorate, again silently appreciating the elegance of its Scandinavian design, so unlike the unsightly concrete buildings that were found throughout the city.

He felt a surge of pride as he walked into the building. He had come a long way to earn his spot at Yasenevo in Special Services, Counterintelligence. As a man who started at the Committee for State Security, the KGB, without family connections, without influential friends, he had climbed to his present position through a willingness to work harder and longer than his colleagues.

He spent the early morning working on paperwork, and he was surprised when he was summoned to General Lebedev's office just before lunch. Baranov felt no anxiety—he had no reason to be rattled by the summons—but the meeting was curious. He had little contact with Lebedev of late; he had been occupied for weeks with routine matters and had done nothing to merit praise or criticism.

Within moments of entering his superior's office, Baranov could tell that the General was in a bad mood. He waved impatiently at Baranov to sit down in the chair in front of his desk. Lebedev fiddled with a file in front of him, cleared his throat, and began speaking.

"We have a problem of some magnitude, Colonel Baranov," he said, pursing his lips. "It comes at an unfortunate time. As you know, we're under attack because of the incident with the Korean plane. We're blamed, yet it happened because of the provocation of the American stooges. All we did was to defend our territorial integrity."

Baranov nodded. The downing of Korean Air Lines Flight 007 by a Soviet fighter jet on the first day of September, with the loss of 269 passengers, had been denounced by the United States and other Western nations. Because of the civilian deaths, Moscow had faced widespread condemnation—unfairly, in the opinion of everyone at Yasenevo and of Baranov's friends. Hadn't the Korean pilots ignored warnings that they were in Soviet airspace? And it was more than likely that KAL 007 was on a spy mission—the Americans had been probing the air defenses of military sites in the Kamchatka Peninsula and Sakhalin Island for years.

Lebedev was upset, his face flushed with anger. "And now another aggression, one designed to further embarrass us. A scheme by the Zionists. It's not enough that the Jews whine and complain about their precious so-called human rights. Our Jews are treated like any Soviet citizen, no better and no worse, but they always want more."

Baranov kept quiet and waited for Lebedev to continue. Had the

General brought him to his office to rant about the Jews? That couldn't be it—there had to be another reason.

Lebedev opened the file and glanced at its contents for a moment, grimacing. "Do you know who Professor Ivan Savchenko is?"

"I do not, sir."

"He's one of our leading physicists. Last week he traveled to Prague for consultations with other scientists, accompanied by his daughter, Tatiana. His security detail was led by Molchalin, the incompetent Molchalin. A few days after he arrives in Czechoslovakia, his daughter disappears into thin air. And where do you think she reappears?"

"I don't know."

"Israel. She appears in Tel Aviv at a news conference on television this morning. The *zhyd* paraded her around in public, with an American politician, one of their congressmen, gloating over it, claiming that she had fled repression. It is a humiliation."

Baranov shifted uneasily in his chair. He sensed that he was about to become entangled in this mess, the kind of disastrous assignment that derailed careers.

"As you can imagine, we have many questions to answer. Many questions. That's why I called you here today, Sergei Mikhailovich. You will go to Prague. You will find out what happened. Assess the failure in security. Find the subversive elements in Prague who helped the Zionists. Find whoever else is responsible. They must be dealt with harshly. The full weight of the law. Do you understand?"

"I do." Baranov did indeed understand. He did not want this assignment, but he knew better than to protest. He immediately understood Lebedev's maneuver: if the General failed to clean up the mess for Moscow Center, Baranov would become the fall guy, the sacrificial lamb for the Department. He was expendable—never in the inner circle of Department K, tolerated but not welcomed.

"You're the right man for the job." Lebedev smiled, his anger diminished for the moment. "You read and speak Czech according to your file."

"I can get by," he conceded.

"They say you think several moves ahead at the chessboard. That skill should serve you well in this case."

Baranov remained silent. He did not doubt that it would be part of Lebedev's defense if he failed: "See, we put our cleverest man on the case. For whatever reason, he wasn't clever enough." Baranov knew his colleagues considered him an annoying intellectual, and that he was mocked behind his back as the Grandmaster.

"Where is Professor Savchenko?" he asked. "I would like to interview him, if that is possible."

"That will not be necessary." Lebedev closed the file folder he had been fiddling with and handed it to Baranov. "He has been interrogated already. He claims ignorance. Knew his daughter was unhappy, but never imagined that she would defect, and certainly not to the Zionists. You will see from his statement that he is not being truthful nor particularly cooperative."

"Perhaps he can be encouraged to cooperate?"

"I thought that, too. But he is a sick man. Cancer. The doctors say he has six months, at best. It gives us little leverage. What does a prison sentence mean to a man so near death? He already has his sentence. He dies in the prison infirmary, instead of a hospital." Lebedev's face hardened. "The file includes his statement and that of Molchalin, the fool in charge of Savchenko's security. You will learn little from them. You will find the truth of the matter only in Prague. You must leave for there immediately. The trail grows colder every minute, and I'm convinced that some of those behind this outrage are still there. The Jews who helped. Perhaps others. A conspiracy has conspirators. I'm counting on you, Colonel, to hunt them down and bring them to justice. Is that clear?"

"It's clear, General."

"This Department has a reputation to defend," he said. "I'm relying on you to uphold it by producing results, and doing so rapidly and ruthlessly. Report your progress to me. Only to me. Review the file I've given you and then leave for Prague." He looked at his watch. "You should reach Prague late this afternoon. Voronin, the second-in-command at the *rezidentura* there, has been alerted to your arrival. There is no time to waste."

* * *

Back at his desk, Baranov reviewed the folder Lebedev had given him. It contained brief statements from Professor Savchenko, Georgi Molchalin, head of the security team assigned to guard the professor, and Oleg Voronin, the KGB's second-in-command in Prague.

Savchenko claimed his daughter had been sick over the weekend with headaches and nausea. When he had returned to the hotel on Monday at lunch, she was missing from her room. He was surprised but thought that she might have been feeling well enough to go sightseeing on her own. When she hadn't returned by dinnertime, his concern grew. Finally, later in the evening, he had alerted Molchalin.

In his statement, Molchalin claimed that he had no reason to suspect anything was amiss. He and his team had focused on protecting the professor, and while they had kept an eye on the daughter, there had been no directive to keep her under constant watch. Once informed of Tatiana Savchenko's disappearance, he had his team begin looking for her in the vicinity of the International Hotel, where they were staying, and had asked Voronin at the embassy to alert the StB to be on the lookout for her.

Baranov could imagine the frantic search that ensued, but by then, Tatiana Savchenko was long gone. Her father had been lying, of course, covering for his daughter. He claimed she was happy, that she would have no reason to defect. But she had, and he was complicit.

Colonel Voronin, the KGB liaison with the StB, claimed that there had been no unusual activity by any of the hostile foreign intelligence officers in Prague. Nor had informants connected to the dissidents and other subversives reported anything out of the ordinary.

The incompetence of the men assigned to watch Professor Ivan Savchenko and his daughter, and the bumbling of the Czech intelligence officers, was clear. Molchalin had been too respectful; he should have demanded that a doctor attend to Tatiana Savchenko once she was reported ill.

If Molchalin was lucky, his failure meant a demotion and assignment to some Godforsaken post in Siberia. If his failings were deemed more serious, Molchalin would be cashiered. He would struggle to find work. The comfortable flat, the car, the holidays to Crimea, all gone. His wife would leave him. It was better than the old days, of course, when his punishment would have been a pistol shot to the head.

Baranov turned back to the file and read Savchenko's statement again. His story was absurd on its face—he had to have known what his daughter was planning. But why would the Zionists bother to smuggle Tatiana Savchenko out of Czechoslovakia? For propaganda purposes? For a news conference with an American politician? No, Baranov suspected the payback involved the father, and what he could tell the Zionists about the Soviet nuclear program. The tradeoff seemed obvious, and no doubt it was why General Lebedev didn't want any further investigation of Savchenko, at least not by Baranov. A connection between the defection and the passing of nuclear secrets would represent a failure of such magnitude that it would end careers at the most senior levels. No one at Yasenevo, or at the main State Security headquarters in Dzerzhinsky Square, wanted that.

He looked up to find his colleague Fedorov watching him from his desk across the office. Fedorov gave him a slight nod. Baranov wondered whether he knew about the assignment to Prague. Fedorov was one of the friendlier co-workers.

Baranov had never been popular in the Department. He was different. He knew about the nicknames. *Satan Eyes. The Grandmaster. Professor Baranov.* He wasn't one of the boys. Considered aloof and standoffish. A reluctant drinker. He spent too much time reading, borrowing books from the library. Too much time training with the weights in the gymnasium. A stickler for the rules. He knew what they said about him, and he didn't care.

Since he was a child, his eyes had been a problem—one blue, one gray. It was a genetic anomaly, heterochromia, one he shared with Alexander the Great, one observed and described by Aristotle. For the ignorant or superstitious, though, it was seen as something sinister. He remembered how, as a child, he had heard the whispers about Stalin, and his webbed left foot, the mark of the devil.

He ignored the rumors, that he hid a Jewish background (not true, as far as Baranov knew), that his father was a prominent member of the Party (also false), that Baranov didn't know how to go along to get along (true, an impediment to his career prospects). He had little patience with office politics. Nor did he care for the strong-arm tactics of the gorillas of Department K, those officers who seemed to enjoy solving problems violently.

Why did he stay? He had asked himself that question almost from the start of his time in State Security, and the answer was simple. He had grown up poor, without connections, without a Party bigwig as a father (Mikhail Baranov had been a tailor) and Sergei Baranov decided that he would not follow him into an early grave because of too much cheap vodka, too many unfiltered cigarettes, and grinding overwork. When he was a child, his teachers had noted that he had a head for numbers and that he showed considerable skill at chess.

Baranov loved the clarity he found in the sixty-four squares of the chessboard. He had studied the moves of the Russian masters—Mikhail Botvinnik, Yefim Geller, Mikhail Tal, Viktor Korchnoi, Garry Kasparov—and the eccentric American Bobby Fischer. Baranov had closely followed the match between Fischer and

Boris Spassky in Iceland in 1972 when Fischer's victory had surprised the chess world.

He had excelled in his studies at Moscow State. When he was encouraged by one of his professors to apply for a job at the Ministry of the Interior, Baranov had taken his advice. To his surprise, he had been chosen for State Security, and he hadn't regretted that decision. Until today.

On the other hand, he could make his name with this case. Roll up the network that engineered Tatiana Savchenko's defection, and he would be State Security's Man of the Hour, destined for promotion, for a luxury car and a dacha and the other perquisites that came with moving up in the organization.

Baranov had a starting point, thanks to the American congressman and his boasting during the news conference. Tatiana Savchenko had taken the train from Prague to Vienna, and she must have come in contact with numerous people en route. Then, there were the border guards and customs officials. Someone would remember something. If he could establish the identity Tatiana had employed to leave, he could work backward, figure out who in Prague had helped her.

He found his notebook and began to write down the questions that needed answering. After he had filled two pages, he went through and read them slowly. He fought against the temptation to arrive at any initial conclusions. It appeared to be a Mossad operation, but was it? General Lebedev assumed that it was the Zionists. True, the Jews were crafty and clannish, but did the small circle of Jews who remained in Prague help in her defection? Were the Americans involved? He would know soon enough—or at least he believed that he would.

Baranov glanced at his watch. It was time to leave for the airport. He shoved the folder into his leather briefcase, a gift from his uncle, waved goodbye to Fedorov and headed to the parking lot.

He felt a growing sense of confidence. General Lebedev's implicit judgment was correct—Sergei Baranov *was* the smartest officer in the Department. Now, he would prove it.

Sixteen

By the time Claire had crossed the Vltava River by way of the Palacky Bridge, it was nearing twilight. She picked up her pace; she needed to reach Jan Klima's place before the sun had set. She couldn't afford to be blundering around in the dark, looking for his address.

As she made her way, Claire had been careful not to make eye contact with any of the men and women she passed by. She kept her scarf on, hiding her hair, hoping to blend in. If she could have made herself invisible, she would have. It seemed to be working—she had been ignored by everyone she encountered on her way. And she hadn't spotted any uniformed police.

When she reached the outskirts of Smichov, she stepped into a doorway and quickly checked her map. She still had further to go, perhaps a mile or so. The surrounding buildings had the same run-down, worn-out feel of those in Piri's neighborhood. As she walked down a narrow side street, two boys and a girl kicked a soccer ball, crying out in excitement as they played. An old man shuffled past her, a newspaper tucked under his arm. A moment later, she experienced the sweet malty smell of the Staropramen brewery, which was a few blocks away, as it wafted by her.

The light was beginning to fail as she reached Ostrovskeho Street, which according to her map would lead her to Jan Klima's address on Radlicka Street. She found herself sighing in relief. It had been a long walk, and her feet hurt. She pulled her coat—Tatiana Savchenko's coat—around her. It had grown cooler with nightfall approaching. Now, if only Rafe's cousin was home.

The address Rafe had given her was near the end of Radlicka Street. When she reached it, she opened the unlocked door to the apartment building. Next to the stairwell was a door with a small sign with the word *Vrátný* on it. Rafe had said that his cousin lived on the first floor; she knocked once, and then twice, on the door, and was greeted by silence. She was about to turn away when she heard a lock rattling, and the door swung open.

The thin young man who stood there seemed familiar, and then she remembered him from the antique store when she had caught a glimpse of his face when Rafe was talking to him. He had a smudge of what looked like blue paint on his chin, and a jagged white scar on his right cheekbone. He gave her a wary smile. Claire saw the resemblance to Rafe immediately in his eyes and nose.

"Jan Klima?"

He didn't respond.

"I'm Claire Markham. Rafe told me I could come here if I needed help."

"Yes, I'm Jan," he said. He nodded to her and stepped aside to let her enter the room. It was dark and closed in, with a card table, two chairs, and a narrow cot. There was a hot plate on the table. In the far corner, she spotted two easels with paintings. A stand-up lamp with one light bulb illuminated the nearest canvas, which was a portrait of a middle-aged woman. The far painting was in the shadows. There was a palette, a set of brushes, and tubes of paint on a small table next to the closest easel. She smelled turpentine and another odor she couldn't immediately place. "This is my studio," he said. "And where I live. I'm the custodian for this building."

"Some things have happened," she began. "Some unexpected things. I can't stay where I had hoped to, so I need your help. Someplace to stay. Just for the night."

Jan nodded. "Rafael explained. Please sit. I will make tea. You like tea, yes?"

She found herself drawn to the paintings and moved closer to them. The portrait was well-executed, a blonde woman in a ball gown with an ornate gold necklace and gold earrings. The other painting was unfinished and intriguing—two spectral figures, ghost-like, floating above a bridge. They were waving poles with red flags, one flag with a white hammer and sickle, the other with a black swastika. The dark sky above them was filled with stars. When she looked closer, she realized the bridge was the Charles Bridge, with its line of dark statues. Claire had never seen anything quite like it, a mixture of the realistic and surreal. It reminded her of Salvador Dali's work.

"We must approach this calmly," Jan said as the teapot began to whistle. He motioned for her to sit on a folding chair. "It's best that you tell me only as much as is needed. We'll have our tea, and I will think about what is best to do."

Jan handed her a glass of tea and apologized for not having cream.

She told him she preferred her tea that way, and he smiled. "How can that be? Aren't you English?"

"I live in New York. I fell out of the habit of cream in my tea." She gestured toward the far painting. "Your painting, the one that isn't finished, is quite different. Striking."

"Then you like this painting?" He seemed surprised.

"I do," she said. "But it's quite sad. The ghosts. The flags. A comment on your country's sad history, I imagine."

"This city is filled with ghosts," he said. "I can see them around me, and so they are what I paint. But in the eyes of the authorities, my paintings are subversive, decadent. I paint them here, in my dungeon, but when I am done, I hide them elsewhere. Only one canvas here at a time. That way, should they come here, it keeps the loss to only one."

"And the portrait?"

"There is always a market for flattering portraits. With the crowns I collect for them, I buy the paints and canvas for my real work. This arrangement is *nesmyslný*, absurd, but I can't help myself." He shrugged. "I'm like a smoker who knows he should quit but can't. At least not for very long."

"It's not absurd," Claire said. She was surprised at Jan's directness. "Thank you for offering to help. How is it that your English is so good? So fluent?"

"Rafe did not tell you?"

She shook her head.

"My father was a diplomat who had been posted in London, and then Paris. This was before I was born. He wanted me to follow in his footsteps, and so he insisted I learn French and English. And of course, we were taught Russian in my school."

"What did Rafe tell you? About why we came to Prague?"

"He said you were helping a dissident leave the country. That either of you might need assistance if there were complications."

"There have been complications," she said. "I was to stay one night in Zizkov with a young woman and then leave today, but she went to the police when she learned of the defection of the dissident and connected me to it. I just got away in time. I was going to get an emergency passport at the British embassy, but I can't go there. Not safely. The police must know my plans by now and they could be waiting for me there."

"We can't have that, can we?" Jan took a sip of his tea. "What more can you tell me?"

"There is a contingency plan," she said, and then hesitated. How much could she tell him? Could she trust him? Then again, she didn't really have a choice in the matter. "A rendezvous. Arranged before. I missed the time and place today, but I can go there tomorrow. My contact will have papers and money and a way for me to get out of the country."

"You can't stay here," he said. "One of the tenants would report you. I know the one who has been ordered to spy on me. She is always snooping around. Snooping, that is the word?"

Claire nodded.

"But there is a place where you can stay. A flat of a friend who is out of town. Much nicer. Fewer people around." He stood up. "It's time that we go."

* * *

Jan took her arm once they were on the street. "We will pretend to be a couple," he said. "Just to be safe. If the police are looking for a single woman, it should fool them."

"How far do we have to go?" Claire didn't want to complain, but she was exhausted from the long walk from Piri's neighborhood and the anxiety of the day.

"Tereza's flat is in Mala Strana. Not far."

A pair of workers in rough clothing passed them. Her nostrils filled with the malty smell from the brewery again. They came to a stretch where the streetlamps flickered, leaving sections of the street in the dark. Jan steered her up a side street and then stopped, pointing to a wall covered with graffiti on the other side of the street.

"That's the Lennon Wall," Jan said. "After he was murdered in New York City, someone painted the wall to look like a gravestone, and then lyrics from his songs and political slogans began to appear. The government has painted over some of it. They recognize that people are protesting through what they paint on the wall. They don't want the message to spread, and for us to follow the lead of the Poles."

She nodded. She remembered the shock she had felt when John

Lennon was killed by a deranged fan on New York's Upper West Side. She had cried at the sudden senselessness of it, the violence directed against a man who had so embraced the idea of peace.

They continued their walk for another ten minutes until they reached a quiet residential neighborhood of buildings with Baroque facades and red tile roofs. At a two-story house with flowerpots on the window sills, Jan led her through an archway into a courtyard. At an imposing door, he reached above the molded door header and located a key. He fiddled with the lock and opened the door. They climbed a narrow stairway to the second floor, where he used the same key to open another door. He stepped inside and flicked on the light. Claire was surprised at the modern decorations. The flat had high ceilings, tasteful dark furniture, and floor-to-ceiling drapes. There was a small kitchen with shiny appliances and a compact refrigerator. In the living room, she noticed a painting of ghost-like angels floating above a huge Christmas tree that was decorated with lit white candles and ribbons. It hung above a white leather couch and dominated the room.

"Is that your painting?" she asked.

He nodded. "Tereza always loved that one. It reminded her of Christmases she spent with her grandmother in Brno. I gave it to her two years ago."

"You gave it to her?"

Jan shrugged. "She liked it very much."

"Will my staying here place her in jeopardy? If the authorities ever found out?"

"Tereza's father is a powerful Party member. He would protect her if it ever came to that, which it won't." He looked around the flat. "His family lives well. They can shop at the Tuzex stores, where they can buy all the best items from Germany, and France, and Sweden." He smiled. "Orwell had it right: 'All animals are equal, but some animals are more equal than others.'"

"You've read *Animal Farm?*"

"I have, and *1984*. A friend from my University days had copies. You can be sure I read them quickly because having the books in your possession could mean going to prison." He tapped his right temple with two fingers. "I remember quite clearly the pig Squealer, and how he justifies the perversion of socialism. We are ruled by Squealers, today."

"Thank you, Jan, for helping me," she said. "I don't like troubling you with my problems. Tomorrow I'll meet someone who can help me with travel papers and money."

He looked at her gravely. "Do you know this someone?"

"I don't," she confessed. "I know it will be a woman. And the time and place where we will make contact." Before she could say anything more, Jan raised his hand.

"No more details. It's better that I don't know. Please stay inside. Don't answer the door. I'm sorry. If the neighbors see you, a stranger, they might report you. I will bring you food."

"Won't they be suspicious of you coming and going?"

He shook his head and smiled. "At one time, Tereza was my

girlfriend." He blushed. "I still stop by from time to time. We're good friends. The neighbors know me. It's been a while since my last visit, but they'll figure that we're back together." He paused. "Can I ask you a question?"

She nodded.

"I understand why Rafe would get mixed up in this. He's always broke, and he's not too picky about where the money is coming from. And he's reckless. But why would you?"

"Why did I do this? I wanted to do something that would make a difference. I wanted a change. I had some difficult times in my personal life. Someone turned out to be completely different than I thought."

"A man." He studied her face.

"Yes. I thought he was someone that he wasn't."

"You ended it?"

She shook her head, surprised that she was sharing the story with a complete stranger. "I wish I could say that I did. He told me that I was crowding him. That I wasn't fun anymore. A list of all of my deficiencies. It was difficult."

"I'm sorry."

"I didn't handle it very well. I wrote him a long letter, telling him how I felt. He didn't respond. He wouldn't take my phone calls. Finally, a good friend told me to face the facts. He was a selfish man, and he had used me. I was better off without him. It took me some time to accept that. I had been in love, you see, and that can blind you to the truth. Not that there weren't many good things about Hal."

"Love works in strange ways," he said. "Not as we would like."

She remembered the day Hal broke it off with her. He had talked about how stale their relationship had become, how there was no excitement, no passion left for him. She had been stung, had wanted to ask him whether it was that surprising for a child of divorce to crave stability in her personal life, but had stayed silent. She realized that Hal was doing her a favor—if they had reached a dead end in their relationship, she needed to get on with her life. Only later did she discover that he had begun seeing someone else before their breakup.

"And now I have a question for you," she said.

"It's only fair that I answer."

"The woman who denounced me to the police. Who betrayed me. I don't fully understand why she did. They never would have connected her to me. Piri could have let me walk away, but she didn't. Why? Can you tell me why she would do that?"

"Sadly, I can. At an early age, we learn to denounce before we are denounced. We live under a system based on the fear of being next. Piri couldn't be absolutely sure that she was safe from exposure."

"It's like something out of Orwell."

"Yet it's all too common. I was denounced by a friend once. I know how that feels. I don't forgive him for what he did, but I understand why. He followed the Law of Self-Preservation."

* * *

Jan left her in the flat and went out, returning twenty minutes later with food—fresh bread, sausage, some cheese, and bottled beer. Claire found that she was famished, and she ate more than she normally did.

"I must go," he said. "I'll return in the morning. You'll be safe here."

She thanked him again and bolted the door shut after he had gone. She felt a wave of fatigue wash over her. She believed him, that she was safe in the flat—at least for now.

What would they have done to her if they caught her at Piri's? Would they have arrested her, held her in a cell, interrogated her? They had to be angry. Tatiana Savchenko's defection had embarrassed the Czechoslovak government and must have infuriated the Russians. A propaganda coup for the West. Would they have expelled her from the country? But what if they decided to charge her? Prosecute her as a spy?

She wasn't a spy, she told herself. Spies stole secrets. All Claire had done was to loan her passport to a desperately unhappy woman in the name of religious freedom, a young woman who only wanted to emigrate to Israel, a woman who longed to worship freely. That Claire had been part of a scheme to fool the Czechoslovak authorities didn't make her a spy.

None of it seemed real. In New York, she would have been sitting at her kitchen table with a cup of coffee and finishing the Sunday

New York Times, taking her time reading the paper, perhaps even starting the crossword puzzle in the magazine. It had been a mistake to have said yes to Singer—she realized that now. What had started as an exciting adventure had turned into something nightmarish. What had she been thinking? It was Singer and Townsend's world, not hers, and a few days of training wasn't enough to prepare her for that reality.

She walked around the flat. The bathroom had a tub, shower, and washbasin. The fixtures were sleek—no doubt imported from France or West Germany—and there were bars of scented soap at the washbasin. She undressed and stepped into the shower. The warm water felt wonderful after her long day. She dried herself with a thick Turkish towel. It didn't seem possible that she had been on the run from the police just hours before.

Claire wasn't sure she was going to be able to sleep, but when she lay down on the queen-sized bed, she found herself beginning to doze off. For the first time in days, she did feel safe, tucked away in a corner of the city with only Jan Klima aware of her hiding place. She was thinking about him, his laconic smile and the scar under his eye, as she drifted into sleep.

Seventeen

Baranov stopped at his flat in the Presnensky District only long enough to pack a small suitcase with a change of underwear and a few shirts. At Sheremetyevo Airport, he showed his passport and identification at the Aeroflot desk and took the next flight to Prague. It was dark by the time his plane landed at Ruzyne Airport. A driver was waiting for him there, but not Oleg Voronin of the KGB station in Prague, the primary liaison with the Czechoslovak Security Service. Baranov was surprised that Colonel Voronin hadn't bothered to make the drive to the airport to meet him. What was Voronin thinking? Was his absence meant to send a message? A calculated insult?

Baranov didn't let his anger show in front of the driver, a young probationer from Leningrad. He would wait and confront Voronin directly. It was not an auspicious start.

Once at the Soviet embassy, a spacious mansion in the diplomatic quarter of Bubenec, Baranov found a sullen Voronin waiting for him. The Eleventh Department's man in Prague had a round face, thinning salt-and-pepper hair, and a slight paunch. He was noticeably anxious. Voronin had been living the good life, and the Savchenko disaster threatened that comfortable existence, the spacious flat, the long lunches, the leisurely pace in the office. The events of the past few days had to have come as a shock to him—Czechoslovakia was considered a safe posting, all things considered. It was a place you could hide from the often-toxic office politics of Yasenevo and Lubyanka. As long as you demonstrated a firm hand in dealing with the Charter 77 types, the local intellectuals and agitators, there was little oversight from Moscow. With the hardliners ruling from Prague Castle, and with the bully boys of the StB at your beck and call, there was no need for tact or delicacy when it came to dissidents.

"We're at your disposal, Colonel Baranov," Voronin said, with arms folded across his chest. No high-ranking officer in the *rezidentura* ever welcomed the arrival of an officer from Counterintelligence. It could only mean trouble. Baranov could quickly end Voronin's tenure in Prague with a report to Moscow that implicated him in the Savchenko disaster. They both knew that.

Voronin was eager to establish his innocence. "As you know, we were not involved in protecting Dr. Savchenko or his daughter," he said. "That was Molchalin's responsibility. He and his men came with the professor from Moscow. We were not asked to provide any support. Molchalin didn't even stop by the embassy as a courtesy."

"Molchalin has been recalled to Moscow," Baranov said. "He will be dealt with there. But if you think that you can escape culpability, you're wrong." He stared at Voronin, aware how his differently colored eyes disturbed most people. Voronin was no exception—he looked away. "You are also responsible. Whatever happens in Prague reflects on you and your management of the relationship with the StB. There's no escaping that."

210

"I must protest. I won't be made a scapegoat for other's mistakes."

"What of your mistakes? You and your StB colleagues failed to warn of a major plot by the Zionists and the Americans, an operation conducted under your very noses. How could this happen without you getting wind of it? How can that be? You cannot evade responsibility. And based on the report you sent to Moscow, you have no idea who was involved, or how they can be brought to justice."

Voronin shrugged. "We're not mind readers. It wasn't any of the Americans based at their embassy. We have their operatives under close surveillance. They weren't in contact with the Savchenkos. I'm confident of that."

"Confident enough to wager your career on it?"

Voronin had no immediate answer. He tugged at his shirt cuffs, considering his response. "The Americans could have recruited others for the operation. I will concede that. But I think it was the Zionists behind this. Mossad. The first we knew of the defection of the Savchenko woman was when she appeared in Tel Aviv. It seems logical that it was the Jews. They're the ones who benefit from this."

"Let's assume you're correct," Baranov said. "Then the Israelis would need to bring agents here. They would need local people supporting them. And they would have to make contact with the daughter. There's a network involved in such a scenario."

"I agree. Had I been informed on a timely basis that she was missing, we could have alerted the airport and border control. As I said, we're not mind readers, nor miracle workers."

Baranov studied Voronin's impassive face; he had a point. Molchalin hadn't informed Moscow Center or the Prague station on Monday evening that Tatiana Savchenko was missing, perhaps hoping that she might turn up in the meantime. A stupid blunder. If the Mossad had engineered her defection, it was doubtful that any of their agents had remained in Czechoslovakia. But there might be Czechs or Slovaks who had assisted, and finding them would be Baranov's focus.

"We haven't been idle," Voronin said. "We have interviewed all of the workers at the hotel where Professor Savchenko and his daughter stayed, the International. Nothing of use. The girl was supposedly sick and didn't leave the room for two days."

Baranov frowned. "She could have left on Saturday for all we know. We must try to establish a timeline. That will help us find the local collaborators who assisted her."

Voronin remained silent. They both knew that Baranov had to produce results—arrests, confessions, an explanation of how Tatiana Savchenko had evaded her minders.

"Our Czech colleagues brought in known troublemakers from the University for questioning yesterday," Voronin said. "They focused on the Jewish students. The interviews produced nothing of value. They all denied any involvement. The StB's informants corroborate that—no unusual activity on the part of any of the dissidents."

Baranov moved closer to Voronin and lowered his voice. He spoke slowly, enunciating each word. "I will not fail," Baranov said. "Do you understand me?"

"I understand fully, comrade."

"If I discover that you are working against me, you will find yourself on a flight to Irkutsk before the end of the day. I've been given complete authority in this matter."

"I will do whatever you ask of me. I have every reason to want you to succeed. You must see that."

"I do. This will be your opportunity to repair some of the damage to your reputation," Baranov offered his hand to Voronin, and he reluctantly shook it. Baranov wondered if he persuaded Voronin that their fates were linked. "First things first," he said. "Inform your counterpart in the StB that I expect full cooperation and as many men to assist as I need. Tell me, who is their most competent officer? The one with the most productive informers?"

"Pavel Cerny. He spent time in Moscow being trained as an interrogator. He's part of the counterintelligence apparatus. Cerny has sources inside the Charter 77 movement, and a few of the so-called dissidents are under his control. He's smart. One of the few of theirs with more brains than brawn."

"I will need to meet him. We've no time to waste."

"There is one aspect of this affair I do not understand," Voronin said. "Why would the Zionists spend so much time and effort on this woman? With all due respect, she's a nobody. Another whiny Jew." He rubbed his chin. "They ought to take the entire lot of them and ship them to Israel. Good riddance, I'd say."

"I'm here to investigate," Baranov said. "Not to speculate. Take me to meet Cerny now so we can begin work."

* * *

They drove from the embassy to StB headquarters on Bartolomejska Street in silence, a silence which suited Baranov. It gave him time to think about what he needed to do next. He had a rough plan of action. The driver stopped at No. 4 Bartolomejska, and when Voronin led the way into the building, the uniformed guards saluted him.

Cerny proved to be a tall man with coal-black hair and brown eyes. He carried himself like a soldier, and his handshake was firm. His Russian was clear with only a slight accent. Baranov nodded to Voronin; he could see why he had recommended the man.

"What can you tell me about the defection?" Baranov asked. "What are you hearing?"

"I've talked to our most-reliable informers," Cerny said. "They had heard nothing about any local operation involving this Russian woman. I do not believe any of the dissidents have the organization or resources to have planned and executed this scheme. It appears to have been a Zionist plot, and so we have turned to the Jews in the city. We've brought several of the Jewish students known for anti-state sentiments in for questioning. So far, nothing. If subversive elements in Prague helped in this operation, we will find them and bring them to justice."

"I'm here so that we can accomplish that," Baranov said. "You will assist me. Directly. Colonel Voronin has assured me that we will have the full cooperation of your colleagues in State Security."

Cerny and Voronin exchanged glances. "I understand," Cerny said.

"We will need some luck," Baranov said. "Do you play chess, Captain Cerny?"

"I do. Badly."

"Our adversaries have played a very bold game. Too bold. They will have made mistakes. A stranded pawn. A missed move. We must find where they have been sloppy. If it is the Mossad behind this, the errors will be of arrogance. They will believe that they are smarter than us."

Cerny led them to a private office that had been prepared for Baranov. It had a dark wood desk, a swivel chair, and two telephones. Baranov sat down and pulled out his notebook.

"We will begin with the trains to Vienna," he said. "According to the file, the American politician boasted of a 'daring escape' by train and an assumed identity. We can't know if he is lying, to throw us off the trail, but it's all we have to work with. We need to trace the route she took. Inform the appropriate officials at the Czechoslovak State Railways that in the morning we will begin interviewing all of their personnel involved in trips to Vienna—conductors, waiters, porters, ticket-sellers. Anyone with contact with passengers. We need a schedule detailing when the Prague-Vienna trains arrive and depart, and when we can talk to the workers. We will show them the photo of the woman. If any of them remembers her, it may give us something. Was she alone? Did she travel with someone else?"

Cerny nodded. "I'll make the arrangements, Colonel." He saluted and left the office.

"We have a flat nearby prepared for your stay," Voronin said. "We will have your bag sent there. Do you wish to go there now?"

"You can leave the keys," Baranov said. "I have a long night ahead of me. I will see you in the morning."

He decided he would spend the evening with a cup of strong coffee reading the StB reports on the interrogations of the Jewish students, and any other dissidents that had been questioned. First, however, he needed to call General Lebedev's private number, his number at home. Lebedev's voice was noticeably slurred when he answered. He must have started drinking earlier in the evening. Baranov explained that he was at StB headquarters and had begun the investigation.

"Our Czech comrades have been very cooperative," Baranov said. "As has Colonel Voronin. I believe that we will get to the bottom of this."

"I'm confident that you will, Sergei Mikhailovich. Much depends upon your success. You will immediately report any progress to me."

"I will be in the field tomorrow, General. As soon as practical, I will provide an update."

He turned to the files on the desk after completing the call with Lebedev. He had been confident on the phone because that was what was expected of an ambitious State Security colonel, but he wondered if he was on a fool's errand—looking for wind in a field as the old saying went. He wouldn't become discouraged. He had to narrow his search as quickly as possible. At least Cerny appeared competent. He could run interference for Baranov with the locals. It was no different than a difficult chess problem, he told himself. You looked at the moves as far ahead as you could and thought through all the angles, all the countermoves.

Eighteen

Summer had dawdled too long over her Turkish coffee and sweet brioche roll and arrived at the Main Post Office on Jindrisska Street ten minutes late for her daily phone call back to London. She figured Freddie North wasn't going anywhere—she pictured him in his office in a cloud of smoke waiting for her call—so a slight delay wouldn't matter. After stopping by the statue on Charles Bridge two days in a row, and not finding the mysterious Claire waiting for her, Summer hoped that Freddie might tell her she could stop visiting the rendezvous spot. That would be fine with Summer; she found the cloak-and-dagger aspects of this particular side gig to be slightly ridiculous.

There was some static on the international phone line to London, and Summer had to strain to hear Freddie. She pictured the smoky office, Freddie with his feet up on the desk, the ashtray already crammed with finished cigarettes.

"Good news," he said. "I've got a job for you lined up, my dear. I need to get back to the promoter today. It's a folk festival in Brighton. Starts on November 20th. Can I tell him yes?"

"Sure," Summer said. "I'm cool with it."

"It's in Brighton."

"I've got it. Brighton. Tell the man 'yes'. It'll be a blast. I'll be back in London in a few days and we can talk then."

After they said their goodbyes and she hung up, Summer stepped out of the phone booth, her mind racing. She hadn't expected to hear Freddie use the code word. She had thought she was going to get paid twice—the small amount from the concerts, and the much larger payment from Townsend—for doing nothing more than singing her songs and drinking beer and walking across Charles Bridge twice. It had been a fun time, a blast. Her concerts had gone well. She had given them the old standards, "If I Had A Hammer," "This Land is Your Land," and "Turn, Turn, Turn!" and the audience had sung along in accented English. She had played some more recent songs, like "You've Got a Friend" and "Both Sides Now," which the crowd listened respectfully to, and since it was a concert for peace, she always played John Lennon's "Imagine," and "Blowin' in the Wind." For her last song of the night, she always finished with "Me and Bobby McGee."

She had two more days in Prague. A show that night, and then the next day she would sing at a farewell lunch. A peace and friendship lunch, Anton Sykora had called it, celebrating her visit to Prague.

With Freddie using the word "Brighton," something must have gone wrong. Townsend had made it clear that he would turn to her only if all "other arrangements" had failed. That meant Claire had run into some sort of trouble, and she might need help in leaving the country.

When Summer took the assignment, she knew, in theory, that it might get messy; she just didn't think that would ever happen in practice. She would be careful. If there were any signs of the police at the meeting spot, she would keep walking.

She wondered if Townsend would increase her payment for the extra risks she would be taking—the equivalence of hazardous duty pay. It wouldn't hurt to ask when she next saw him in West Germany. After all, she was the one heading out onto the thin ice.

She had about two hours to kill before the rendezvous at the bridge. She decided she would walk along the Vltava River embankment, enjoy the late morning sunlight, and make her way to the Charles Bridge just before one o'clock.

* * *

Claire greeted Jan's return to the flat in the morning with relief. He brought a light breakfast and they ate rye bread with jam and butter and drank tea lightly sweetened with honey.

They agreed that Jan would meet her at Tereza's later in the day after her rendezvous with her contact. He had daily chores at the apartment building to complete, and he didn't want any of the tenants to complain to his supervisor.

"If I'm not back by two o'clock, you should leave," she said. "If I'm arrested, I won't tell them about you. I promise."

He remained silent, his eyes fixed on her.

219

"I want to thank you for what you've done," she said and surprised him by hugging him and kissing him on the cheek.

"You're very kind," he said. "I'm sure that I will see you later for a proper goodbye."

Claire wore her sunglasses and a scarf over her hair, hoping to blend into the crowd of tourists on the Charles Bridge. She passed through the Stare Mesto Tower and walked slowly toward the center of the bridge. She wondered if the police were already looking for her. What had Piri told them? Had they figured out the ruse that had allowed Tatiana Savchenko to escape? Did they know Claire was still in the country? If they did, had they distributed Claire's photo?

A few minutes before one o'clock, she made her way to the statue of John the Baptist, and stood on the north side of the bridge, closer to Castle Hill. The massive figure loomed above her, the statue's finger pointing toward Prague Castle. She found herself wondering whether any of the Czechs saw the saint's gesture as a rebuke of sorts to the atheistic regime that ruled their country.

A constant stream of tourists and visitors streamed by the spot she had chosen. She waited nervously, turning to look out over the Vltava and the far embankment to the north, turning her back so her face couldn't be seen. In the distance, the medieval battlements of the castle loomed over the Mala Strana below. A tour group clustered nearby around the most famous statue on the bridge, that of St. John Nepomac. Below, on the river, she spotted a small boat being rowed by a thin man. She wished for a moment she could trade places.

From the far side of the bridge, two policemen in uniforms sauntered toward her. She averted her eyes, holding her breath, waiting until she thought they might have passed her. When she turned around, they were on the other side of the bridge, questioning a ragged-looking man.

Townsend had told her that the Charles Bridge contact would be a young woman who would carry a black handbag, and would signal that all was well by holding it in her right hand. If it was in her left hand, it meant she had been followed, and Claire was not to engage with her.

She checked her watch—it was one minute before the hour. How long could she stay there without attracting attention? Just as she heard a single church bell tolling, a girl with long blonde hair cascading down her back, a guitar in her right hand appeared out of nowhere. Was the guitar in her right hand the signal for safety? She couldn't be certain, but the woman smiled at her reassuringly.

"Claire," she said. "The third day I've stopped by here at one o'clock, and I was about to give up on you. You need to come with me, now. Smile like you know me."

The woman had a beautiful, musical voice. Claire nodded. "You're Summer?" she asked.

"I am, in the flesh." The woman motioned for Claire to follow her. "I'm here to sing some songs, hence the guitar. And now, it seems, to help a damsel in distress." She stopped for a moment. "I have your photo in my pocket. Do you need to see it? Or have I said enough for the cloak-and-dagger thing?"

"That's enough," Claire said, struggling to keep up with Summer's long stride. "Where are we going?"

"A place where we can talk."

They walked through the Tower and turned south. Summer led the way to a green park bench on the embankment. They sat down, and Claire looked around to make sure they couldn't be overheard. There didn't seem to be anyone watching them.

"So how are things?" Summer asked her.

"I'm in a bit of a jam. The police came looking for me yesterday. The woman I was staying with betrayed me. I was lucky because I was out on a walk or they would have arrested me."

Claire knew that she was talking too fast, and the blonde woman reached over and touched her hand.

"It's all cool, now," she said. "Our mutual friend, Jack Townsend, sends his best. You can tell me as much or as little as you like."

"Did he tell you why I'm here? Why I came to Prague?"

"He was a bit vague, but I got the general drift. Helping a dissident. That was enough to know that you might piss off the government. Which it sounds like you have."

"I'm afraid so. How long have you known Townsend?"

"Not long," she said. "We traveled to Germany together before I drove here. He's different. I like him, though. He's cool. No bullshit."

Claire shook her head. "I can't go anywhere near the embassy to get my emergency passport. I missed my flight to London last night."

"That's taken care of. I brought the papers you need. Where are you staying now?"

"A flat in the Lesser Town. It's not far from here."

"Can we go there? We can't go where I'm staying because I have a minder. Miss Nosek. Nosek the nosy. She tries to tag along whenever I go out. It's clear that she's there to watch me and report back to the authorities."

"Won't they wonder where you are?" Claire asked.

"No problem. I've established that I'm a free spirit. I'll tell them I met a cute boy, and we spent the afternoon drinking wine."

"At the flat, there will be a friend. A man who is helping me."

"A Czech?" Summer asked. "Do you trust him?"

"Yes, I trust him."

* * *

They walked through the streets of the Lesser Town, pausing once or twice to make sure they weren't being tailed. Gray clouds had begun to form overhead, and it looked like it would rain. Claire could feel herself relaxing. Townsend's contingency plan was working, and there was something calming about Summer with her laid-back California vibe—and Claire smiled, because the word "vibe" fit Summer's affect perfectly.

When they reached Tereza's building, Claire led the way up the narrow stairway. Inside the flat, Summer looked around with a nod of approval. "Not bad," she said. "Where's your friend?"

"He'll be here later."

Summer sat down on the floor and laid her guitar on its back. She quickly loosened the strings and reached inside the opening. She felt around and grunted. "Got it," she said. A moment later she pulled out a passport, a piece of adhesive tape hanging from one end. She ripped off the tape and opened the passport.

"Her Britannic Majesty's Principal Secretary of State for Foreign Affairs requests and requires in the Name of Her Majesty all those whom it may concern to allow the bearer to pass freely without let or hindrance, and to afford the bearer such assistance and protection as may be necessary," she read aloud. "The passport holder is a woman named Carol Jordan who looks exactly like you in the photograph." She handed the passport to Claire.

Claire examined it carefully—she recognized the photo; Townsend had taken it when they were preparing for the first trip. She flipped through the pages, studying the visa and stamps on the interior pages. She wondered—was it a forgery? Or a passport of a woman named Carol Jordan that now bore Claire Markham's photo?

"There's more I owe you," Summer said. She reached into her front pocket and produced a wad of bills. "Here, some local currency. Quite a bit of it, in fact. Maybe a thousand pounds' worth."

"Thank you," she said, putting the money in her pocketbook along with the passport.

"So what now? I'm driving back to Germany in a day. Townsend thought you could travel with me. Or you can use the passport and fly back to London."

"Could we leave now?" Claire asked. "Flying might be chancy. They screen the passengers closely from what I've heard. I hate to ask, but the sooner I leave Prague the better."

"I've two more gigs left, one tonight and one tomorrow afternoon, a farewell lunch. I don't think canceling either would be smart. We should wait. Play it cool. If we split now, that might make them suspicious."

Claire took a deep breath. "I think I'll wait and go with you."

"Super! You're my girlfriend, along for the ride. I've got a pair of jeans that should fit you and a tie-dyed shirt and we'll cut your hair, and to the world you'll be a cool swinging chick from London. 'England swings like a pendulum do.' A perfect disguise." She looked around the flat. "Can you stay here until we leave tomorrow?"

"I'm not sure. With the new passport I could go to a hotel, but I'd rather not. I'll need to ask my friend if it's all right to stay another night."

"This friend? Are you sure of him?"

"Jan is the cousin of the man I was traveling with." She glanced at her watch. "He should be here shortly. I trust him. You'll see."

"Jack Townsend said you're an antiques dealer. Is that on the level?"

"It is. I manage a small shop in New York. And you're a singer? Townsend told me nothing about you."

Summer held up her guitar, which she had been fiddling with as they talked. "I can play this. I'm a singer, for real. My agent, Freddie, sometimes books me for side gigs. Errands. Delivering things. Acting as a courier. The money's good, so why not?"

"Who for?"

"Most times he doesn't tell me. Freddie used to work in the government in intelligence. I assume the jobs are for some of Freddie's former colleagues. They pay well enough, and Freddie has kept my immigration status clean, so I can stay in England. It's all cool."

"Don't you worry? The risks you take?"

"Up to now, it's been fairly tame. This is the first time I've crossed into the East. All my other errands have been in France and Portugal and Germany. Believe you me, I asked for a lot more money to do this one. But I'm enjoying it, to tell the truth. It's been a trip. I liked fooling them, the police and the border guards. They had no idea. They thought I was a hippie folk singer." She plucked one of the guitar strings and then strummed a chord. "Seems to me, you're the one with the high-wire act. I'm just here setting up the net to catch you."

* * *

A light rain began to fall outside, with thunder rumbling in the distance. From the front window of the flat, Claire could see the cobblestones glistening in the rain and pedestrians scurrying down the street, umbrellas aloft. Then she spotted a thin figure, hatless in the rain, making his way toward the building and entering the courtyard. It was Jan, and she was surprised at how happy that made her.

She found a towel in the bathroom and met him at the door to the flat; she gave it to him so he could dry his hair. He stepped inside and thanked her.

"I made contact," she told him. "I have a way to leave. New papers."

"Good."

Claire stepped aside so he could see Summer standing behind her. "And this is Summer. She's the one sent to help me."

Jan nodded at her warily and kept drying his hair.

"But I can't leave just yet," Claire said. "Summer can't leave until tomorrow in the afternoon and I'm going to travel with her. She has a car, a Volkswagen Beetle. Would it be possible for me to stay here tonight?"

He hesitated. "The longer you are here, the more likely that the neighbors will suspect something and report us."

"I can go to a hotel," she said. "Wouldn't that be better?"

Jan frowned. "It's true Prague is a city of more than a million," he said. "You might think it would be easy to hide among all those people. But that's not the case for one simple reason—they have us spying on each other, informing the police of anyone or anything suspicious. A hotel would be a bad choice. They report their guests to

227

the authorities. We need to find an isolated place for you for the next day or so, where there aren't many neighbors."

"And where might she find that?" Summer asked.

"I know one place. My family's summer cottage. It's west of the city, outside Podebrady. Perhaps sixty kilometers. It's nothing fancy, a very simple *chata*. During the week, there are few people around. I can take Claire there this afternoon, and you could go there tomorrow, collect her, and drive on to Germany."

Summer nodded. "I like the idea. Keep her out of sight and out of mind."

"What do you think, Claire?" Jan asked.

"It makes sense," Claire replied. "One of the neighbors here might have already noticed strange people coming and going from this flat."

"We must not lose any time," Jan said. "I will borrow a vehicle for the drive. Give me an hour."

* * *

After Jan had left the flat, Claire and Summer watched from the front window as he walked up the street. The rain had let up, and Claire was relieved to see that the street remained empty, with no one following Jan. She hoped it meant that their presence had gone undetected.

"He doesn't have to take more risks on my behalf," she remarked to

Summer. "I know he's been in trouble with the police before. I'm surprised he's doing this."

"I'm not," Summer said. "He digs you. That's obvious. And he's cute, I'll admit. Not my type, mind you. I don't go for those skinny artistic ones. Too serious, and they typically don't have two nickels to rub together. How can they show you a good time when they're broke?"

"I don't think you mean half the things you say."

"I'd much rather have a rich boyfriend than a poor one. Is that a federal crime? Most girls feel that way, they just won't admit it publicly." She adjusted the strap on her guitar. "He's very skinny."

"I think he'd rather spend his money on paint and canvas than on food."

"An artist. A romantic. That's as bad as falling for the lead guitarist."

"I haven't fallen for him."

Summer laughed. "But you find him attractive."

Claire felt herself blushing. "Even if I did, I hardly think that now is the time."

"It's always the time for love."

Claire shook her head. "At the moment, I'm not worried about a boyfriend. I'm worried about getting home."

"If something happens, it happens," Summer said. "It couldn't hurt."

"We're leaving in a day."

That produced a smile from Summer. "I've never let that get in the way of love," she said. "Why should it?"

She pulled Claire to her and hugged her. "I'll wait here with you until skinny Jan returns. Then I'll have to leave because the show must go on."

Nineteen

Jan remembered those long winter nights in the dormitory at the University, drinking cheap beer or wine and chain-smoking cigarettes, debating philosophy and music and politics. They were careful when they discussed the regime, making sure that everyone in the conversation could be trusted, although you could never be certain who would inform and who would not. That was how they had all lived in the time after the Prague Spring, after the crackdown, when students and artists and intellectuals feared a visit from State Security.

One cold November night, Jan had joined an epic debate over the notion of free will, a debate that was fueled by copious amounts of red wine and plum brandy. His friend Lukas, a self-described skeptic and materialist, had scoffed at the idea that destiny or fate or any other supernatural cause lay behind human actions. "We make the decisions, not God or some superior force," he proclaimed after they had finished their second bottle of wine. "I alone decide, and whatever happens follows naturally. It won't occur if I don't elect to do something. I'm the cause and the agent. There's no such thing as chance." Jan didn't put up much of an argument, but he wasn't quite sure that Lukas had it right. Didn't chance play a bigger part in life than Lukas thought?

He remembered the debate long after he left the University, and how random events, how chance, often pushed him in a direction he hadn't expected. His father's death. The painting class he took in his second year at University that convinced him that art was his calling. Then, he had gotten himself into trouble in the years that followed by painting the scenes in his head, the subversive scenes that came to him unbidden. That compulsion—and that was what it was, he had decided—wasn't rational; it seemed to surface from some deep place in his subconscious. But was that truly under his control? He didn't want to become an enemy of the state, and yet that was the inevitable result of his actions. Even now, when continuing to paint the ghosts of Prague could cost him, he continued, incapable of stopping, of doing the smart thing.

He hadn't willed Rafe to show up with his dangerous request. Was that fate? Or just bad luck? Lukas would argue that Jan could have refused to help, that he made a conscious choice. The truth was that he had responded instinctively. He hadn't thought it through, calculated whether it was worth going back to prison. He tried to conjure up how he had felt during his eighteen months in the labor camp at Hermanice, a brush and a paint bucket in hand. His captors had thought assigning him to whitewash the barracks walls a clever humiliation, a way to put him in his place, an artist reduced to house painter, forced to fill in blank surfaces. How he had missed the smell of paint and turpentine. The feeling when he would apply the first dabs of paint on a bare, fresh canvas. The sense of anticipation, and then the excitement as the work took shape and what he had seen only in his mind became concrete. Did he want to be cut off from that? To be caged again?

He knew it was a mistake, a stupid romantic gesture, but he wanted to help Rafe, his cousin, his dashing English cousin. When Claire arrived at his door in Smichov, and he heard her story, he knew that he would keep his promise to Rafe and that it might not end well. It was more than likely that the StB would hunt down anyone involved in sheltering her. But perhaps he would be lucky, for once, and escape notice and the consequences.

It was clear that Claire couldn't stay another night in Prague. Hiding her outside the city in their summer cottage near Podebrady, far from inquisitive eyes, was prudent. It had the added benefit of letting him spend more time with her, alone. He had been surprised by the immediate attraction he felt for her. She had an appealing manner, reserved and yet vulnerable, with a hint of mystery about her. More than once he had caught her staring at him and she had quickly looked away. Did she sense the same attraction? She would be gone in a day—not the most promising conditions for a romance.

Now he had to move quickly, to borrow a vehicle for the trip to the west, and to warn his mother about his situation. He had to create some distance between them, so that later, if need be, she could deny any knowledge of his actions. Jan quickly scribbled a note to her, explaining that he would be at the summer house, that he needed to leave the city for a few days to collect his thoughts, and that she might want to visit her friend, Hana, in Brno. He would ask a friend to deliver the note to his mother. She would understand the message—something had gone wrong for him, and that he needed to make himself scarce. By suggesting the visit to Brno, he was warning her that the police might come looking for him, and he didn't want her caught up in his troubles. He was confident that she would act on his note after she had destroyed it. Such was life in the Czechoslovak Socialist Republic.

* * *

Jan returned later in the afternoon in a battered blue Skoda sedan. A young woman with long dark hair and lips painted a vivid red sat in the passenger seat next to him, and Claire felt a twinge of jealousy, which she knew was ridiculous. She had no claim over him, even though she believed there was a strong mutual attraction.

Jan introduced the dark-haired woman to Claire and Summer as Lenka, a friend. She looked Claire up and down before nodding at her. "Jan says you are Rafe's friend," she said. "From England. That's so?"

"Rafe and I have worked together," Claire replied. "And I'm English, yes, but I live in New York."

"I'm loaning my car to Jan so he can drive to his *chata*," she said. "Because he asked."

"Lenka has offered to help us," Jan said. "She understands that it's a delicate situation."

"Thank you," Claire said.

Jan explained that Lenka could attend Summer's last performance and then guide her to the Klimas' summer cottage. "You'd never find it without assistance," he told Summer. "Lenka knows the way. After you arrive at the cottage to collect Claire, Lenka and I will drive back to the city."

"Awesome," Summer said. She kissed Claire on the cheek. "I'll catch you on the flip side," she said. "Stay safe." She turned to Lenka. "Walk me back to my place. I can introduce you to my minders as my new friend. That way it'll be more natural when you show up tomorrow."

After Summer and Lenka had left, Claire got into the passenger side of the car. "Thank you for doing this," she said quietly to Jan.

He shrugged. "I'm no hero. What have I done? I found a new place for you to stay. An additional night's lodging, that's all. It means I can look Rafe in the eyes when I see him next and know I did what I said I would."

"And Lenka? Another girlfriend? You seem to have many young women eager to help out."

"Lenka is just a friend. Another painter." He put the car into gear and pulled out into the street. "I'm no Casanova," he said. "I'm not like Rafe with all of his girls. His birds."

"I couldn't speak to that. I hardly know Rafe."

"It's true that you're not quite his type. I can see that."

"I'm not?" she asked. "What type is that?"

"He likes a party girl, not someone as smart as you." Jan blushed. "Of course, I don't mean that you're not pretty."

"I like the compliment about being smart more," she said.

"There's no question about that."

"I'm not so sure. I'm not so smart that I haven't gotten myself into quite a bind."

"A bind? What is a bind?"

"Trouble. I never should have agreed to this crazy scheme. To what I've done. It's like being trapped in a bad dream and not being able to wake up."

"Another day," he said. "One more day and that bad dream will be over."

By the time they reached the outskirts of Prague, the sun had begun to peek through the cloud cover. The grimy prefabricated concrete apartment buildings, the *panelaks*, gave way to fields and small villages along their route, Highway 67. Jan asked Claire about her and Rafe's visit to Prague, and she found herself relaxing as she told him about their sightseeing and shopping expeditions in the city.

After an hour of driving, Jan took a winding one-lane dirt road through the woods and slowed to turn into a driveway. Almost immediately they came to a clearing with a one-story building. Jan parked the Skoda next to a large pine tree and turned off the engine.

"We could have gotten here sooner," he said. "But if I drove faster, above the speed limit, the traffic police might have stopped us."

The cottage was surrounded by dense woods of spruce, pine, and oak, with a stand of birch trees close by. As they exited the car, a light wind moved through the tops of the pine trees, and Claire was struck by the simple beauty of the place. She took a deep breath, delighting in the fresh air, the scent of the pines.

"The *chata* was a reward to my father for his service to the regime," Jan said. "The faithful diplomat. We spent many happy weekends here. After he died, and I got myself into trouble, I feared that they would take this away from my mother. Thank God, they didn't. A friend of my father, a senior official in the Foreign Ministry, interceded on her behalf."

"Do they do that? Punish the family?"

"They do. It's quite an effective means of control. Who wants to drag their family down with them? My mother has never complained about my foolishness jeopardizing her. She wants me to be careful for my own sake. She would never tell me to stop creating my 'subversive' paintings—but she does warn me against attracting the attention of the authorities."

"But you haven't been careful, though, have you? Agreeing to Rafe's request. Helping me."

"Ah, what could I do?" he asked with a smile. "A chance to annoy those bastards who rule over us from the Castle? And to bedevil the Russians? It was irresistible. I couldn't turn Rafe down. And maybe it wasn't the wisest choice. But I don't regret it, certainly not after meeting you."

Twenty

It had taken longer than he had expected, but Baranov had remained confident that at some point there would be a break in the case. A clue or stray bit of information would shed light on the mystery of Tatiana Savchenko's defection. One thing would lead to another, and in the end, Baranov would have his solution—he had experienced it before. He had to be patient, even as he was painfully aware of the minutes and hours passing.

Captain Cerny had photographs of Tatiana Savchenko couriered to the StB officers in Breclav and Ceske Velenice, the crossing points by train into Austria. He tasked them with interviewing the border guards and customs officials about whether they had seen a woman matching the photograph. Cerny promised that Baranov would have word from the border by mid-afternoon.

The first break, however, came closer to home. Baranov and Cerny went to the central train station, the Hlavni Nadrazi, on Wednesday morning, where they waited impatiently for the arrival of the morning train from Vienna. The first conductor they questioned shook his head when he was shown Tatiana's photograph. He was sure he hadn't encountered her. They had more luck with a different conductor, a thin, middle-aged man named Marek.

"I remember her," he said. "I do. An Englishwoman. She was traveling with a young man. They came from Vienna, the morning train."

"Are you sure?" Baranov asked. "She was with a man?"

"I'm sure."

"What was this man like?"

"A businessman. Well-dressed. He spoke Czech without an accent."

"The train *from* Vienna? Not *to* Vienna?"

"I only saw them on the inbound train."

"You're sure? Not the outbound?"

Marek shook his head. "I remembered them distinctly because the man was quite friendly. He asked me to recommend some restaurants in Prague. Would he ask that on the way to Vienna? I think not."

"You say they were English? Did you see their papers?"

Marek shrugged. "I see hundreds of tourists. I'd bet a week's pay they were English. They spoke English to each other."

Baranov was puzzled. It made no sense; Tatiana Savchenko could not have been on a train from Austria to Prague. He showed the photo to Marek again. "You're sure it was this woman?"

"It was her," he said. "I'm certain of it. She was quite lovely. I've got an eye for the lovely ones. Always have."

Baranov thanked him, and he and Cerny retreated to a coffee shop in the departure hall. They sat with cups of Turkish coffee and Cerny lit up a cigarette.

"What do you think?" Baranov asked.

"It doesn't make much sense," Cerny said. He blew a smoke ring to the side. "This man Marek is sure he saw the woman in the photo. It couldn't have been Savchenko, not coming from Vienna. She only traveled in one direction. And Tatiana Savchenko's Russian, not English."

"He could have been confused about which train she was on. I can see that happening. It's a routine job. One trip blurs into the next."

"Marek seemed confident that the woman he encountered was English."

"He didn't examine her papers," Baranov replied.

Cerny stubbed out his cigarette. "Seems like a coincidence—a woman who looks like Savchenko happens to take the train to Prague. An Englishwoman."

Baranov drummed his fingers on the tabletop. "Let's for a moment consider that Marek's correct on all counts. He encountered the couple on the train from Vienna to Prague. The woman resembled Savchenko. She is English. Is this a coincidence? Or part of the plan? Was the woman meant to look like Tatiana, chosen for her resemblance? This Englishwoman travels to Prague, and Tatiana takes her place on the return trip—she uses her passport and visa and returns with the young man. They're just another couple of British tourists. Tatiana passes for the Englishwoman. It's even possible the officials at the border remember them from the first leg of their trip.

They have familiar faces. Whoever planned this might have been counting on that."

Cerny nodded. "And there's no reason to stop them or question them at any length."

"Exactly. Tatiana Savchenko hides in plain sight. I think this may be how they did it. And if we can discover who these people are—this English couple—we may have something. No, we *will* have something."

"Do you think the Zionists recruited them? Perhaps they are English Jews."

"Anything is possible. The conductor said the man spoke fluent Czech. If I were running this operation, I would want someone who spoke the language, who could blend in, who could make arrangements. I would look for a man with some charm, who could smooth the way at the border."

* * *

They returned to StB headquarters on Bartolomejska Street where Baranov and Cerny wolfed down slabs of pork on dark bread and washed their lunch down with tea. At Baranov's direction, the StB turned to compiling a list of visitors with British passports who had stayed at hotels in Prague in the past week.

"There are only four luxury hotels in the city," Cerny explained. "The

Alcron, International, Esplanade, and Jalta. They are the ones that cater to foreign businessmen."

"Then we will start there," Baranov said.

Within an hour they had the list. It wasn't long, and he and Cerny whittled it down to a few names by eliminating older tourists and businessmen. Two seemed particularly promising—Rafael Klima and Claire Markham—a couple traveling on business who had stayed at the Jalta Hotel. Baranov and Cerny drove to Wenceslas Square to interview the hotel personnel. They had immediate success. The concierge remembered the couple well, particularly the man, who spoke excellent Czech. It was the couple's second visit to Prague in the past two months. They had stayed at the Jalta both times and had checked out the day before Tatiana Savchenko surfaced in Israel. The woman, Claire Markham, was buying antiques and Klima was acting as her guide and translator. The concierge gave Baranov the names of the three antique stores that the two had visited.

"They came here once before," Cerny said. "Do you think they made the arrangements then? Met with local subversives?"

"It's possible," Baranov said. "Whoever planned this is quite clever. The first trip was a rehearsal for the second. Convince your colleagues at Bartolomejska Street that this couple is harmless. After a few days of surveillance, it becomes clear that they are above reproach, spotless. No need to assign officers to tail them. There are hundreds if not thousands of tourists who come from the West to your city every day. You can't follow them all."

From the Jalta, they went to the antique shops that the couple had visited. They learned nothing of importance at their first two stops;

Klima and Markham had shopped there but had done nothing suspicious. At the third store, however, the store manager, a Mr. Svoboda, mentioned that Klima had met with another man at the front of the store while their purchases were being packed for shipment.

"Miss Markham was a lovely person," Svoboda said. "The man was rude. Quite arrogant. Just because you speak Czech doesn't make you an expert on the value of art objects."

Cerny thanked him, and they returned to the car. Baranov was growing more confident that they had uncovered the mechanism for Tatiana Savchenko's defection. She had taken Claire Markham's place on the return trip, accompanied by Klima. He asked Cerny to drive back to the Jalta. There, he showed the photo of Tatiana to the concierge. She paused and then identified the woman in the photo as Claire Markham.

Baranov had to admire the scheme. It was simple but elegant in its construction. There was nothing about the couple to raise suspicions. They had used the train instead of flying because the scrutiny of passengers, especially foreign tourists, was more relaxed. A canny move.

Had Klima's meeting at the antique shop involved a local conspirator? That was another lead to run down because he assumed the StB had a file on the Czech-speaking Rafael Klima. Did he have relatives in Prague? Close friends? How often had he visited?

What of Claire Markham? The scheme had to call for her to leave Czechoslovakia immediately after the defection. A passport in another identity? A flight to the West from Ruzyne? He asked Cerny to dispatch officers to the airport with the photo of Tatiana Savchenko so they could question the passport control officers there.

A young, stern-faced female officer from the StB archives arrived with two slim files on Rafael Klima and Claire Markham. Baranov read through them carefully, looking for patterns and connections. There wasn't much to go on; in one field report, he learned that they had acted like typical Westerners in Prague on a business trip, mixing in visits to the traditional tourist sites with shopping in antiques stores.

But in Rafael Klima's brief file there were two other pieces of paper, and they offered what Baranov needed. One was an informant's report on Klima's visit to his relatives in Prague, his aunt Nadezda and cousin Jan, in 1980. According to the informant, Jan had taken Rafe to a disco where they had partied until two in the morning, returning to the Klima flat.

He asked Cerny to procure the files on Jan and Nadezda. "I'll go myself," Cerny said. "Speed up the process."

He returned twenty minutes later and sheepishly admitted failure—the officers in the archives believed the files on the Klima family had been misfiled and began an immediate search for them.

Baranov rubbed his eyes and suppressed a yawn. He had only slept a few hours since his arrival in Prague, and he was relying on strong coffee to stay awake, if not completely alert.

"I do have something else to report, though," Cerny said. He hesitated. "Something quite strange. A friend of mine, a cop in Zizkov, says a young Hungarian student came to the station, claiming that she had a woman staying with her who might be a spy,

245

somehow connected to the Savchenko defection. This happened the afternoon of the news conference in Israel. The woman was named Claire, and she was English. The police went with the Hungarian girl to question this woman, but she wasn't at the flat. They searched the neighborhood but couldn't find her."

"What made the student suspicious? What made her think that she was connected to the plot?"

"When she told the Englishwoman about the news conference in Israel, and that the StB was questioning students from the University, the woman became visibly disturbed, her hands trembling. What's more, the woman had an appointment at the British embassy to claim an emergency passport. She told a flimsy story about a jealous Czech boyfriend who was trying to keep her in Prague by holding her passport."

"Where is this student now? What is her name? We must question her."

"Her name is Piri Szabo. She's studying engineering at Charles University. However, she's gone. Flew to Budapest yesterday. Her father is a Party official there."

"Do you think she was part of this?"

"She told the police that she had only recently met the Englishwoman. She thought that she was helping her extricate herself from a romance that had gone bad."

Baranov snorted. "If this Szabo woman is blameless, why did she take off for Hungary? She is connected with Claire Markham, and I'll wager it was not a chance meeting. My colleagues in Budapest will get to the bottom of this."

The pieces of the puzzle were beginning to fit together. Baranov felt that he could explain the mechanics of the plot with some certainty. Even better, he had the names of the foreign couple at the center of the scheme.

He knew that he had better brief General Lebedev before he telephoned the KGB station in Budapest and asked for their help in questioning Piri Szabo. He couldn't very well request the interrogation of a Hungarian citizen—one whose parents might have influence in Party circles—without alerting his superior. The story he would tell would be vague, that this woman might have some knowledge about Tatiana Savchenko's defection, that Baranov didn't believe that she was part of the scheme. He wasn't ready to share any more with Lebedev, not until he had more evidence.

When he reached General Lebedev by phone, the conversation was brief. Lebedev agreed to the questioning of Piri Szabo but pressed Baranov about the pace of his investigation. No doubt Moscow Center was demanding answers Lebedev couldn't supply. Baranov was relieved when the General quickly ended the call.

He recognized that he had to show more progress. Whether it was the Mossad, or MI6, behind the defection, he had to assume their agents were long gone. The best he could hope for was to document the operation and then find and arrest any local subversives who had helped execute it. He could at least claim credit for that, and it might be enough to satisfy General Lebedev, if not the General's superiors. Lebedev would no doubt sacrifice a few pawns—the hapless

Molchalin and perhaps the overly complacent Voronin—but with luck, Baranov could stay clear of any blame.

Twenty-one

Hawes woke at dawn on Wednesday and dressed quickly. He had a hasty breakfast in the hotel dining room of poached eggs, cheese, and cold ham slices washed down with two cups of tea that he diluted with ample amounts of cream. When he returned to his room and stood by the large window, lost in thought, he realized that it had begun to rain outside. The city had begun to stir below. A man in a long raincoat strolled past, black umbrella held high, carefully stepping around the puddles that had begun to form on the sidewalk. Two women wearing scarves hustled aboard a streetcar.

Hawes checked his watch. It was eight o'clock, still too soon to call London where it was an hour earlier. He would have to wait. He didn't want to walk in the rain, but he was restless, and couldn't bear the thought of waiting in his room with nothing to do but brood.

Well, he had time to kill. He remembered a joking claim once made by a grizzled Army sergeant in his unit—it was all right to kill time because eventually time would kill you. When was that? 1945? Hawes had heard that as you grew older, memories would suddenly pop up, unbidden. The sergeant's name was Baxter, Bill Baxter, and the rumor in the barracks was that his middle name was Makepeace, that he had been named after William Makepeace Thackeray. Hawes shook his head. It was strange that on a rainy morning in Vienna he was thinking about William Makepeace Baxter, a man who would be in his eighties if he was still alive.

Hawes borrowed an umbrella from the Hotel Imperial's concierge and set out on foot. It was windy on the street and the air had a chill to it. A hard rain began to beat down upon his umbrella, and gusts of wind sprayed water onto his suit. He didn't want to go back inside, but it was a nasty morning for a walk. When the wind gathered more force, threatening to break the umbrella, he stepped inside a doorway. He looked around—the weather had chased people indoors. The abandoned streets matched his mood. A gray sadness. A sense of failure. And Vienna was a place replete with bad memories.

He walked back to the Hotel Imperial, and once in his room, took a brief warm shower. He dried himself off thoroughly and changed into fresh clothes. He sat at the hotel desk and scribbled down what he was going to say to Tobias Kent when he reached him on the phone. He checked the clock—it was time. He reluctantly picked up the receiver and placed the call to London. It was going to be an awkward conversation; he would be putting his friend in a difficult position. What choice did Hawes have? To help Claire Markham, he had to pursue every avenue.

When Tobias answered his call, Hawes quickly explained that he was in Vienna and that his colleague in Prague had encountered some difficulties, one that he would rather not discuss on an insecure line. "I'm at wit's end," he added. "I don't know what's going on. It would help if I could speak with someone from my old shop at the embassy here in Vienna. Someone senior."

"Do these difficulties have to do with the matter we discussed the other day?"

Hawes wasn't going to lie to his friend. "They do, sorry to say."

"I must say that I'm disappointed."

"No more than I."

"This puts me in an awkward position, to say the least."

"I recognize that, Tobias. I would never call you unless I had no other choice."

"I'll see what I can do. I'd prefer you not come to the embassy. Where can you meet?"

Hawes told Tobias that he could be found at the Café Landtmann beginning at one o'clock.

"Very well," Tobias said. "Your contact will ask you if you know the results from the Liverpool-Sunderland match."

"What were they?"

"An upset. Sunderland, one nil."

* * *

The morning's hard rain had tapered off into a light drizzle by the time Hawes arrived at the Café Landtmann. He took a seat where he could watch the front door, and ordered tea and Topfentascherl,

251

a cheese-filled pastry. He knew he had been drinking too much tea, but he hadn't been bothered by any chest pain. He leafed through a copy of *Die Presse* while he waited.

Hawes recognized Nathan Kidd immediately when he entered the café. They had been contemporaries at SIS, first meeting when the agency's headquarters had been at 54 Broadway. Some had considered them friendly rivals, but Kidd had been more ambitious, more political than Hawes, who never had any desire to climb the career ladder. Hawes developed a reputation for speaking his mind and taking chances. It was no surprise that he ended up leaving SIS; he wasn't built for bureaucratic infighting. Kidd, on the other hand, seemed destined for bigger and better things.

Kidd's rapid rise through the ranks came to an abrupt stop when he backed the wrong side in an internal dispute over a reorganization of the headquarters staff. Banished from Century House, Kidd first was posted to Bonn Station, and then on to Saigon, Rome, and—the last Hawes had heard—Lisbon.

Hawes was glad to see Kidd; he silently thanked Tobias for sending someone he knew, someone from his past.

"We can dispense with the Liverpool results," Kidd said. "I never much cared for football. I'm a rugby man, myself."

"Didn't realize you were in Vienna."

"A reward for good behavior." Kidd tapped a cigarette out of the package and lit it with a burnished silver lighter. He took a long drag and sighed. "I allow myself one a day," he said. "It's been quite a while, Feliks. I heard that you'd retired. Cottage somewhere in East Sussex. Living off your ill-gotten gains."

"Not yet. Still in Redhill. I'm planning to stay in harness for a tad longer. How is Olivia?"

"Quite well, thank you. She's struggling with the idea of being a grandmother. She says it makes her feel ancient. And your son, Nigel. He's at Oxford, is he not?"

"He is, licking his wounds after the election. Even he was shocked by how badly they lost."

"When your fearless leader is Michael Foot, and you're saddled with that absurd manifesto, what do you expect?" Kidd asked. "The longest suicide note in political history. Unilateral nuclear disarmament. Abolishing the House of Lords. Taxes through the roof. You didn't have to love the Iron Lady to know that wouldn't wash." He paused and shrugged. "We could have met at the embassy."

"That was Tobias' call. He thought it would be better this way."

"No wonder that he has thrived at the Foreign Office. He knows when to keep his distance. When to keep things informal. Unofficial. He wouldn't tell me over the phone why you needed a private audience, so I guess it's something nasty. A managing director being blackmailed after a wild weekend in Vienna with a rent boy? Do you need help with the police to hush it up? Something like that?"

"Not quite."

Hawes told Kidd in broad terms about the operation, about the defection of Tatiana Savchenko, and how things had gone awry. "So we're at sixes and sevens. I contacted Tobias because I have no window into what's happening in Prague. You do."

"We do. On the other hand, you've let the side down with this escapade."

"I'm not going to make excuses, but my client left me high and dry. Unexpectedly."

"Did they?" Kidd asked. "A man of your experience?"

"What can I say? In retrospect, perhaps I should have refused to turn over the girl until I had tied off all the loose ends."

"We wondered what had happened," Kidd said. "In the news conference, the American congressman said the Russian girl had escaped by train to Vienna. We assumed that the Mossad was behind the operation. They left no traces here. Uri Avraham at their embassy claims it was all the doing of this New Exodus Project, a private group. The Austrians are furious with him, pointing out that they're a neutral country and plan to stay that way. Uri swears that he and his colleagues had nothing to do with it. Well, it's what I would say if I were in his shoes. A bit of a surprise to find you mixed up in it."

"A mistake to take the job. I was hired by the director of the New Exodus Project. They financed the operation; let me run it with no interference. It went smoothly—we extricated the Russian woman without setting off any alarms. The problems started with that damn news conference."

"Shouldn't you be turning to your Israeli friends for help?" Kidd asked. "While Miss Markham may be a British subject, she's in this predicament on behalf of Tel Aviv, not London."

"There's not much they can do at this point, even if I was willing to involve them, which I'm not," Hawes said. "We have an embassy in Prague. People there who might be able to assist. It's in your best interests to lend a hand."

"Is it? And why is that?"

"Because if she is arrested, and the Czechs decide to make her an example, the London tabloids are going to make a big deal of it. Young Englishwoman persecuted by the Reds. Her only crime is helping a Jewish woman escape from behind the Iron Curtain. Weeks of headlines. What is Her Majesty's Government going to do about it? I hardly think you want that."

Kidd shook his head. "I think your girl would be seen as a less attractive figure if it was known that she was operating at the behest of the Mossad. Since Lebanon and the massacres at Sabra and Shatila, the Israelis aren't as popular as they once were. Some even consider them a bit villainous."

"Are British hands clean on Lebanon? If MI5 had been doing its job, the Palestinians wouldn't have been able to shoot down the Israeli ambassador in broad daylight at the Dorchester. But that's beside the point, Nathan. Claire Markham was working on behalf of the New Exodus Project, as was I. Reputable organization, based in Washington, known for helping Jewish dissidents leave the Soviet Union."

"But carrying the water for Mossad on this one, yes? How on earth did you get mixed up in this? I thought you worked the corporate angle, keeping managing directors safe and sound. Checking security systems at headquarters. That sort of thing. I would have thought that your reckless days were over, long past."

"You know me, Nathan. How could I pass up a chance to embarrass the bastards at Moscow Center?"

"For Christ's sake, Feliks, it's been twenty years since you left Her Majesty's employ. And now you decide to mount a rogue operation against the Reds? Unsanctioned?"

"It seemed like a good idea at the time," Hawes said. "Isn't that what the second-story types say to the Bobbies when they're caught? Consider what we accomplished. We got the girl out. I imagine Moscow Center will blame the Czechs and vice versa. Confusion to our enemies. I'd think London would be happy with that. From what I hear, the Czechs' First Directorate has been rather bold the past few years. Recruiting Labor MPs to spy for them, agents all over London. To say nothing of their training the PLO and the Syrians in terrorism tactics at that special center outside Brno. So you should enjoy the idea of boxing their ears."

"Not like this. Not with the potential for an international incident involving a British national. Two Brits, if you're added to the count."

"I can't change the past. Help me salvage the future. I don't know what's going on in Prague, and anything your people there can find out would be of immense help. There's a contingency plan to get Claire Markham out of the country."

"This is my last posting," Kidd said. "One more month, and then I'm done. Finis. Olivia can't wait. I can only offer you limited assistance. Unofficially, of course. I'll do what I can, but I'm not going to expose our people in Prague to any heightened scrutiny by the StB, nor am I going to leave a paper trail for the internal watchdogs to sniff out. Nothing in writing. I'll make a few discreet calls to Prague, and I'll let you know what I can find out."

"I appreciate that. Whatever you can do." Hawes wrote down his hotel and room number and handed the slip of paper to Kidd.

Kidd shook his head. "For Christ's sake, if she's still at large, do whatever you have to and get the girl out of the country as soon as humanly possible."

* * *

When Hawes returned to the hotel, he found Rafe and Viktor waiting for him in the lobby. Viktor shook his head slightly, a sign to Hawes that he hadn't shared any information with Rafe.

"What's going on?" Rafe asked. "I bumped into Viktor, and he won't tell me why he is here."

"It's about Claire. She didn't arrive at the British embassy as planned. Didn't catch the flight to London she was supposed to." Hawes rubbed the bridge of his nose. "We don't know why."

"It must be because of that damn news conference on television."

"We don't know that."

"But you know something. Viktor wouldn't be here if you weren't working on something."

"You should go back to London," Hawes said.

"I plan to stay here," Rafe said. "I'll stay until I know what's happened to Claire. I feel that I owe her that, and you owe me the courtesy of telling me the truth. What are you doing to help her? You can't just abandon her."

"We haven't."

"Really? I was afraid this was going to happen. I even gave Claire my cousin's name and address in the event *your* arrangements failed."

"You did what?" Hawes asked, incredulous.

"You heard me. Someone had to look out for her well-being. I know that Jan can be trusted. Can you say the same of whoever you hired in Prague?"

"You're an utter fool," Hawes said, his face reddening. Viktor placed a hand on his forearm to restrain him. "You may have jeopardized Claire by involving him."

"Or maybe I saved her," Rafe said. "Jan is clever. If she was able to reach him, he'd move heaven and earth to help her."

"There's no point in jumping to conclusions, one way or the other," Viktor said. He had been silent up to that point. "There is a contingency plan for this development, Rafe. One you aren't privy to. Claire hasn't been left without a lifeline."

"Is that so?" Rafe asked. "There's a fall back plan for her?"

"There is," Hawes said. "And Viktor and I will share it with you if you'll calm down for a moment. It's designed to give her another way out of the country. It's a sound plan. I've never left any of my people out in the cold, and I never will."

Twenty-two

The Klima's modest cottage was primitive by American standards. Jan explained that over the years his family had expanded it, room-by-room. He and his father had done the carpentry on the weekends. The cottage had a compact kitchen, a dining area, two attached bedrooms, and a fireplace in the main room.

Propped up against the wall was a portrait, an oil painting, of a red-haired woman who looked to be in her thirties. Jan saw Claire looking at the picture.

"My mother," he explained. "It's from a photograph of her that was taken when she and my father lived in Paris. It's meant to be a birthday present for her. I've been hiding it from her here."

"She's quite beautiful," Claire said. "It's different from your others, but you use color and light in the same way."

"It's not a conscious choice," he said. "It's how I see things."

Jan suggested they go for a walk before the sun went down, so he could show her a small nearby pond. Claire followed him through a winding path in the woods, startling several rooks, which flew away, their wings flapping. The path led to a stand of pine trees, and just

261

beyond, the pond. A soft wind stirred ripples on the surface of the water. Prague seemed a million miles away—not a two-hour drive.

"It's so peaceful here," she said. "A sanctuary."

"I swam here as a boy," Jan said. "It's not very deep, but the water can be cold. I haven't been here in a year. It hasn't changed."

"Thank you for bringing me."

"I thought you might appreciate it."

* * *

Jan cooked dinner for them with ingredients he had brought from the city. Claire found that she was famished. She hadn't eaten since breakfast. He made tomato soup and a mushroom omelet with a side of peas, and for dessert, they had apple strudel Jan had purchased from his favorite bakery in Smichov.

They ate slowly, finishing a bottle of red wine, and Jan asked her about Gramercy Antiques, and how she had chosen her career.

"I loved art history," she said. "It seemed natural, working for an antiques dealer. I loved researching the history of the old things in the shop. I always wondered about who had owned them. Their history."

"History can be a dangerous thing," Jan said. "It's why they hated my paintings, why
they confiscated them. The Ghosts of Prague. Ghosts in Wenceslas Square dancing above the Russian tanks in 1968. Ghosts circling the

huge Stalin Monument as it was demolished in 1962. Imagine that, the world knew of Stalin's crimes in 1956, and it took our leaders, our Squealers, that long to admit that he was a criminal."

"What happened to them? The paintings?"

"They told me that they had burned them."

"That's terrible."

"They didn't get all of them. My mother hid two and brought them here to our summer cottage. And there's the one I'm painting now that you saw at my flat."

"The ones that are here, may I see them?"

Jan hesitated and then nodded. He unlocked the door to one of the bedrooms and emerged a moment later with two canvases under his arm. He placed them on the table, face up, so she could see them. The larger painting was of a building with a second-floor balcony and floating in the air nearby was another spectral figure, painted in soft gray tones. She thought it might be the place where Jan Masaryk, the Foreign Minister of Czechoslovakia, had fallen to his death in 1948. Most Czechs believed he had been pushed out the window by the Soviets; the official story was that he had committed suicide.

"Is this Jan Masaryk?" she asked.

"His ghost. You can see why they would destroy it if they ever found it."

The second canvas was of Prague's Spanish Synagogue with multiple ghosts—men, women, and children—rising toward the sky above its Moorish dome. She felt herself tearing up, moved by the image. She knew that the Germans had deported most of the Jews of Prague to the Theresienstadt ghetto and from there to the death camp of Auschwitz.

"This is beautiful," she said. "But it is hard to take. So sad."

"I don't do many of these paintings now," Jan said. "I paint portraits. The wives of Party leaders. A politician or two. The money comes in handy. I can buy more paint and fresh canvases. And the informers only know about the portraits, not these."

"And that is how you ran into trouble. An informer."

He nodded. "A man I thought was a friend. It's a common story, to be betrayed like that. He told them about my ghosts. They came to our house and arrested me and took my paintings as evidence. They took me to StB headquarters in Old Town, what they call *Kachlíkárna*, or the Tile, because of the tiles on the outside of the building. It's next door to what was the Church of St. Bartholomew, it was once a convent, of all things. They converted the nun's quarters into cells with solid metal doors. And while the walls were quite thick, you could still hear when they were torturing someone, their cries."

"And did they…?"

"They roughed me up, but they didn't need to torture me. No need for a confession because they had the paintings. Proof positive of my anti-state activities. They kept me in jail and then tried me. When the judge saw my ghosts, I knew there was no hope for a fair trial—I could see it on his face. A picture is worth a thousand words, yes? My defense attorney tried to convince me to plead guilty, but I refused. I was sentenced to two years for subversive activities against the

Republic. At Hermanice, the labor camp, I was assigned to a work detail that whitewashed the walls of the barracks. The guards thought that was hilarious. I was released after eighteen months, the longest months of my life."

He stood up, and took their plates to the sink and began to wash them. She studied the paintings, struck by their originality and authenticity—the connection to the painful history of Prague and its people. Jan finished drying the plates and silverware and returned to the kitchen table. He took a sip from his wineglass.

"Why don't more of us speak up?" he asked. "Why aren't there more dissidents?" Jan shook his head. "I would ask instead—why are there any? Do you know the cost of opposing the regime? If you challenge them directly, you're more than likely to end up in jail. Or you will lose your job. You will lose your vacations at the lake. You will lose your flat and will be forced to move to inadequate lodgings far from the city. Your children will be excluded from the best schools, from going to University. In short, you will have ruined your life. And for what? Things won't change here as long as the Soviets have tanks and soldiers here, backing up Husak.

"There's a joke I've heard. A man shows up at the Bulovka Hospital in Prague. He demands to see an ear and eye doctor. The nurse asks him whether he wants to see an ear, nose, and throat expert, and he shakes his head no, only an ear and eye doctor. She thinks perhaps he's crazy, so she sends him to one of the resident psychiatrists, who asks the man what his symptoms are. The man says, 'I hear all these wonderful things from the government, but I don't see anything like them. My ears and eyes must be failing.' The psychiatrist shrugs and says, 'I'm sorry to say, I can't help you. There is no cure for socialism.'"

"But you have resisted." She motioned to the paintings, now stacked against the wall.

"I'm an artist. How could I stop doing that? I couldn't paint the way they wanted me to. Happy farm workers. Determined factory workers. Sentimental lies. When I first began painting what was in my mind, it was like taking a drug. I couldn't stop. I couldn't help myself, even when I knew it would end badly. It is a hard thing to do, to resist that compulsion. I've been trying."

"You're helping me."

"I shouldn't be. It's a mistake, and I know it's a mistake. I've stayed away from politics. I told myself it was for the better. I did not want to go back to Hermanice. Do you know what it is like to be caged? To feel as if you are squandering your life, that your best years are being wasted?"

"I've never risked anything," she said. "I've been sheltered from this sort of thing. I haven't suffered anything more than a broken heart from a man who lied to me. That's all."

"Pain is pain," Jan said.

*　*　*

He piled wood carefully in the fireplace and lit a fire. They sat on the floor and talked. Outside, the wind had picked up and rattled against the windows. She shivered.

Jan asked her about Tatiana Savchenko's defection and the part Claire had played in it. She told him about how they had prepared for the operation, and how the news conference in Israel had disrupted her plans for leaving Prague. Then, he had more questions for her.

"Why have they gone to all this trouble for this woman?" he asked. "She is not a famous person. Who had heard of her before? Not a dissident, or a refusenik. Why send you and my cousin to Prague?"

"That's what this foundation, the New Exodus Project, does. They help Jews in the Soviet Union emigrate to Israel. This was a special case because the Russians wouldn't let her leave through the normal channels."

"Why was that?"

"Her father was political. They were punishing him by blocking her emigration."

"And that is what they told you?" Jan shook his head. "I don't believe that. There has to be another reason. One they did not reveal to you."

"I refuse to be that cynical," she said.

"No, I'm not cynical. I'm a realist. Living under the thumb makes you that way. Here is what I think. There has been a fair sum invested in her defection. It was planned. My cousin told me he was well paid. The woman, Piri, was paid to shelter you for the night. Who spends like this without a return on that investment? We don't know what it might be, but they will expect a return."

"You sound like a capitalist. A return on investment?"

He gave her a thin smile. "Perhaps you're too much of a romantic,

Claire. I like that about you. We need dreamers. But it makes you vulnerable to manipulation. This man Singer. Who is he? And the Englishman, Townsend? When you describe them, I don't picture them as humanitarians."

"You think I've been terribly naïve, don't you?" she asked.

"You have a good heart, Claire. You trust people. It's not that way for us. We must be cynical about the motives of others."

"And yet you've trusted me. Protected me."

He shrugged. "Maybe I'm a bit of a romantic, too." He stirred and rose from the floor. "I will sleep in the first bedroom," he said. "I use it as a studio, so there's the smell of paint. I'm used to it."

Claire rose to her feet and moved next to him until their bodies were just inches apart. She kissed him on the lips, surprising herself by her boldness. He responded with another long kiss. "Let's go to bed," she said. "I want you to make love to me."

"Are you sure?" he asked.

"I am sure," she said, and took him by the hand, leading him to the bedroom.

The bed was narrow, with a single pillow and blanket. She kissed Jan again on the lips and began unbuttoning his shirt. He pulled her onto the bed and helped her undress. She found herself shivering from the cold, and he covered their now naked bodies with a blanket.

She ran her hands through his hair and covered his face and neck with kisses. She gasped with pleasure as he entered her, and she pulled him close, her fingernails raking his back. He murmured her name as they made love and cried out when he reached climax.

For the first time in days, she felt safe, lying in his arms, the sound of the fire crackling, while the demands and cares of the outside world seemed to recede.

"I don't do this," she told him. "Sleep with someone I hardly know. But this, being with you, feels different. You're different."

"I was attracted to you from the beginning," he said. "I didn't know if you were interested. I don't have much to offer a woman these days. I have no money. No prospects."

"But you've had girlfriends. Lovers."

"Not as many as you might think. And you—you must attract the attention of many men."

She laughed. "Not as many as you think. I have been wary of romance. That's what a bad love affair will do."

He pulled her closer. "I'm sorry you were hurt."

"I wish you could come with us," she said. "Cross into Germany. Have you thought of leaving? Emigrating to the West?"

Jan nodded. "I have. They've let some of those who signed the Charter leave the country. They might let me. But I'm an only son, and my mother depends on me. When she's gone, I will try."

"Then, I wish you could come with us at least as far as the border."

"I wish I could. But a citizen of the great Czechoslovak Socialist

Republic must have a permit to enter the border zone, and I would never pass muster for that honor."

He fell silent, and they lay there together. Claire thought about how sudden their romance had been—she had known Jan for two days, and yet she felt that he understood her. He was more of a mystery—gentle and sensitive, and yet he had an impulsive and reckless side that had led him into trouble.

They had been quiet now for several minutes, and she broke the silence by asking him what he was thinking.

"What am I thinking? *Lepší jedno dnes, než dvoje zítra.* 'Better one today, than two tomorrows.' It's true. One today with you…" His voice trailed off for a moment. "I won't think about tomorrow."

She studied Jan in profile, his eyes closed and a wistful smile on his lips, and wished she could somehow stop time, freeze that moment. Jan was right, they had their one today, and there would be no tomorrow for them.

Part Three

Twenty-three

For a few moments after she woke up, Claire wasn't sure where she was—the narrow bed and light pinewood walls surrounding her were strange and unfamiliar. Then she realized she was in the Klima summer cottage, and she remembered that she had spent the night with Jan. None of it seemed real to her, the tension and fear of the past few days, and the suddenness of the intimacy with Jan. It was almost as if there was another Claire Markham, a different woman, who had been plunged into a strangely exciting but dangerous world.

She could hear Jan moving around in the kitchen. She wrapped the blanket around her naked body and stepped to the door. He was dressed in a black T-shirt and jeans, his feet bare. His back was turned to her, and she had to call his name twice before he responded.

"Come to bed," she said.

She waited for him in the bed, surprised at her desire, her sudden need for his body. He joined her without saying anything, and she helped him pull his clothing off. They made love again, slowly, and she clung to him, pulling him closer and closer to her. They moved together in rhythm, and she found herself gasping from a mounting tingling sensation that climaxed in waves of pleasure.

Afterward, she nestled in his arms, and he kissed her lightly on the lips. Claire gently touched the scar under his eye. "How did you get this?"

"In prison. A fight. Not one that I wanted, but one that was necessary. They left me alone afterward. The doctor who stitched me up wasn't very good."

"It's distinctive," she said. "And you're a very handsome man."

"I'll finish making us breakfast," Jan said. "I found some clean clothes for you in the dresser." He pointed to a wooden chair in the corner with a folded light red blouse, and blue jeans.

Claire dressed quickly and found the clothes fit her better than she had expected. She wondered whose it was—a lover from the past? When she sat down for breakfast—*palačinky*, crepe-like pancakes rolled with strawberry jam, and hot milky tea—it was her first question.

"They were Tereza's. She left them here."

"Was she here often?" Claire tried not to sound jealous.

"At one time, we planned to marry. We spent many weekends here before my troubles. But after I was expelled from the Union of Painters and Sculptors, and after I was sentenced for my crimes, we ended it. As a Party member, and with her father in the government, she couldn't associate with me, let alone marry me. She was building socialism, after all, and I was a reactionary. When I was sent to Hermanice, Tereza took up with another man, a man well regarded in Party circles. They married while I was in prison, but he was jealous and abused her, and she left him. They live apart now."

"She treated you quite shabbily."

Jan shook his head. "Should she have thrown away her life for me? I don't blame her for the choice she made. Tereza was being practical. I admire her for that—it's something I never quite got the hang of. Being practical."

"How do you feel about her, Jan?"

"Once I loved her. But as Tereza never failed to point out, I loved painting more. Or more accurately, I loved painting what I wanted to paint. If I stuck to landscapes and portraits, we could have had a conventional marriage. We are friends, now, but I made my choice and it wasn't her."

She wondered about her feelings toward Jan. They had spent relatively little time together, and yet she felt a deep connection. He listened to her in a way that Hal never had, nor any of her previous boyfriends, and he was willing to share his history and his feelings as if he had nothing to lose.

After breakfast, they went for a walk in the nearby forest. The pine trees reminded her of Vermont. She felt the morning wind on her face and hair. They stopped in a small glade and sat for a moment.

"Will we ever see each other again?" she asked.

"I would like to visit New York one day soon," he said. "You could show me the museums."

"I could. We could go to the Museum of Modern Art, and the Guggenheim. And if you want to see more classical art, there's the

Metropolitan Museum. We could spend days going from museum to museum, and stopping for coffee and ice cream in between."

"I would like that. Very much. And I'll keep an eye out in the antique shops for magic carpets so I can come see you."

* * *

Summer had hoped for an uncomplicated final day in Prague. She was eager to get on the road, to collect Claire, and turn around and head for the border. But then Anton asked to see her in private. He fidgeted nervously before he spoke. "There is a problem," he said. "Miss Nosek has complained to me. She is concerned that she has not performed her duties as your host appropriately. You have spent very little time with her."

Summer smiled. "She should not be concerned. I've had a great time. Made some friends. Saw the city."

"You don't understand," he said. "This will reflect poorly on me."

"That's ridiculous. I'm not complaining about her, and you've been totally cool. Couldn't ask for a better gig."

Anton shook his head. "Miss Nosek reports to the Interior Ministry. It could cause problems if her superiors take it up with the Ministry of Culture."

"I get it," Summer said. "Where is Marjeta? I'll smooth things over, don't worry."

"She went back to your rooms. And thank you, Miss Summer."

Summer found Marjeta sitting on the steps of the apartment building where they were housed. She immediately apologized for not being around more often. "I told you I was a free spirit," she said. "Let's spend some time together this morning. I'm heading over to Nove Mesto, to call my agent. Would you like to walk to the Main Post Office with me?"

Marjeta beamed with delight at the idea. It took them twenty minutes to reach Jindrisska Street and the Main Post Office. Marjeta followed her into the large main hall with its glass roof. Summer stepped into the booth and waited as the operator placed her call, smiling at Marjeta, who waited just outside, clearly hoping to overhear what Summer had to say.

"The gig's been cool," Summer told Freddie when he picked up. "Thanks for booking it for me. And for setting up the one in Brighton. That's going to work out just fine."

"Splendid," Freddie said. "I'll pass that along to the promoter. He's looking forward to meeting you once you're back."

"I just have a farewell lunch this afternoon," Summer said. "Then I'm driving to Nuremberg. I'll call you when I get there. Oh, and I've met a very nice girl from London. Name of Carol Jordan. She's been touring Prague, seeing all the sights. I've offered her a ride back when my gig is over here."

"Kind of you to do so," Freddie said. "Drive safely. No speeding."

"In that old Beetle? I couldn't speed if I wanted to. Bye-bye, Freddie."

She turned to Marjeta after leaving the phone booth. "Will you sit next to me at the luncheon today?" she asked. "My last one. I wish I could stay longer, but my agent, Freddie, has booked me for shows in England. Freddie is a sweetheart. Always looking out for me. He's more than an agent, he's a friend."

* * *

Claire heard the sound of the Volkswagen, the engine running rough, before the Beetle lurched into view. Summer was driving with Lenka in the passenger seat. She and Jan went to greet them.

"The damn farewell luncheon dragged on forever," Summer said. "I made my apologies and took off. Finally ditched Comrade Nosey, and we drove straight here." She looked around, taking in the cottage and the nearby forest. "Quite pretty. It's off the beaten path, that's for sure."

As they stood by the Beetle, a light breeze stirred the nearby pine trees. Claire found herself distracted, marveling at the beauty of their surroundings.

"There's something wrong with the engine," Summer said. "The temperature gauge showed red most of the way from Prague, but I didn't want to risk stopping. Then, the damn thing started smoking. I'm afraid of driving it now, without a mechanic looking at it. I learned that the hard way. When I was living in L.A., my boyfriend kept driving when his engine was overheating and he fried it. Not the smartest guy."

She turned to Jan. "Can we get a mechanic for the car"

"He will have to come here," Jan said. "It will be very expensive."

Summer exchanged a look with Claire. "We can pay. In pounds. Or crowns."

"Crowns are best." He paused. "I have a friend, Tomas. Lenka knows him. He's a mechanic who does work on the side. For a price."

"Can you call him?" Summer asked. "Ask him to come?"

"We can drive to Podebrady," Lenka said to Jan. "Call him from there."

Jan glanced at his watch. "Twenty minutes to Podebrady. It will take Tomas perhaps ninety minutes from Prague."

There was an awkward moment when Jan turned to Claire and she thought he might kiss her on the lips. Instead, he smiled and winked. "We'll be back before you know it."

Claire and Summer sat drinking more tea in the kitchen. Claire found herself watching the dirt road that led to the cottage, already missing Jan.

"How did you sleep?" Summer asked. "You looked quite relaxed. And you're wearing different clothes. What's going on?"

Claire blushed. "The blouse and jeans were left behind by one of Jan's friends. It was a relief to change into clean clothes."

"You're not fooling anyone," Summer said. "The way the two of you look at each other. I don't think Lenka is too happy about it."

"I can't do anything about that."

"No, you can't. And you shouldn't." Summer rummaged through her backpack and found a glass-bead necklace and large hoop earrings. "You should put these on," she said. "They'll make you more of a hippie chick. Traveling with me, you have to look the part."

Claire reluctantly put on the earrings and the necklace. Summer studied her for a long moment. "It's a change. But you'll need to smile more. We're troubadours! Bohemians!"

"What will the real Bohemians think? A California bohemian?"

"I'm not really from California. I tell people that, but I'm from Ohio. Not a cool place, and it's easier just to say L.A. You're selling the dream. Sunny Southern California. Malibu. Hollywood. The Beach Boys and the Eagles."

"Do you think about going back to the States?" Claire asked.

"Why? At least in London, I'm somebody. An American folk singer. Not that many of us there."

"Couldn't you do that in the U.S.?"

"Too much competition. I'm not good enough. I don't kid myself."

They were interrupted by the return of Jan and Lenka, the Skoda pulling into the clearing by the cottage. Summer took Claire's hand and gave it a squeeze. "Don't worry. I'll occupy Lenka so you can spend some private time with Jan, say goodbye."

Jan's friend Tomas, the mechanic, arrived in a shiny green Skoda, beeping the horn as he rolled into the clearing, parking next to Lenka's car. He and Jan chatted briefly before Tomas took a grimy canvas bag filled with tools and walked over to the Volkswagen. Summer climbed into the driver's seat of the Beetle and started the engine. Tomas shook his head and waved at her to turn the engine off.

He spent ten minutes at the back of the Beetle with the engine exposed, a wrench in one hand and a greasy rag in the other, working away. Finally, he shook his head. "Thermostat," he said. "It's bad."

"Can you fix it?" Claire asked.

Tomas said something in Czech to Jan.

"The thermostat needs to be replaced," Jan said. "He doesn't have the part. He'll have to return to the city to get it."

"What about Podebrady?" Claire asked. "It's much closer, isn't it?"

Jan and Tomas conferred. "Tomas is sure that he can get the thermostat in Prague. He doesn't know anyone in Podebrady. We'd have to find a garage, hope they have a Volkswagen thermostat, and would be willing to sell it to us. That's a crime, of course, selling state property."

Lenka said something to Jan, and he nodded. "Lenka and I will go with Tomas to get the part in Lenka's car. Tomas will leave his car here. He'll need more money for the spare part. That's how the real economy works here. You pay under the table. If you're an electrician, a plumber, an auto mechanic, you find work on the side, illegally. The saying is 'he who doesn't steal, robs from his family.' The system corrupts us all."

"We must go," Lenka said. "We need to be back before dark."

"One minute," Jan said. "I need to talk to Claire." He motioned for her to follow him into the cottage. He closed the door behind them and took her in his arms and kissed her. "I've wanted to do that all afternoon," he said.

"Lenka doesn't like me," Claire said. "She's jealous."

Jan shook his head. "She is protective. She worries that helping you will cause trouble for me with the police."

"She's jealous. Trust my female intuition on this."

"A friend, Claire, not a lover."

"Then she is a friend who would like to be a lover. I wish you would stay. Can't she and Tomas go to Prague and get the part without you?"

He smiled. "Driving to and from is the least I can do when I'm asking favors of both of them. And I've been away and I need to stop by my building."

"I wish you would stay."

"There's a saying, *Snesl bych ti modré z nebe.* 'I would take the blue from the sky for you.' That's how I feel about you, Claire. But we must be practical. What you need now is a Volkswagen thermostat, and that's what I'm going to get for you."

Twenty-four

It had been four days since Claire Markham had handed over her passport to Tatiana Savchenko, three days since she missed her flight to London, and two days since Hawes had Freddie North pass along the code word to Summer Devine. Hawes knew that with every additional minute and hour Claire spent there, the odds of her making it out of Czechoslovakia worsened. She wasn't trained to evade the net that had to be closing in around her.

He sat down with Viktor after an early breakfast, and they had a brief but pointed conversation. Hawes believed that it was time to stop by the Czechoslovak embassy and obtain visas, which were available the same day of application. They needed to be ready to cross into Czechoslovakia to assist Claire and, he hoped, Summer. Viktor shook his head.

"I don't like this, Feliks. It's a bad idea. What can we possibly do? We're both too old for the field."

"Are we? I don't agree. If anything, we're at an age where we'll draw less attention."

"Do you plan to use your own passport?" Viktor asked.

"I do. My name shouldn't ring any alarm bells. I left the Service more than twenty years ago. Sure, there's a dossier with my name on it at Moscow Center gathering dust in the archives somewhere. The Czechs wouldn't know me from Adam."

Viktor shook his head slowly. "I'll do as you ask, but if we go in, I doubt there's much we can do. Not now. It won't be easy finding them."

"If Summer calls Freddie again, I can get a message to her. Have her call me directly."

"I know you feel responsible," Viktor said. "But you shouldn't blame yourself."

"I am responsible. And I'll be damned if we watch this from a distance."

* * *

An hour after his discussion with Viktor, Nathan Kidd called Hawes from the Hotel Imperial lobby and suggested they meet in the bar for a drink. "I have news to share."

Kidd had already stubbed out two cigarettes in the ashtray and was puffing away when Hawes joined him. The waiter brought Hawes a beer and a second gin and tonic for Kidd.

"I thought it was one a day," Hawes said, looking at the ashtray with a slight smile.

"Depends on the day. Today calls for more than one."

"What's the news?"

"Nothing about the girl. But it seems that you've stirred up the proverbial hornet's nest. Lots of cable traffic between Moscow and Prague. From what we can gather, Moscow Center has sent a man from counterintelligence to handle the matter. Chap named Baranov. A colonel. That suggests they're taking this quite seriously. They don't see the StB as particularly competent. Do you know the joke about the Czech State Security? 'Why do StB officers work together in groups of three? You need one who can read, one who can write, and a third to keep an eye on the two intellectuals.' It's true, by the way. The StB is filled with not-so-keen thugs and more than a few sadists. The Russians would never trust them to figure this out by themselves."

"How good are your sources?"

Kidd stared at him. "We've pieced this together from some low-level contacts. One of our chaps in the embassy has a Czech friend in the Foreign Ministry. There's been grousing about interference from Moscow. We're quite in the dark about what Baranov is up to, but I imagine he's there to conduct a thorough investigation. I hope to God that you don't have any assets in Prague other than the girl. No Czechs, I mean. You can imagine what the KGB and StB would put them through."

"No locals," Hawes said. "One Hungarian student, but I'm not worried about her. She knows very little." He took a sip of his beer. "There's no word on Claire Markham? Not even rumors?"

"Nothing. I doubt they'd announce an arrest, but our people haven't heard about it."

"She may still be in the wind, then. Good."

"This is far from an ideal situation, Hawes. What do you plan to do?"

"I have a contingency plan. It's been put into motion. With any luck, it should work."

"Are you in contact with the girl?" Kidd asked.

"Not directly. By design."

"And if they catch her?"

"Then it will be up to Tobias and the Foreign Office mandarins. A diplomatic solution. I don't think the Russians would want to go public. Too embarrassing. The bird has already flown the coop, and they wouldn't want to draw attention to that fact."

"The woman. Claire Markham. Did she ever work for MI6? MI5?"

Hawes shook his head. "No connection to any intelligence service."

"A civilian?"

Hawes ignored the implied rebuke in the question. "The plan worked, Nathan. The bloody circus act in Tel Aviv is what queered things. Claire would be on this side of the border, free and clear, but for the political grandstanding."

"You go to bed with hornets and you can expect to wake up stung."

"I've been stung. The question is how to make things right."

"Well, I've helped as much as I can. To do more than pass along what Prague Station turns up, I'd have to go through the proper channels. London. You don't want that, do you?"

Hawes shook his head.

"Neither do I," Kidd said. "What I can do, I will. If we hear anything more about Miss Markham, we'll let you know."

"I appreciate that, Nathan."

Kidd drained his glass. "You know, I regret I didn't leave Century House when you did. My brother-in-law wanted me to come to the City, join his trading firm. Or I could have done security work. I would have made a packet either way. Olivia and I could be living outside of Palma. She's always loved Mallorca."

"You could still do that."

"On what I can expect from my pension? Not quite. At the time, when you left, I thought you were making a mistake. I envy you, now."

"Not today," Hawes said. "I don't believe I'm in an enviable place today."

* * *

After Nathan Kidd left the bar, Hawes sat finishing his beer. He was startled when Benjamin Singer walked over and slid into the seat opposite him. Hawes shook his head. "I'm surprised to see you," he said. "I thought shame would keep you away."

"It's not what I wanted," Singer said. "I'm sorry it went this way."

"That circus in Tel Aviv has had consequences. For Claire."

"I know. I heard from Rafe."

"The irony is that I'm angrier with myself than with you. I blamed myself for taking the job. I was too eager to get back in the game. Run a meaningful operation. I ignored the red flags. Your people never worry about burning bridges. I knew that, and I went ahead with the operation. And now Claire may pay the price for my arrogance."

"I'm sorry for my part in this mess," Singer said. "There have been other consequences. The New Exodus Project is dead. The Soviets will never deal with us again. As far as they're concerned, we're just an arm of Mossad."

"How wrong would they be?" Hawes asked. "Based on the past week, can you dispute that claim?"

"Until this episode, I had little to do with them. I might occasionally share information with them, but nothing more. I kept my distance until now."

"Until now? What changed?"

"They convinced me of the importance of bringing Tatiana Savchenko to Israel. That while it might require compromising the New Exodus Project, it would be worth it. That access to Professor Savchenko was of vital importance to our national security. After all, what's the point of liberating Jews from the Soviet Union if there's no Jewish homeland for them to go to? If our enemies gain the upper hand. You know what the Arabs say, 'Palestine from the river to the sea.' Where does that leave us?"

"You're the ones with the upper hand, from all that I can see."

Singer shook his head slowly. "It appears that way, but I know better. I was in Sinai with a tank battalion in '73 during the Yom Kippur war. Ten years ago, almost to the day. The Egyptians fought better than we had thought possible. They had those damn RPG-7s. Crude but effective against armor. We took heavy losses. It was a desperate time. Running out of ammunition. Without Nixon and the airlift, who knows what would have happened? We learned from that. We can't let up on developing our own weapons, or making sure we have friends in America."

"And you believe them? About the importance of Savchenko and his information?"

"I do."

"If he was so damned important, why didn't the Mossad do their own dirty work?" Hawes asked.

"Not everyone in Tel Aviv agreed about the urgency or the relative risks. There was no consensus on employing the Mossad. Thus, the New Exodus option."

"But the news conference. Why couldn't you wait? Claire Markham would be in London, safe and sound, if it weren't for that grandstanding politician. I just needed one day. If you could have waited one more bloody day, she would have been out of the country, free and clear. Moscow Center would have figured it out in the end, of course. But that wouldn't have mattered."

"The damage has been done," Singer said. "We can't do anything about it, now. We have to salvage what we can."

"I will do what I can," Hawes said. "I've never run an operation without a contingency plan. Something always goes wrong. I didn't anticipate this turn of events, but I have an alternate way for Claire to return."

"Your contingency plan. What are the particulars?"

"With all due respect, it's best that you don't know."

Singer remained silent.

"I don't trust your masters," Hawes said. "Your Congressman. Whoever else you answer to."

"It's not like that," Singer said. "Getting Claire out of Czechoslovakia isn't political for me. It's personal."

"That may be so. But now there are other people involved. I won't jeopardize them. The fewer who know, the safer they are. I learned the hard way to never take anything for granted. I was here, in Vienna, in 1956. There was an American diplomat, a turncoat who had defected to the East and then changed his mind. I went to Budapest to assist his escape, along with an American journalist who was his childhood friend. The uprising was underway, and in the confusion we got him across the border. Then, I made a mistake. I let my guard down once we reached Vienna. We were betrayed by one of our own. The Russians hunted down the diplomat and killed him. My fault."

"I can help," Singer said. "Logistics. Money. I can call in some favors. Tell me what I can do."

Hawes paused to finish his beer. "I understand that you want to help, Benjamin. But we're well past the time where you could. The contingency plan has been set in motion. We'll know soon enough whether it has worked or not, and for Claire's sake, I hope to God that it does."

* * *

The Czechoslovakian embassy in Vienna was located in the Penzing District in the Palais Cumberland, once the summer chateau of Empress Maria Theresa. Hawes and Viktor made separate visits to get their tourist visas; Hawes went early in the afternoon and Viktor waited until later in the day. Hawes filled out the form, paid a fee, and sat in an uncomfortable wooden chair until a bored clerk called his name and handed him his passport and visa.

Back at the hotel, the front desk clerk gave Hawes a message—Freddie North had called. Hawes immediately called him back.

"I received a collect call from Summer," Freddie said. "She has one final performance, and then she plans to leave Prague. She'll drive back to Germany this afternoon in the Volkswagen. She told me not to worry, she had a London friend along for company who would make sure she didn't doze off while driving. A girl named Carol Jordan."

"Thank you, Freddie. That's tremendous news."

"Glad to be of help. I made her promise to contact me once she has reached Germany."

"I'm going to drive to Nuremberg," Hawes said. "Should be there in the early evening. When she calls you, tell her to meet me at the Grand Hotel."

Twenty-five

He was bone-tired and thankful for the seemingly endless cups of Turkish coffee the StB secretaries kept bringing him. Baranov had managed only a few hours of sleep, and he needed to remain alert. What was the dark saying—plenty of time to sleep when you were dead?

Baranov returned to the embassy to call his colleagues in Budapest. He wasn't sure how secure the telephone lines at StB headquarters were, and he didn't want his conversation monitored or recorded. He knew the officer tasked with interrogating Piri Szabo, a man named Ivan Petrovich Zolotov. They had met in Moscow at a boring internal seminar on embassy security. Zolotov had joked with Baranov about the presenter, a portly bureaucrat with a decided stutter.

When he reached Zolotov on the phone, he learned that the interrogation had been productive.

"We've handled her carefully," Zolotov explained. "Her father carries some weight in the Party. But the girl was very cooperative. I guess Daddy made it clear how deep in the shit she was."

She had been subjected to several hours of intense questioning and gave what Zolotov believed was a full confession. Her story seemed credible. She had been approached in London by a Hungarian emigre, Viktor, who had introduced her to another man who made her a lucrative job offer. Upon her return to Prague, she would be paid handsomely for hosting an Englishwoman, Claire, for a night and then accompanying her to the British embassy. They had paid her half in advance, and Piri had seen nothing wrong in making some money on the side. The cover story the men told her was laughable—the Englishwoman was fleeing her abusive Czech lover and Piri was providing safe harbor. The trip to the embassy the next day was to obtain an emergency passport so Claire could leave the country.

"Szabo said she had no reason to doubt the story," Zolotov said. "But she became suspicious after she heard about the Savchenko defection, and when State Security turned up at Charles University asking questions. That's when she went to the police."

"The story was fishy from the start," Baranov said. "That was clear. She figured that she could avoid blame if she informed on the Englishwoman."

"She swears that she knew nothing about the defection."

"And you believe her? You don't think she's part of a cell?

"There's nothing in her past involving anti-State activities," Zolotov said. "She's just greedy. Bringing blue jeans back to sell on the black market. The men in London who recruited her told her fairy tales, and she didn't care as long as she got paid."

"These men? Were they Israelis?"

"No, she said the one who first approached her was definitely Hungarian. Then, the man who gave her instructions was English. A man named Townsend. She said he was older, maybe in his fifties. He spoke some Hungarian, but with a strong accent."

Baranov wondered what to make of the news. An Englishman recruiting accessories to the plot? Was MI6 involved? A joint operation with the Mossad? It was confusing. The two intelligence agencies were far from friendly and any collaboration would be reluctant at best.

"What about the Englishwoman, Claire Markham? Any details?"

"Szabo said she was very anxious. Guilty. Szabo thinks that her questioning of Claire spooked the Englishwoman into leaving the flat. She figures Claire made a dash for the embassy, and then perhaps the airport."

Baranov thanked his colleague for his help and suggested he release Piri to the Hungarian police. He doubted the AVH would be gentle with her—they had a well-deserved reputation for brutality—but perhaps her father had enough clout to keep her out of the hands of State Security.

Her interrogation had been productive. Piri Szabo had been recruited to play a given part, and by going to the police, she had disrupted the plan for Claire Markham's departure from Prague. Perhaps only a temporary disruption, but it had flushed the Englishwoman into the open, and that might mean she had contacted others in the city, other collaborators.

When he returned to the Tile, Baranov asked Cerny to contact the border control officers at Ruzyne Airport to ascertain whether Claire Markham had taken a flight to the West. "It's more than likely we'll find that she flew out to London on Tuesday."

"Before I do that, I have something to share," Cerny said. He had a file folder in his hand and a broad smile on his face. "We found the file on Rafael Klima's cousin. Jan Klima." He paused. "I think you will find it very interesting."

As Baranov leafed through the dossier, Cerny remained standing, eagerly awaiting his reaction.

"Excellent," Baranov said aloud, once he had scanned the documents. Rafael Klima's cousin had been convicted of anti-state crimes and had served time in prison. He had been educated at Charles University and by all accounts had been considered a promising painter. But then, according to the file, at some point he had begun painting decadent and subversive paintings and when he had been warned, refused to stop. His social circle included artists, writers, poets, and political dissidents. Since his release from prison, the only work he could find was as a maintenance man in a residential building in Smichov where he occupied a basement flat.

"This begins to make sense," Baranov said. "I would bet that Rafael Klima made use of him in this scheme. At the least, Jan Klima will know something. Let's find him, bring him here for questioning. Start at his flat. If he's not there, find his friends named in his dossier.

298

They may lead us to him. Interrogating him becomes our top priority."

"I will go to Smichov myself," Cerny said. "We will find him."

* * *

It wasn't until very late in the afternoon that Jan Klima arrived at his flat on Radlicka Street. When the StB officers closed in, Klima took off, running up the street. He ran directly into Cerny, who knocked him down to the pavement. Klima didn't say anything as Cerny handcuffed him. His flight alone suggested guilt, and he had an air of resignation about him on the trip to StB headquarters.

Cerny began the interrogation with Baranov observing from the corner. Jan sat in a chair, facing Cerny, with a small table between them.

"Do you know why you are here?" Cerny asked.

Jan shrugged. "What does it matter what I know or don't know? Tell me."

"Your cousin, Rafael Klima. He is a spy for the Zionists, and you have assisted him."

"Rafe? A spy? That's absurd."

"He came here to Prague with a woman, Claire Markham. She is also a spy."

Jan shrugged. "I don't know who that is. Rafe isn't a spy, he's an interpreter."

"You met with him at an antiques store on Narodni Street, where he gave you instructions."

"Hardly. He's my cousin. I went to say hello."

"You are lying. You have conspired with the enemies of the state."

"I'm a janitor. I clean the windows, take out the trash, stoke the boiler with coal. I stay out of politics."

"Then why did you run from us? If you are innocent of wrongdoing, why did you run?"

Jan didn't respond.

"You should tell us the truth now," Cerny said. "It will go much easier for you."

"I'm telling the truth."

Baranov sat in the corner and watched and listened. He knew Klima could see him out of the corner of his eye, and Baranov hoped his presence added to his anxiety. Baranov stood up and told Cerny that he would take over the interrogation. He took his place in the chair opposite Jan. He had a file folder with him, which he placed on the tabletop.

He didn't say anything at first. He just kept his eyes fixed on Jan's face, hoping to intimidate him, to rattle him. Then he began asking questions, in Russian.

"What do you think you're accomplishing by lying to us? A hero, are you?"

"I'm no hero," Jan replied. "What do you want from me?"

"I see from your file that you have a subversive history."

Before he could answer, Baranov felt a tap on his shoulder. It was Cerny, who asked Baranov if he would join him in the corridor for a word in private.

Baranov closed the cell door and turned on Cerny. "Why have you interrupted the interrogation?"

"One of our officers talked to a Mrs. Prazak, who resides in Klima's building. She has provided information in the past. She saw Klima and a dark-haired woman leave the building yesterday afternoon. She thought it was strange at the time because she was in the hallway and heard them speaking in English."

"It could have been Claire Markham."

"That's what I thought," Cerny said. "Did she go to Klima for help after she left Piri's flat?"

"We will find out in short order."

The two of them re-entered the cell where Klima waited.

Baranov sat down and shook his head. "Your file says that you were released from Hermanice and had agreed to refrain from anti-state activities. You have broken that promise. The state prosecutor will not look kindly on your actions." He sighed. "You are a young man.

Do you wish to spend the next ten years in prison? You know what it is like in a labor camp. You will be broken there."

Jan remained silent.

"You have repeatedly lied to us. We know that you helped Claire Markham. Where did she go? How was she planning to leave the country? Train? Bus?"

Jan shook his head. "I can't help you."

Baranov sighed. "You will tell me. It is only a matter of time. You have made your choice." He stood up and beckoned to Cerny. "You know what to do. Call me when he is ready to cooperate."

* * *

Jan resolved to hold out for as long as he could. To buy time for Claire. He would focus on resisting, minute by minute, and soon the minutes would add up. He had no illusions about what would eventually happen—he would reach his limit for pain, and he would tell them something. He resolved to reveal as little as possible.

They brought him to a different cell, smaller with dark walls, and tied him into a chair.

He tried picturing Claire, the hollow of her neck, the freckles on her back, her lips. He wanted to keep those images in his mind, to block out what lay ahead in that squalid little room.

"Who are you working for?" his interrogator asked. A small man in an ill-fitting uniform, he had a ruddy complexion and dark eyes. "The Jews? The Israelis?"

"I'm not working for anyone," he said.

The officer slapped him in the face, hard enough to bring tears to Jan's eyes. "We are not idiots." He had a Slovakian accent. "Who are you working for?"

"I'm telling you the truth. I'm not working for anyone."

Another slap. Then a punch to the gut, and Jan doubled over in pain.

The man administering the punishment showed no emotion. He wasn't angry with Jan. He and his colleague were simply doing their job, applying the techniques that were known to quickly produce names, or answers, or confessions.

"Where did the Englishwoman go?"

"What woman?"

The punch to the cheekbone that followed stunned Jan, dazing him. He stayed silent, keeping his eyes closed, hoping to stall for time. Another slap to the face followed, hard enough to cause him to open his eyes.

"Who else are you working with? What are their names?"

He wondered how much punishment he could take before he broke. He had to delay them. That was the only hope for Claire and her American friend. He knew that eventually he would tell his interrogators what they wanted to know, but he had to postpone that moment. How much time could he buy them? Another two hours? Perhaps three? He knew he should give them something.

"I'm not working for anyone," he said. "I did a favor for my cousin. I gave a friend of his, this Englishwoman, a tour of the city."

His interrogator turned and looked over the corner of the cell. Jan recognized the man there—it was the officer who had arrested him on Radlicka Street, Captain Cerny. The officer nodded. A moment later Jan groaned at the hard punch to his stomach. He felt like he might vomit.

A slap to the face. Another officer untied him from the chair and stood him upright. The red-faced officer began to beat Jan on the legs and arms with a rubber hose, the blows stinging painfully. He kept at it for several minutes, pausing between swings, making Jan flinch before the blow arrived. Jan tried to think of Claire, but the pain was searing, burning—it couldn't be ignored. He fell to his knees, dizzy, and then suddenly everything went dark.

He fought his way back to consciousness. He was lying on the cold concrete floor. How long had he been out? He had lost all sense of time. At least, the beating had stopped. His arms and legs throbbed with pain.

The two uniformed officers standing in front of him, impassive, studied him. They lifted him from the floor and held him up by his arms.

Jan managed to croak a few words, telling them that he was willing to talk if only they would stop. He was ashamed of his weakness, but he couldn't take another beating. He decided he would give them some answers, enough to keep them from hurting him, but slowly.

"She told me that she was in trouble," he said. "She was very pretty. So I helped her."

"And why do you make us do this?" Jan squinted through his swollen eyelids. It was the Russian who had begun questioning him before. He gestured toward Jan's face.

"I'm no informer," Jan said.

"I take no pleasure in ordering this treatment," the Russian said. "It is degrading. But you have forced us to employ these measures because of your stubbornness. Now, we must talk to each other like civilized men." He paused. "Sit him down."

The two State Security officers pushed Jan into his seat. They placed a small table and a chair directly in front of him.

"I am Colonel Baranov," the Russian said, sitting down in the empty chair. A different officer appeared with two glasses of tea. Baranov took the glasses from him and carefully placed one down on the table and motioned for Jan to take it. Jan sipped some of the tea, surprised at how grateful he was for that simple act of kindness. The Russian stared at Jan for a long moment. "Do not attempt to deceive me. If you lie to me, they will beat you again. We know what Claire Markham did. We know she came to Prague as part of a Zionist plot. So please, no more fictions about your giving her a tour of Prague. Tell me about your involvement."

"I found a place for her to stay Tuesday night," Jan managed. "A friend's flat."

"What did she tell you she was doing?"

"She said she had helped a young Jewish woman leave the country. A matter of conscience."

"You've been deceived. This was a scheme by the Zionists to defame the Soviet Union."

"It was a favor for my cousin."

"Then what happened?"

Jan hesitated, making a rough calculation of how long he had been in the Tile—it had been several hours since he had been detained. If Tomas had fixed the Volkswagen, Claire and her friend would be well on their way to the border.

"She left. She didn't tell me where she was going, and I didn't ask."

"I see. Quite convenient." Baranov rose to his feet. "You will tell your story to Captain Cerny in detail, now. You will give us names. I warn you that we will check everything you say. If we discover that you have lied, it will not go well for you."

Twenty-six

The sun had begun to set, and Claire waited impatiently for Jan's return. She kept checking the clearing by the front of the cottage where the Volkswagen and Tomas' shiny Skoda sat parked. When she glanced at her watch, she was dismayed to see it was well past six o'clock. Where was he? Had they not been able to find the spare part, the thermostat, after all? What could be keeping him?

"Stay cool," Summer said. She put a reassuring hand on Claire's shoulder. "They'll get here."

Summer spread a roadmap out over the top of the kitchen table. She studied it for several minutes, muttering to herself. Claire remained silent, her eyes never leaving the clearing.

"There are two border crossings into West Germany," Summer said. "I crossed at Rozvadov. There's another one, further south, at Zelezna Ruda. I think we should go back the way I came. With any luck, the border guards will remember the Bug with a painted peace sign and remember me, too, and wave us through."

Claire forced herself to stop looking through the window and to focus on Summer. "How long a drive will it be?"

"Maybe three hours. We're some fifty kilometers west of Prague, and we have to drive on some rural roads."

"Are you sure it will go smoothly? I didn't enter the country with you."

"You didn't. No problem. You're an English friend who came to my show in Prague and I offered you a lift. There's no reason for them to be suspicious. Hey, you'll be wearing my necklace and earrings. Just smile at them. Flirt a little. Pretend you're a California hippie chick." She grinned. "Do you know how many California hippie chicks it takes to screw in a light bulb?"

"No," Claire said, willing to play along.

"Ha! None. California hippie chicks screw in hot tubs."

Claire found herself laughing, more at the mischievous look on Summer's face than at the joke.

A minute later they heard the sound of a car, and then Lenka's Skoda rolled into the clearing and came to a stop. Claire and Summer hurried outside. Claire felt a sudden chill when she saw only Lenka and Tomas in the front seats of the Skoda. Where was Jan? Why hadn't he come? She found herself rushing over to the car.

A grim-faced Lenka exited the vehicle, and with crossed arms, stood facing Claire. Tomas ignored them and immediately headed over to the Volkswagen, flashlight in hand.

"Where's Jan?" Claire asked.

"He didn't meet us where he said he would, at the garage," Lenka said, glaring at Claire, making no attempt to disguise her hostility.

"We had dropped him off at his place. Tomas and I purchased the thermostat and we drove back to Smichov when Jan didn't return. One of the neighbors told us that he had been taken by the police."

"My God. That's terrible," Claire said. Jan taken by the police? She had a hollow feeling in her stomach.

Lenka shook her head. "Someone must have informed on him. Somehow they learned about Jan helping you. He will be sent back to prison. All because of you." She paused. "I told him not to get involved, that it wasn't worth it. But he felt that he had to."

"Are you blaming Claire?" Summer asked. "That's not fair."

A look of disgust crossed Lenka's face. "I do blame her, and I blame his reckless cousin. Jan's an artist. He's not political and he shouldn't have gotten involved. And now they have him. Do you know what they will do to him? They will beat him. I know Jan. He will resist, and they will punish him harshly. For what? People he hardly knows?"

"If that's how you feel, why didn't you turn us in?" Summer asked.

"I thought about it. But if I did, Jan would never forgive me." She turned to Claire. "I'll be here for him long after you're gone. I have always cared for him. You have come here and ruined everything."

"We didn't mean to," Claire said. "I told him that he could stop, that he shouldn't put himself at risk."

"The knight in shining armor. He couldn't resist." Lenka faced Claire directly. "Did you sleep with him? Is that why he protects you?"

"I don't see how that's any of your business," Claire said.

"So you did."

Summer stepped between them. "This isn't cool." She turned to Lenka. "We can't waste time arguing. If they've arrested Jan, we can't stay here for very long."

Lenka shrugged. "They will be looking for *her*," she said, pointing at Claire. "Jan would never tell them you are here, but you must get out of the country."

Summer nodded. "I'm sorry about what has happened. Thank you for driving out here."

"I did not do it for you or her. Jan made me promise the other day that if he was arrested I would continue to help you."

Tomas called out to Lenka in Czech. He turned to them, with a wrench in one hand and a dirty part in the other. They talked briefly.

"Tomas says that he has replaced the thermostat," she said. "He wants you to try the engine."

Summer got behind the wheel and started the car. The engine turned over and then she pumped the gas pedal and it roared to life. She looked over at the gauges and nodded. "No overheating. I think it's fixed."

"Thank you, Tomas," Claire said. He bobbed his head in response.

"We will leave," Lenka said. "You must go, too."

"Not yet," Summer said. "We'll wait until the morning."

"Why is that?"

"I don't want to blunder around on these roads in the dark and get lost. And I don't want to arrive at the border crossing late at night. We'll leave first thing in the morning. Arrive there just before lunch."

Lenka shrugged. "That's a mistake, but you do what you think is best."

"I'll need to make a phone call," Summer said. "To tell my agent in London that I'm driving to Germany."

"Go to Podebrady. There are hotels there for the people who come to the spa. You could make an international call from there, but they will want to see your passport." Lenka paused, considering her words. "You can expect no more help from me. I've done what I promised Jan. You're on your own now."

* * *

At first light, Summer made her way to the bedroom where Claire slept, curled up and vulnerable, safe for the moment. She hesitated before waking her. Summer was surprised by the sudden tenderness she felt for Claire, a woman she hardly knew. But Claire needed her. She might not be tough enough to do what might need to be done that day on her own. Summer had the toughness. She had lived by her wits before.

There had been times when Summer didn't know where her next meal was coming from, but she had always found a way to get what she needed. Claire had never struggled like that, had never had to fight her way out of a corner. Why would she? She came from a world of money—that had been apparent to Summer within five minutes of meeting Claire. A silver platter girl. Pretty and smart and taken care of.

Summer quietly left the bedroom and heated some water for tea. She glanced at her watch. They would leave for Podebrady in ten minutes. She would find a hotel and call Freddie North and wake him up with a message for Jack Townsend. Summer had assured Claire that crossing the border would be easy, but Jan's arrest had changed things. They would have to pass through the first checkpoint twenty kilometers from the border, and then through border control at Rozvadov. She had begun to worry that the police might be looking for the Volkswagen. What if Jan had talked?

Claire appeared at the door to the bedroom, yawning and rubbing her eyes.

"How did you sleep?" Summer asked.

"Not well. I kept thinking about Jan. I finally fell asleep and got a few hours."

Summer motioned her over to the kitchen table and offered her a glass of tea. "We'll drive to Podebrady. I'll call my agent. He's my connection to Jack Townsend. We may need Townsend's help later today."

"What about Jan?"

"There's nothing we can do for him. I imagine that they're treating him roughly. Lenka seemed convinced that he wouldn't talk. As long as he doesn't tell them about me and our plan to drive to Germany, then we have a fighting chance."

312

"I feel terrible about what's happened. Lenka is right—it's my fault. They must have found out about Jan helping me."

"We don't know that. Lenka assumed that, but she could be wrong. The police may have picked him up for a different reason. He's been playing hooky from his job, hasn't he?"

"He has. But what about Lenka? She's the only other person who knows about us."

"I'm sure she's making herself scarce."

"I hope you're right," Claire said.

They finished their tea and collected their belongings for the trip. Claire looked around the cottage for a long moment before she closed the door. She would never be back. Summer was already in the driver's seat in the Volkswagen, leafing through a guidebook with an unfolded map. She looked up when Claire climbed into the passenger seat. "I've got a plan," Summer said. "We'll stop in this town called Bor in the early afternoon. It's before the highway checkpoint on E50 on the way to Rozvadov. The guidebook says there's a medieval chateau there with a moat and tower. There's also a historic church. We'll stop there and take in the sights and wait to see if Jack Townsend shows up to help us get across the border. Maybe a different vehicle. Who knows? He has to have some tricks up his sleeve."

"You're asking Townsend to join us there? How far is it from Vienna?"

"He was supposed to meet me in Germany yesterday, so he should be close to the border. Jack got us into this jam, so he should get us out. Or send someone."

"And if he doesn't?"

"Then we'll figure out a way to do it by ourselves."

There was very little traffic on the way to Podebrady. They stopped at a hotel near the center of town, and Summer and Claire went into the lobby together. The hotel operator connected Summer to Freddie's home number. The phone rang ten times before he picked up with a muttered oath.

"Who the hell is this?"

"Your favorite singer."

"Summer, where are you? We expected you last night. You had us all worried that you'd had an accident on the way."

"You were worried? That's sweet. Sorry for the confusion. We're headed home today after a slight delay. We're planning to stop in a little town near the border called Bor. Will spend the afternoon there."

"I see," Freddie said.

"There's a chateau there, according to the travel guide. Let our friend Jack know I'll take some pictures for him. I know he takes a keen interest in my wanderings. So don't forget to mention that."

"I'll do just that. He's in Nuremberg and I'll give him a call."

"He's in Nuremberg? Why that's just a hop, skip, and a jump from where we'll be. The picturesque town of Bor. Tell him also that we've had more car trouble."

"I'll be sure to pass that along to Jack. He might want to meet you there."

"That would be lovely," Summer said. "Maybe he can do something about our car. Hope to see you in London in a few days."

"Sure, love. Do take care."

* * *

They had traveled twenty miles when they encountered engine trouble—the gauge starting to flirt with the red zone. Summer pulled the Volkswagen over to the side of the road and they sat for a while, waiting for the gauge to return to normal.

"This is going to slow us down," she said. "We'll wait for a little bit, let the engine cool down, and then try again."

Claire held her breath when Summer started the Volkswagen and began driving again. She kept looking over at the engine temperature gauge. For the next hour, it stayed below the red, and Summer turned to her.

"Can you drive a stick?" she asked.

Claire nodded.

"Great. Take over for a while. I need a break. There's very little traffic."

She brought the car to a stop by the side of the road and hopped out. Claire took her place in the driver's seat. Summer settled herself into the passenger seat and cradled her guitar on her lap.

"Just don't strip the transmission," Summer said. "The car has to stay in one piece until we reach Germany."

Claire struggled with the clutch and changing gears, but after fifteen minutes she began to feel more comfortable.

"Is there a song I can sing for you?" Summer asked,

"Something from James Taylor, maybe?"

"Sweet Baby James." Summer strummed the guitar and began singing.

Claire drove for another hour before they changed places. Summer was at the wheel when they took the turn off E50 to Bor. She explained that they needed to stop for gasoline. They drove a few miles until Claire spotted a small building with gas pumps and Summer pulled the Volkswagen into a small parking lot.

The teenaged gas station attendant had reddish-brown hair and a slight sprinkling of freckles and spoke a fractured English. Summer chatted with him as he began refueling the car. To Claire's dismay, an older vehicle with the word POLICIE on its side pulled into the station. An older man in uniform got out of the car and walked over to the gas pump and said something to the attendant, who turned to Summer.

"Policeman has questions. You tourists? Yes?"

"We are," Summer said. "We're on our way back home."

"He like to see passports," the red-headed boy said.

"Sure," Summer said. She handed her passport to the policeman, and Claire followed suit.

The policeman studied the photo in Summer's passport and glanced over at her. He repeated the process with Claire and seemed satisfied. He said something to the red-head.

"Where you go?" their interpreter asked. "Border?"

"Rozvadov."

That needed no translation. The policeman nodded and said a few brusque words.

"He says okay," the boy said. "He say not many Americans."

Summer waited until the police car had disappeared from sight before she got back into the car. The attendant waved to them as they drove off, headed to Bor.

"We're cool," Summer said. "A local cop, curious about a VW with a peace sign." She stole a glance at the clock on the dashboard. "We're right on time. We'll walk around the town, look at the church. Kill some time."

"Do you think Townsend will come?"

"Freddie will give him the message. Jack won't leave us out on a ledge by ourselves."

"You're very sure of that."

"I'm pretty good at sizing up people. Jack Townsend is the sort of man who does his duty."

"How can you be so calm about all this?" Claire asked.

"No point in getting uptight. My grandmother used to talk about how everyone has a Book of Life, and how we're the authors of that book. She'd tell me I could decide what my chapters would look like." Summer smiled. "This is one of the exciting chapters."

Twenty-seven

The greatest chess grandmasters had the gift of foresight; they could look at the board and project many moves in advance. They could see the logical sequence, the likely responses, and the exchange of pieces that would lead to eventual victory. When he was fourteen years old, Baranov lost a match to a twelve-year-old prodigy who had that gift. Later, when he reviewed the game, Baranov realized how overmatched he had been from the start. For the first time, he confronted his limitations as a chess player.

While he could never compete with a player of that caliber, Baranov worked to improve his ability to anticipate his opponent's moves. He became a better player. It proved to be excellent preparation for his career in counterintelligence. Thinking ahead. Putting yourself in the place of your adversary.

He had to admire whoever it was in the Mossad or British Intelligence who had designed Tatiana Savchenko's defection. They thought ahead, like a grandmaster. The plan had exploited the weaknesses in the border control system. It had kept each phase of the operation compartmentalized—the Hungarian student Piri Szabo knew very little beyond the simple instructions she had been given. Nor did Jan Klima have much worthwhile information to offer—his cousin had been deliberately vague in his dealings with him, and Jan's role had been to shelter Claire Markham for a night.

Baranov had been surprised when Cerny reported that Claire hadn't taken a flight out of the country from Ruzyne Airport, at least not under her own name. Where and when did she leave? He would have the Interior Ministry review Wednesday's border crossing records and find the time and place she departed Czechoslovakia—in his final report to Moscow, that mastery of detail would demonstrate Baranov's thoroughness. All loose ends accounted for.

He had delayed calling General Lebedev without significant progress to communicate. Now, he could assert with confidence that he had uncovered the role of an English couple—Rafael Klima and Claire Markham—in Tatiana Savchenko's defection. Further, he had identified at least two of their confederates—one Czech and one Hungarian.

General Lebedev listened in silence when Baranov reached him on the phone. He didn't say anything for quite some time, and Baranov wondered if the line had gone dead. Then Lebedev spoke. "An English couple? You say the woman gives her passport to Savchenko, and the man accompanies her across the border? I can see that trick working with the incompetents our socialist comrades employ in their border police. But so far, you've caught only small fry. This is a Zionist plot. Where is the evidence of the Mossad agents behind this outrageous provocation? The English couple had to be under their control."

"We continue to hunt down the local conspirators," Baranov told him. "I believe that we will uncover the connections to Mossad."

"How soon?"

"Within days."

"We need hard evidence of Israeli involvement. My God, man, they held a news conference in Tel Aviv. You need to demonstrate that this was a Mossad plot, not the work of amateur do-gooders, this New Exodus Project, as they claim. You will transmit a full and detailed report to me today."

"Sir, we are at a point in the investigation where time is of the essence. Permission to delay the report until tomorrow afternoon? I believe you will be very pleased with the progress we can make in the interim."

The line went silent again. Baranov wondered if he had pushed back too hard.

"I will give you until then," Lebedev said. "This oral report will have to suffice." He paused. "I'm dispatching two officers tomorrow to assist you. Colonel Krupin and Captain Sobol. They will be in Prague by midday."

Baranov immediately saw the move for what it was: Lebedev wanted to claim personal credit for progress in the case. With three counterintelligence officers assigned to the investigation, Baranov's leading role could be downplayed.

"Thank you for the assistance," Baranov said. "Please have them report to Colonel Voronin at the embassy. There are several leads in Prague they can work on, and I will leave instructions with Voronin."

"You will not brief them yourself? Where will you be, Colonel?"

"If I can spare the time, I will. But it's likely that I'll be on the move, in the field."

Lebedev seemed mollified by his answer and broke off the call with an abrupt goodbye.

After the call, Baranov sat and thought for a long moment. He had half-a-day before Krupin and Sobol arrived in Prague. He knew Krupin all too well; he was lazy but politically connected and would report Baranov's every move to General Lebedev. Sobol presented a different problem. He was known for his rough tactics, and more than one colleague had complained privately about his sadistic tendencies. Baranov would need to keep him far away from Jan Klima and any other prisoners.

He decided it was time to enlist Colonel Voronin's help in sidelining Lebedev's reinforcements. Baranov had one of the StB men drive him to the Soviet embassy. He found Voronin in his office, shuffling through a stack of papers on his desk. Voronin waved at him to sit in a solid wooden chair positioned in front of the desk.

"I must thank you," Baranov began. "Captain Cerny has proven himself to be quite capable. It was an excellent recommendation on your part. We have arrested one of the cell members here in the city."

"Have you?" Voronin was wary.

"We have. I will note in my report that you and the *rezidentura* have been of great assistance." Baranov leaned forward. "There may be another break in the case. We are looking for additional confederates and for evidence of Zionist involvement. You could provide further help in this search."

"I could?" Now, surprise on Voronin's face.

"It is important that my investigation not be impeded."

"Impeded? What could impede you?"

"Moscow is sending two officers from Counterintelligence to assist me. Krupin and Sobol. They'll arrive tomorrow. Briefing them will pull me away from the investigation at a crucial time. And that's how you can help. I hoped you could act as a liaison with these officers. I would regard it as a personal favor."

Voronin didn't immediately respond. Baranov watched him closely as the older man considered his request—Voronin hadn't risen to second-in-command for the KGB in Prague without some skill in office politics. He would understand why Baranov might want to avoid interference from Moscow.

"What would you have me do?"

"I'm concerned that I may have missed key details in my brief interviews of railroad personnel. My Moscow colleagues should repeat those interviews. And they should question the employees at the International Hotel for a second time. I'll have Captain Cerny provide an interpreter from the StB to accompany them."

"I see," Voronin said. "I think that we can keep your colleagues busy. At your request, Colonel Baranov. At your direct request."

Captain Cerny had news when Baranov returned to the Tile. There
had been no sign of Claire Markham at the airport. Baranov found
that curious—how had she left the country? He doubted that she
would have risked a trip by train, so she must have escaped by bus or
car.

Cerny had returned to Jan Klima's apartment building and learned
more from the old lady there who was a low-level informant. She told
him that a young woman and a man wearing the stained-coveralls of
a mechanic or tradesman had come looking for Klima just minutes
after his arrest. The old lady recognized the woman, a friend of Jan's
named Lenka.

When Baranov turned to Jan Klima's file, Lenka Cizkova was listed
as a member of his social circle. He didn't waste any time in asking
Cerny to bring her in for questioning. Could she be part of the
plot? It seemed unlikely, but he had been surprised before by what
the associates of a suspect could reveal when interrogated. It took
Cerny a few hours to find the woman—she was at a café near Charles
University that Klima's circle frequented. She didn't seem surprised
when the StB men took her into custody. She had asked to be allowed
to call her mother, but Cerny had ignored her request.

Baranov had them put the woman in a cell by herself for thirty
minutes. If he had the luxury of time, he would have kept her
there alone for longer to soften her up, but he couldn't wait. In the
meantime, he read her thick StB file. Lenka Cizkova was considered
politically unreliable. She had worked as a waitress in a shabby

restaurant frequented by students and musicians. According to one informant, she had some contact with visitors from West Germany, and had smoked pot with them on two occasions. She had a messy personal life, with several boyfriends.

He recognized the type, the rejection of authority, the risk-taking. Drinking, sexual escapades. No doubt there was a missing or overly harsh father to blame. She might be hard to break. She might welcome punishment.

He wondered if she would look at him, at her interrogator, and make a similar snap judgment—that he was a security type, a man driven by a need for order. Obedient and dutiful. There was truth to that characterization, yet he was different, curious, able to examine things with a clinical detachment. It was what separated him from his colleagues in counterespionage when it came to solving problems.

As it turned out, he didn't have to subject her to an extended interrogation. He had them bring her from the cell to Baranov's makeshift office. She got to the point quickly and began by offering a bargain.

"I'll tell you what you want to know," she said. Her Russian was quite good, Baranov noted. "If you'll promise to release Jan Klima. He is blameless."

Baranov shrugged. "You are hardly in a position to negotiate."

"I can tell you where the Englishwoman is."

"What Englishwoman?"

"She calls herself Claire. You want to catch her, don't you? That's why you arrested Jan."

"Would you like a cigarette? A cup of tea? Coffee?" Baranov was stalling for time. He hadn't expected this young woman to offer him a major break in the case.

She shook her head.

"This woman, Claire. Have you met her? Is she in Prague?"

"I've met her. I know how she plans to leave the country. If you let me see Jan, if you promise to release him, then I will tell you what I know."

"Or I will compel you to tell me."

"Perhaps. But that will take some time, which you don't have if you wish to catch this woman."

He studied her for a moment, measuring her up, her carelessly-combed dark hair and bright red lips. He thought he understood what motivated her. She loved Jan Klima. Was it reciprocated? Baranov doubted it. Klima was a classic loner, wrapped up in his painting. A man who saved his passion for his canvas and that emotional distance undoubtedly made this woman want him even more.

"Why has your Jan protected this Englishwoman?"

"He's very loyal."

"To a woman he met a day ago?" Baranov saw something in her face.

Resentment? Jealousy? He decided to push on. "Or is Claire his lover? He protects her because they are lovers. Is that it?"

Lenka glared at him. "That's absurd. She means nothing to him. It was a favor to his cousin. Will you release Jan if I tell you about her?"

For the first time, Baranov understood why Jan had so doggedly resisted during his interrogation. He had fallen for Claire Markham. Could that be so? They had only known each other for a few days, but they were young, and judging from her photograph, she was attractive. Danger could be a powerful aphrodisiac. That had to be it.

Baranov wasn't a stranger to romance, although he had only been deeply in love once, as a student. He remembered the heady first days of the relationship, his intense near-obsessive focus on the girl, Mila. He couldn't get enough of her—how she looked and moved so gracefully, how her hair smelled slightly of vanilla. Mila had been quite independent, determined to have her own career as a physician. That had driven them apart, for Baranov had wanted a traditional wife, a woman who wouldn't work long hours, who would be there to cook dinner and raise his children. The relationship ended when Baranov decided to apply for a job with State Security. How could it not? Mila hated the idea of him working for the KGB. In the years that followed, Baranov had a few brief affairs—careful to keep them quiet—and once or twice had spent time with a woman who was happy to share her bed for small gifts of cash. But he hadn't found anyone who he could envision making his wife.

"I will strike a deal with you," he said. "I will let you see Jan. He will not be mistreated. If what you tell us leads to finding this Englishwoman, we will consider releasing him, or at least reducing the charges he will face."

Lenka started to say something, and then stopped. She nodded. "I agree."

He and Cerny accompanied her to the cell where Jan Klima was being held. When Cerny unlocked the cell door, Lenka stepped in and gasped. Jan was sitting on the narrow cot, his face swollen and bruised. She went to him, murmuring a few words in Czech, and held his hands in hers.

"I'm all right," he said.

"Lenka has agreed to cooperate with us," Baranov said. "You should follow her lead."

"I've told you all I know."

"Very well," Baranov said. He turned to Lenka. "I have kept my word. You have seen him."

"What time is it?" Jan asked Lenka. "It's Friday, yes?"

"It's Friday morning," she said.

"Did Tomas fix things?"

"He did."

"That's enough," Cerny said. He took Lenka by the elbow and led her out of the cell. Once back in Baranov's office, Lenka accepted a cigarette and a cup of tea. She took a deep drag on the cigarette before she spoke.

"The Englishwoman is not alone. She has a traveling companion."

Baranov tried not to show his excitement. "A Czech?"

"An American. A folk singer who was in Prague for a few shows. A peace activist. I don't know how they met, but they are planning to leave together, to drive to the West."

"When? When are they leaving?"

"This morning."

"Where do they plan to cross? The German border? The Austrian border?"

"They didn't say. I think they will try to get to Germany. It's closer."

"Who is Tomas?" Cerny asked. "You told Klima that he had fixed things. What does that mean?"

"Tomas is a mechanic," she said. "The American girl has a Volkswagen. A Beetle. Tomas fixed the thermostat. They would have left on Thursday, but the engine was overheating."

"A Beetle. What color?"

"Light gray. A peace sign painted on the side."

"The American, do you know her name?"

"Summer. She never said her last name."

"What does she look like?"

"She is fair. Long blonde hair."

Baranov turned to Cerny. "Alert all of the crossing points into West Germany and Austria. A description of the Volkswagen. Two women. One dark-haired, the other a blonde. English and American.

They must be detained." After Cerny had left, Baranov looked over at Lenka. "You've been quite helpful. Is there anything else you can tell me?"

"That's all."

"You may go, then."

"And Jan?"

"I will keep my word. If you've told me the truth, he will be released."

He sat at the desk, deep in thought, after Lenka's departure. He hoped that she would enjoy her brief spell of freedom. She would end up back at the Tile soon enough; the StB would insist on it. The same fate awaited Jan Klima—Baranov would release him, but State Security would quickly arrest him again. If Baranov was asked, he would recommend light sentences for Jan Klima and Lenka Cizkova. They were pawns, used as a means to an end by the originators of the Savchenko operation. He doubted the Czech prosecutors would see it that way, and they would be unlikely to seek or accept lenient sentences.

Lenka had given Baranov a great gift—he could be just hours away from capturing two Western agents. Who knew what they would reveal under interrogation? How had Mossad recruited them? Were more Czechs involved in the plot? They would talk, he was sure of that. It would be quite a triumph. The dismissive nickname, the Grandmaster, might be transferred into one of respect. He had been given a near-impossible task and had prevailed. Even better, his victory didn't have to be shared with anyone else. By the end of the day, the name of Sergei Mikhailovich Baranov would be spoken with respect in the corridors of Moscow Center.

Twenty-eight

They had arrived in Nuremberg early on Thursday evening. Hawes and Viktor took turns behind the wheel of their rented BMW coupe, and Rafe, who had insisted on coming, dozed in the backseat. Hawes had half-expected the gray Volkswagen Beetle with the peace sign on its side to be parked in front of the Grand Hotel—which it wasn't—and there were no signs of Summer or Claire.

After checking in, they had a subdued dinner in the hotel restaurant. Hawes decided to wait in the lobby in one of the plush chairs where he had a view of the front door; Viktor and Rafe repaired to the bar. Hawes had begun to fear the worst when the concierge told him there was a call for him on the house phone. It was a worried Freddie North, who reported that he had not heard from Summer.

"She's not here," Hawes said. "At this point, all we can do is wait. If you hear from her, call me immediately. I'll do the same."

At ten o'clock, Viktor took his place in the lobby and promised to call Hawes if Summer and Claire appeared. Hawes took the elevator to his room on the fourth floor and went to bed.

In the morning, they met for a glum breakfast, but as they were about to order, the waiter told Hawes that there was someone on the phone for him. Hawes went to the house phone in the lobby to take the call. It was a much happier Freddie.

"She woke me up this morning," he told Hawes. "Mechanical problems with the Volkswagen. Getting it repaired delayed her return. She's driving back today, Friday. She asked me to pass along a message to you. She plans to stop in a little town called Bor this afternoon, just short of the border. I think she wants to meet you there."

"What about her friend, Carol Jordan?"

"Still along for the ride."

"Did she say anything more?"

"No. It's curious." Freddie sounded puzzled. "Why would she make a stop on her return? And ask for you?"

"She must need help navigating the border."

"There's another possibility, Feliks. The secret police may have her, and they're using her to lure you into Czechoslovakia."

"Did she sound under duress? Did she say anything strange?"

"She didn't." Freddie paused. "If I know my girl, she would have found a way to tip me off if she was under coercion. No, I think it was on the level. What will you do?"

"Go and meet her. I can, because I've got a valid visa."

"Good luck, Feliks. Call me when you're back in Nuremberg."

* * *

When Hawes returned to his hotel room to prepare for his trip, he placed a brief call to London to apprise Charlotte of the situation. After he hung up, he wondered if he should also telephone Nigel. It had been on his mind since Summer had challenged him about the state of his relationship with his son.

Nigel didn't fully understand Hawes' Tory worldview. How could he? Nigel had been educated at the best schools, buffered from the harsh realities Hawes had experienced as a young man. Nigel didn't even know the truth behind his parent's courtship and marriage. Anna had made Hawes promise never to tell him, and Hawes regretted that he had agreed to keep the secret.

When Hawes met her in Budapest in 1956, Nigel's mother had been a Duna girl—one of the beautiful Hungarian women recruited by State Security who acted as escorts to Western travelers and businessmen. They were used to collect information, and in some cases, to compromise married men so they could be blackmailed. Anna had been coerced into the role. When she was sixteen, a powerful Party official had spotted her at an outdoor restaurant, and when she had rebuffed his advances, he had threatened her only brother, Gabor, with imprisonment. Anna felt she had no choice but to become his mistress. When this official was purged, State Security had forced her to become a Duna girl. During his stay in Budapest, Hawes had fallen in love with Anna; he arranged for her to leave

Hungary in the caravan of British subjects fleeing the besieged city. Later, in England, they were married.

It was not something any son would want to learn about his mother. Anna felt ashamed of her past. She didn't like talking about her life in Budapest, or her family, and Hawes had honored her wishes. It meant, however, that Nigel never fully comprehended the depth of Hawes' feelings about the Left and its support for the regimes of Eastern Europe.

He dialed Nigel's number and let it ring. He was about to hang up when his son answered.

"How are you?" Hawes asked.

"I'm well, and you?"

"I'm fine."

"This line isn't very good," Nigel said. "Static. Where are you?"

"I'm in Germany on business. I'll be back in London in a few days. I thought you might come down from Oxford, and I could treat you to an early supper."

"Is everything all right?"

"As well as can be. I don't see as much of you as I'd like, and I want to change that. If you're willing. There are a few things I want to talk to you about. I thought we could make a fresh start, in a way."

There was a long silence. "Why don't you call me when you get back? We can settle on a date, then."

"I'd like that, Nigel. Very much."

* * *

Under gray clouds that threatened rain, Hawes drove them from Nuremberg to Waidhaus, the German town just across the border from Rozvadov. They had lunch in a roadside inn, and Hawes explained his plans for the afternoon. They sat at a long table, beers in front of them. The dining room was deserted.

"Summer is a clever girl," Hawes began. "I believe that she's stopped in Bor because she's worried that the StB may be looking for the Volkswagen she's driving. If that's the case, then we'll wait for a bit and I'll bring them back in the BMW."

"And the VW?" Rafe asked.

"We'll find a place to hide it."

"Are there other options? Cross on foot?"

Viktor laughed. "I don't think even James Bond could make it on foot. There's barbed wire, mines, a death strip where they'll shoot you down from the guard towers." He shook his head. "If we had time, we could try to get them to Hungary, and from there to Austria. The Hungarians are more relaxed about Westerners these days."

Rafe frowned and turned to Hawes. "If you're going to Bor, what do we do? Do you expect us to sit here and wait?"

"That's exactly what I expect." Hawes quickly explained that if he had not returned by dark with the women, Viktor should telephone Tobias Kent in the Foreign Office. Hawes handed Viktor a slip of paper with Kent's office and home phone numbers. Viktor should report that he and Claire Markham had been arrested by the Czech police at the border.

"What about the American girl?" Viktor asked.

"She knows to scream for her ambassador. They won't have anything on her."

"Then what?"

"The two of you should take a bus to Nuremberg. Fly back to London. Rafe, you can call my secretary, Charlotte, and give her your address so she can mail you your check."

"That's it?" It was Rafe. "We're supposed to walk away?"

"What did you expect?" Hawes asked.

"Why don't I go to Bor with you? You don't speak Czech."

Hawes rolled his eyes. "By now, any half-competent KGB counterespionage officer has identified you and Claire as prime suspects. They've had four days to put it together. At least Claire has a false passport. You don't. If you come with me, and it goes bad, they'll have all of the key players in the operation."

"Don't be stupid, Rafe," Viktor said. "You're compromised. A paper trail in Prague. Feliks is not."

"Feliks?" Rafe slammed the table with his hand and turned to Hawes. "Your name is Feliks, not Jack?"

"It is," Hawes said. "It doesn't matter that you know, now. My name is Feliks Hawes."

"I'm sorry, Feliks," Viktor said.

"What else don't I know?" Rafe asked.

"You know enough to be a star witness at the show trial they'll hold if they arrest you," Hawes said.

"It's the same for you and Claire if they catch you, isn't it?"

"It won't be as clear cut. I believe that Her Majesty's Government will exert enough diplomatic muscle to make the Czechs think twice about going public. Or they'll trade something for us. Better terms on a major commercial deal. Tickets to the finals at Wimbledon. Who knows?"

"And the American?" Rafe asked. "What's her excuse?"

"She has a decent cover story—she met Claire for the first time in Prague and offered her a ride to Germany. There's nothing to connect her to Claire or to me."

"That's the way you want to handle this?"

"It is."

Rafe sighed. "So Viktor and I cool our heels for the rest of the day. It's Miltonic—'He also serves who stands and waits.' We'll be more than properly pissed if we stay here and drink beer." He shifted in his seat. "I have a good paperback in the car. A thriller. It will help pass the time. If you'll hand me the keys, I'll go fetch it."

337

Viktor waited until Rafe had left the dining room before he spoke. "You're relying on Freddie North's belief that Summer hasn't been turned," he said. "The KGB and Czechoslovak State Security could very well be waiting for you in Bor, ready to spring the trap. Are you quite sure this is the best course of action?"

Hawes was about to respond when he looked out the window and cursed. "It's Rafe," he said. "He's taking the car."

They both jumped to their feet and ran to the door. Hawes went first, stumbling outside to the inn's parking lot. He caught a glimpse of the back of the BMW as it rapidly accelerated, heading east toward the border.

"That little shit," Viktor said.

Hawes cursed. There was a rumble of distant thunder, and the wind picked up—rain was on the way. "What the hell is he thinking?"

"He wants to be a hero." Viktor shook his head. "Should we rent another car and go after him?"

"And compound his error? Just a moment ago you were worried about me walking into a trap. No, we'll have to let Rafe play out this hand. He speaks Czech, and he's glib, and maybe he'll talk their way out of any trouble in Rozvadov."

* * *

Rafe kept slightly below the speed limit as he drove into the town

338

of Bor. He didn't want to attract the attention of the local police. A light rain had started as he had passed through Rozvadov, and he set the windshield wipers on low. He drove slowly, looking for a gray Volkswagen Beetle. No doubt the center of Bor would be called quaint in a tourist guidebook with its whitewashed buildings with green and red tile roofs, but the town looked like it had seen better days. Rafe made out the large cylindrical tower of the Bor Chateau through the BMW's rain-spattered windshield.

He kept an eye out for the Volkswagen as he drove through the town and then came to a Catholic church. Further up the road, he saw the distinctive shape of a Volkswagen Beetle, and he pulled into a space behind it. Two women stood by the driver's side of the car, sheltering under an umbrella. One of them had long blonde hair, and the other was Claire Markham.

"And who are you?" the blonde asked when he approached the women.

"It's Rafe," Claire said. "Jan's cousin. I told you about him, Summer."

"Where's Jack Townsend?" Summer asked.

"He's in Germany," Rafe said. "Waiting for our return."

"He sent you in his place?" Claire asked.

"I borrowed his car. He's no doubt royally pissed, cooling his heels in an inn outside of Waidhaus. I speak Czech. He doesn't. We talked about the best way to get you out, and it seemed logical that I should come."

"They arrested Jan," Claire said. "I wish we had never involved him."

"It's as much my fault as it is yours," Rafe said. "I shouldn't have asked Jan to help. I feel responsible."

"Summer is concerned that the police may know about us and the Volkswagen. That's why she asked for Townsend to come. She thought that he might drive us across the border in a different car."

"You're one of Townsend's people?" Rafe asked Summer, making it sound like an accusation.

"I am. A recent recruit. It's been a bit more complicated than expected, but here we are."

"Townsend has a plan, of sorts," Rafe said. "We should try it. We leave the Volkswagen here, hidden somewhere. I'll drive the two of you to Rozvadov in the BMW."

"Won't they be suspicious that you're returning to Germany so quickly?" Claire asked. "And don't you have stamps in your passport from a few days ago, from the trip to Vienna?"

"I've dreamed up a story," he said, turning to Summer. "My American girlfriend—you—and I had quite a row a few days ago. I left Prague for Vienna and then we reconciled over the phone. I offered to meet you and drive you back. Claire is a friend who came along for the ride."

"That's a story, all right," Summer said. "Quite shaky."

"I can sell it. Romantic roller-coaster. Hippie girlfriend who's a handful, a bit crazy, but I'll wink at the guard and say you're worth it. Trust me, there's a universal understanding among men about that."

"Horny bastards," Summer said, but she was smiling. "You didn't tell me what a charmer he was, Claire. Life of the party. Not at all like his cousin, the very serious Jan."

"He has every reason to be serious," Claire said quickly.

"Let's drive out of town and find a place to hide the VW," Rafe said. "I'll lead the way."

Rafe drove for ten minutes to the south, checking his mirror to make sure Summer was right behind him in the Volkswagen. Soon they were in the countryside, with only an occasional house appearing. He turned down a dirt side road that led into a forested area and came to a stop half a mile down where there was a copse of trees in a nearby field. Summer parked the Volkswagen under the trees. She and Claire hurried back to the BMW and got in, Claire taking the front passenger seat.

"I don't feel bad about this," Summer said. "Ditching the car. Not bringing it back. It's on its last legs."

"Don't worry about Townsend being upset," Rafe said. "He'll write it off on his taxes as a business expense."

Rafe glanced at Claire, studying her for a moment. "You look different."

"Not that different," Claire said. "Just the clothes and jewelry."

"The hair," he said. "You let your hair down."

"I had her do that," Summer said. "She wouldn't let me cut it short. This way, she looks like one of my friends."

Rafe looked at his watch. "We need to burn a few hours before we cross. I can say that you two took a bus to Pilsen, and I picked you up there. With any luck, the shift will have changed and there will be new officers who don't remember me. First, we get past the checkpoint on E50 and then we drive to Rozvadov. We'll wait there for an hour or so and then I'll sweet talk us past the border officials."

"Well, you don't lack confidence," Summer said.

"I don't. Never have. I think it's one of my better qualities."

Twenty-nine

Captain Cerny had suggested that they drive to the StB headquarters in Pilsen, where they would be roughly an hour from the two border crossings into West Germany, Rozvadov to the northeast and Zelezna Ruda to the south. Baranov liked the idea. They could check in with the commanding officers of both border control posts by phone. If the Englishwoman and her blonde American companion turned up, they could have them detained and quickly drive to either place to take them into custody.

Pilsen, an industrial city, had a large complement of StB officers. There had been labor unrest at the nearby Skoda car works in the 1950s, and the Interior Ministry wanted to make sure that any Solidarity-type activism was suppressed. The StB colonel in charge, Josef Varga, looked like he enjoyed the city's famous beer; his round belly strained against his uniform tunic, threatening to pop the buttons. He was eager to please, offering to deploy additional men at Baranov's request.

"A room with several telephone lines," Baranov said. "And tea. That will be all, for now, Colonel Varga." He had taken an immediate dislike to the man.

"As you wish, Comrade Baranov," Varga said. "I insist that you make use of my office."

Captain Cerny telephoned border control at Rozvadov. There had been no sign of a light gray Volkswagen Beetle and in the past two days no one who matched the description of the two women had appeared at the border. Baranov took the phone from Cerny and told the commander there it was a matter of the utmost importance that he stop and hold the women. When they called Zelezna Ruda, Baranov repeated his instructions. The officers there had nothing to report. There had been no female tourists from England or the United States crossing that day or on Thursday, nor any women in the age range of Claire Markham. The Austrian border control posts told the same story.

Baranov didn't know what to think. Had Lenka Cizkova lied to him? What had he missed? Was it possible the women had false passports of another nationality? Would they try to cross the border on foot? Baranov doubted that—the border between Czechoslovakia and West Germany was well guarded, with guard towers, minefields, barbed wire fences, and constant patrols.

He decided to go outside, to clear his head. He told Cerny that he would be back in a moment. It had begun to drizzle, and there was a light mist. Fog had begun to obscure the city streets.

Baranov cursed out loud. If the women had decided to risk an illicit border crossing, the weather was ideal. The fog would reduce visibility. He wasn't naïve. There might be ways to get across the border. A bribe to the border guards to look the other way? A gap in the barbed wire and minefields that the local smugglers knew how to navigate?

Could it be that they had found another escape route? By bus? By train? Did Lenka deliberately misdirect him? He didn't think that she had, but it was hard not to have doubts. There was a noise behind him, and he turned to see a uniformed StB officer standing there, waiting to be acknowledged.

"There is a call for you, sir," the man said. "From Moscow."

It wasn't a good line, hissing and crackling.

"Where the hell are you, Baranov?" It was General Lebedev, shouting into the phone; Baranov held the receiver away from his ear. "That idiot Voronin at the embassy said that you were in the field, but he didn't know where. It was the StB that tracked you down. What the hell is going on? Voronin has Krupin and Sobol questioning the chambermaids at the International Hotel. Is that your idea of a proper investigation?"

"I was not satisfied with the initial interviews," Baranov said. "As Krupin and Sobol are professionals, I thought they might uncover facts that have been overlooked."

"They tell me you're in Pilsen. Why are you there?"

"We have uncovered intelligence suggesting that some of the conspirators are attempting to leave the country."

"What are you talking about?"

Baranov took a deep breath. He had to tell General Lebedev something, but he needed to take care. "We believe that some of the Zionist agents stayed behind after the defection. I'm not sure why at this point. We have information that these agents will attempt to reach Germany through the border crossing at Rozvadov or Zelezna Ruda. We have their general description and have alerted the border posts to detain them. Pilsen is equidistant from these border control posts. The moment these agents appear, I will immediately head to the border."

"Then Colonel Krupin and Captain Sobol should be there with you!"

"As you wish, sir. I will call Voronin, and he will arrange to have them driven to Pilsen." Baranov would indeed call Voronin, but only after he had a report from one of the border posts that the women had arrived. So far, he had effectively sidelined Krupin and Sobel with busy work. He smiled at the thought. By the time Lebedev's men arrived in Pilsen, Baranov would be at the border making the arrests.

"Where is my report, Colonel Baranov? You haven't sent me a report."

"My apologies," Baranov replied. "I'll arrange for it to be transmitted from the embassy as soon as I return to Prague."

"Call me if there are any significant developments. I don't care for these cowboy tactics of yours." Lebedev slammed the phone down, ending the call with a decisive click.

While Baranov couldn't afford to alienate the General, he wasn't ready to file a report. That could wait until he had more to show for his efforts. So far he had bagged an overly-romantic Czech artist and a greedy Hungarian student. He needed the Englishwoman and her American collaborator. Then, he would turn in a final report where Baranov was the main actor, the relentless and persistent investigator who cracked the Savchenko case. He would praise Colonel Voronin for his assistance, and Baranov would make sure Voronin received a copy, which would guarantee its wide circulation at Moscow Center.

What was the saying, fortune smiled on the bold? He knew that if he was going to rise further in the ranks of State Security, he had to be bold. No hesitation. No second thoughts. He was so close to the prize.

An excited Cerny burst into the office.

"The police in Bor say a gray Volkswagen Beetle was seen there earlier this afternoon," Cerny said. "Two women inside."

"Where is Bor?"

"It's on the road to Rozvadov. What's puzzling is that the Volkswagen hasn't shown up at the checkpoint between Bor and the border."

"They're no longer in the VW, that's why." Baranov glanced at his watch. "How long will it take to get to Rozvadov?"

"Forty-five minutes."

"Get us there faster."

Thirty

It had begun to drizzle as Hawes parked the car on a slight rise where they could see into Czechoslovakia and the buildings and boom gate for border control in Rozvadov. There were a few vehicles backed up there, waiting to be cleared by the guards, but the West German side had only a single tourist bus.

Hawes had rented a car from a garage in Waidhaus, an older Mercedes, paying a premium and promising the mechanic that he'd bring it back that night. He took out his binoculars and scanned the landscape, spotting barbed wire fencing and open ground to the north and south of the border crossing. Hawes focused on the larger building. He could see a few uniformed men near the entrance. They were smoking, passing the time, unfazed by the light rain. That was a promising sign—if the border guards were relaxed, then it was possible that they had not been alerted about Claire and Summer.

"We won't stay here," Hawes told Viktor. "The moment we see the BMW, we'll head to the Grenzübergang on our side and wait for them there."

A soft fog began to drift over, first covering the trees in the near distance, and then dramatically reducing visibility.

Hawes lowered the binoculars. "I shouldn't have taken the job in the first place," he said. "That was my first mistake. My second was trusting Singer and the people behind him."

"No fool like an old fool." Viktor grinned and lightly slapped Hawes on the back.

"An old fool trying to prove he still has what it takes."

"You're not to blame," Viktor said. "The plan worked."

"Except it didn't, and that's why we're here." Hawes felt his chest tighten, and he reflexively reached for the bottle of pills. He quickly swallowed one and waited for the tightness to begin to ease.

* * *

When they reached the outskirts of Rozvadov, Rafe suddenly pulled off the road and rolled to a stop near two small houses. He left the engine running, opened the trunk of the BMW and, before Claire or Summer could say anything, left the car. A minute later, Claire watched as he carried a black bicycle to the car, and watched as he loaded it into the trunk. Back in the driver's seat, he pulled away into the road.

"What are you doing?" Claire asked, incredulous at what she had just seen.

"It's an insurance policy," he said, grinning.

"How is stealing a bicycle going to help? Are you mad?"

He spoke quickly. "The most important thing is to get you across the border. You're most directly implicated in the defection. Remember I told you I dabbled with screenwriting in my spare time?" He didn't wait for her answer. "When I saw the bicycle next to that house, it just clicked for me. When we reach border control, it should be quite routine—they'll look at our passports and visas, and wave us on our way. But if I sense that they're suspicious, if they want to search the car or question us, we may have to take matters into our own hands. Summer and I will get into a lover's quarrel, quite a ferocious one. That's when you need to grab the bicycle and pedal as fast as you can for the other side. Don't look back, don't stop for anything."

"You're mad," Claire said. "How can that possibly work?"

"It's getting darker outside, and it's rainy and there's some fog rolling in. If push comes to shove, you can take off on the bicycle. If Summer and I do a good enough job, the border police will have their hands full. You'll be overlooked."

"Even if your scheme works, and I'm skeptical that it can, it leaves the two of you up the proverbial creek without the proverbial paddle."

"They can arrest me, but they don't have much to go on," Rafe said. "Can't prove anything. The same for Summer. She's an American who just happened to meet you in Prague. The two of us are traveling under our real names. It's another reason why getting you across should take precedence. You're using a false passport. That alone will hang you."

"Summer, do you agree with Rafe's idea?" Claire asked. "You stand to lose as well."

"They can't pin anything on me," Summer said. "I'll plead innocence.

How was I to know you would bolt like that? I just met you in Prague, hardly knew you. Didn't like the way you were looking at my boyfriend. That's a story I can stick to."

"They're not going to believe that."

"So what? If you're safely across the border, I don't care. Remember what I said about the Book of Life? Here's where this particular chapter gets exciting. This trip has made me feel so alive, and it's not just adrenaline. It's because what you and Rafe did in Prague matters, and I'm happy that I can help."

"How do you know that it matters?" Claire asked.

Summer laughed. "The bastards wouldn't be after you if it didn't matter. And I hate men like them, always have. I don't believe the Communists have a monopoly on bastards, but they're the ones standing in our way, so I say we do what we have to."

"We're almost there," Rafe said. He turned to Summer. "Remember. You're my American girlfriend, and Miss Jordan is your new friend that you met in Prague. You're not happy with me because you think I've been making eyes at her."

* * *

From the checkpoint to Rozvadov took them twenty minutes, with Cerny driving at top speed, honking at cars to get out of their way. The officers at the checkpoint hadn't seen anyone in a Volkswagen but remembered a BMW with a young man and two women passing through some twenty minutes ago.

"It's them," Baranov said. The sighting of the Volkswagen in Bor had convinced him that Claire Markham and her American companion planned to cross at Rozvadov. They must have found another vehicle and had been joined by a male confederate. If the officer in charge at the border post followed his orders, anyone matching the descriptions of the women Cerny had circulated would be immediately detained. Then again, there was always the danger of laziness or incompetence.

The fog had thickened so much that Baranov finally told Cerny to slow down. "We can't be of much use if you crash," he said.

"I've driven in worse," Cerny said, but he eased back on the gas pedal.

Baranov didn't respond, lost in thought. He was eager to reach Rozvadov—he was convinced that there they would find Claire Markham and her companion, and Baranov would have his professional triumph, one that would be recognized by the highest levels of Moscow Center. He had solved the case through intuition and perseverance and he wondered, for a moment, if some day his investigation would be used as a model to teach new officers. That was within his grasp, just a few minutes away, at the border crossing.

* * *

When their turn came at the Rozvadov border station, a stern-faced officer asked them to get out of the BMW as one of his colleagues began a search of the vehicle. Claire watched as he opened the

353

trunk and removed the bicycle and placed it on the ground. She walked over and lifted it upright and exchanged a quick glance with Summer. She moved toward the front of the car, wheeling the bicycle, calculating how, if need be, she could maneuver it past the red-and-white striped boom blocking the way to the road beyond.

Fog now blanketed the area, and Claire could only barely make out the taillights of a car that had braked at the border post in West Germany. Rafe had been right about one thing—the dark and the fog would make it very hard to see more than twenty feet ahead.

Rafe had their passports in his hand, and he had begun talking to the officer, trying to work his charm. Claire heard him say the words *Americká přítelkyně* and nod toward Summer, and then something else. The officer fought back a smile. Summer gave Claire a slight nod—it seemed to be going well. The officer searching the BMW had finished with the interior of the vehicle and had popped the hood of the car and was looking at the engine with a flashlight. He finished his inspection and closed the hood. Claire wondered whether she should wheel the bicycle back to the trunk.

Before she could move, she heard the sound of someone repeatedly honking a car horn. A moment later, a large black sedan pulled up at the curb, some five car-lengths away. Two men left the car, and one of them started yelling. "*Stůj.* Stop." The men headed toward the BMW.

"Go," Summer hissed at Claire. "Ride, now. Don't look back. Whatever you do, don't stop."

Before Claire could respond, Summer strode over to Rafe and the border security officer and began yelling. "You bastard," she said to

Rafe. She pushed him, her hands on his shoulders. "You cheating bastard."

Claire wheeled the bicycle around the boom gate and got on it quickly and began pedaling. A thick fog hung close to the ground and she prayed that it was acting as a blanket, hiding her from sight. The road sloped down, and she pedaled as fast as she could, her lungs burning with the sudden effort, hurting from the cold air.

She could hear Summer yelling behind her. Then came the sudden sound of a man yelling, amplified by a loudspeaker. Claire heard the word "stop" several times, but she kept pedaling. A bright light suddenly illuminated the mist. She wondered if they would chase her.

She could see the lights of the border post ahead. Claire could make out distant figures, but the swirling fog made it impossible to tell who they were.

* * *

Baranov felt a surge of pride and excitement when he saw the BMW ahead of them, the trunk up, slightly blocking his view. He and Cerny exited the car. As he ran forward, Cerny just behind him, he could see a young woman with long blonde hair flailing at a man, and a border guard trying to separate them. The woman was yelling curses, and she swung her arms wildly.

"Arrest them," he called out, and Cerny repeated his order in Czech. The closest officer grabbed the young man who continued to struggle, and the woman broke free and ran toward the front of the BMW. A second officer helped subdue the man, who they handcuffed.

"There should be two women," Baranov said. "Where are they?"

Another border guard arrived with a rifle. Baranov looked up and saw the young blonde woman running up the road.

"Stop her," he said. "Warning shots, first."

The border guard turned to Cerny for confirmation. He nodded. The guard raised his rifle and squeezed off a round. The sound of the gunfire broke the silence.

The young woman, slowed, hesitating, and turned toward them.

"What is it that she is doing?" Baranov asked Cerny.

"She is making a hand gesture," he said. "With her middle finger."

Baranov felt a sudden surge of anger. To be mocked by this subversive was infuriating. He peered through the fog and could see the woman was standing there, her hand still in the air.

"Stop her," Baranov said. "Now."

The border guard didn't hesitate. The sound of his second shot reverberated, and the figure in the distance staggered for a moment and then fell to the ground. Cerny and border guards didn't say anything.

"You fucking bastard," the young man in handcuffs said. "How in God's name could you do that?"

* * *

At the German border post, Hawes heard two rifle shots, and he turned to Viktor. They could see a searchlight ranging across the landscape hungrily trying to pierce the mist.

"What's happening?" he asked Viktor.

"I don't know."

Hawes felt a deep ache in his chest, and he found he was gasping for breath.

Two armed West German border guards moved in front of them, peering into the dark.

Through the fog, a figure appeared, a slim woman on a bicycle. She pedaled furiously toward them, and when she saw the uniformed men, she slowed her pace.

Hawes and Viktor ran to her, and she stopped and let the bicycle fall to the ground. "Claire," Hawes called out to her. "We're here, you're safe."

She was sobbing, and Hawes moved to embrace her. Before he could reach her he felt a shooting pain in his left arm, radiating to his chest. He clutched his arm and slumped to his knees, surprised at how dark everything around him had become.

He saw Viktor reach Claire and fold her into his arms, and then his vision blurred, and he felt a crushing weight on his chest, and then the darkness closed in on him.

Thirty-one

New York

December 1983

A thick crowd of shoppers had congregated in front of Macy's Christmas windows, and so Claire crossed Broadway at the light on 33rd Street to avoid the crush. It was a crisp day, and the azure December sky above was free of clouds. She loved Manhattan during the holiday season. She pulled her mohair coat closer, suddenly shivering. It would be a long walk, all the way to 59th Street, but she welcomed the opportunity to think as she strolled the twenty-five or so blocks ahead of her.

Claire had agreed to meet Benjamin Singer at the Plaza Hotel that afternoon. She thought Singer had been surprised that she was willing to see him after all that had happened. The Plaza was a strange choice, she thought, for it was in the Oak Room where he and Jack Townsend had recruited her. (Or to be accurate, where Singer and a man she later discovered was named Feliks Hawes had recruited her.) Perhaps Singer thought she wouldn't make a scene there. Or worse, he was oblivious to the memories that meeting at the Plaza might trigger.

When she neared West 59th Street, she looked across to Grand Army Plaza where the chestnut vendors had set up their carts, and tourists were taking photographs in front of the Pulitzer Fountain. She could see the golden statue of General Sherman on horseback to the north.

She told herself to be calm as she entered the hotel. She wasn't quite sure how she felt about meeting with Benjamin Singer. It was confusing. She had every reason to hate him for the sorry ending of the mission, but she had found it hard not to think of him with some affection.

Claire had questions about what had happened in Czechoslovakia, and he was the only one with the answers. He wouldn't deny her that—somehow she was confident that he wouldn't keep anything from her.

Singer stood up when he saw her enter the Oak Room and waited for her by the table, which was next to the windows facing Central Park to the north. He wore a green-gray tweed jacket, a white shirt and red tie, and gray flannel trousers, and his face was lightly tanned. He motioned for her to take the seat across from him, and waved for the waiter.

"How have you been, Claire?" he asked.

"Better," she said. "I took a month off, and then went back to work. Two or three days a week at the start. Mr. Galvin has been wonderful. Very generous with my taking time off. He told me not to rush back."

"That is good. In matters like these, it can take some time...."

"I'm sleeping better. Not as many nightmares. My therapist says that it should get better over time. The further I get from the trauma."

"Everyone reacts differently," Singer said gently.

The waiter arrived, and they ordered—Claire, a glass of sherry; Singer, a Manhattan.

After they were served their drinks, Singer raised his glass: "Cheers!"

"What can you tell me?" she said. "What about Rafe? How is he?"

"He's moved to Toronto," he said. "He decided that he wants to be a college professor, of all things. Linguistics. So he's about to start a graduate program there. Rafe told me he's had enough adventure to last a lifetime. They roughed him up at the border, but no permanent harm. Two weeks in jail. The British ambassador was quite good, threatened to make the whole mess public. They had nothing concrete on him, and the Czechoslovakian government wasn't going to risk jeopardizing tourism with a show trial."

"Thank God."

"Rafe should never have gone back across the border, you know. It was foolhardy, to say the least."

"I disagree," she said. "It was a courageous thing to do. He gave us a better chance. It didn't work out, but he tried to even the odds a bit." She looked away, gathering her thoughts. "And Summer?"

"A tragedy. I'm so sorry about her death. Never in my wildest imagination did I think it would end that way." He cleared his throat. "The Czechoslovakian government claimed it was an accident, that Summer wandered into a prohibited area and was shot by a border guard after ignoring repeated warnings. A very stiff note from the American ambassador and the Czechs made profuse apologies. She was brought back to the U.S. I believe there was a memorial service in London and in Ohio. Summer had many friends. Her parents wanted her buried in Akron, which is what was done."

"I wish I could have been there, at one of the services. She saved me, you know. She distracted the guards at the border. She must have thought the worst that could happen was that they would arrest her."

Singer didn't say anything. They sat in silence for a long time. Then, Claire stirred.

"Seeing people die," she said. "I wasn't prepared for that. To see that in front of me, to have Jack Townsend collapse and die. They say that he had a bad heart."

"He did."

"Viktor told me that his real name was Hawes. Feliks Hawes."

"That's true. He was a good man. Never said anything about his health, about his condition. His death was a surprise. I wouldn't have approached him for the mission if I had known."

She paused. "And Jan Klima? What do you know about what happened to Jan?"

Singer shifted uneasily in his chair. He looked away from her. "Jan? From what we can gather, a secret trial on charges of subversion. He had confessed to helping you, and so there was no question about his guilt. Not in the eyes of the judge. Jan was sentenced to twenty years in prison."

"My God, that's terrible."

Singer paused, studying her face. "The entire episode was an embarrassment for the government. The Czechs had to show the Russians that they would punish those involved harshly. Jan became the scapegoat."

"Twenty years," she said, tears trickling down her cheeks. She took her napkin and wiped them away. "Is there any chance he could get out earlier?"

"I don't know. Perhaps if there is a thaw. Detente or liberalization. A change in the leadership in Prague. I wouldn't want to raise your hopes."

"Jan didn't deserve this," she said. "He had been in prison before, and he never wanted to return. He sacrificed himself for me. For us."

"I take it you got to know him, then?"

"We had two days together. He was a lovely man. An artist through and through. An idealist." She looked down and traced an imaginary pattern on the tablecloth. Then, after a pause, she spoke. "And what of Tatiana Savchenko? My double? How is she?"

"Miss Savchenko has adjusted quite well to life in Israel. She has made a fresh start in life, thanks to you."

"I would like to meet her someday," Claire said. "Will she come here? To the U.S.?"

"Perhaps that day will come. Or you could visit Israel. Would you like that?"

"Not now," she said. "I have a question to ask you. Was it worth it? Her defection. Considering the cost."

Singer rubbed his chin and frowned. "What can I say? I never thought it would end the way it did. There was that unfortunate press conference in Tel Aviv. A bad mistake. I argued against it at the time."

"You argued against it?" She stared at him. "Aren't you the executive director of the New Exodus Project? That's what your card says. If you thought it was a mistake, a bad idea, why was it held?"

"I'm the executive director, but I answer to my board. It was their decision, and I had to honor it. The board thought publicizing Tatiana Savchenko's story would give hope to those Jews trapped in the Soviet Union. We never forget that Israel is the only country in the world where Jews have an immediate right of citizenship. The Russians don't regard Jews as true Russians. They may say that a Jew can also be a Soviet citizen, but the price you must pay is to turn your back on your ancestors, on your traditions, on your faith. And if you do, that's no guarantee the day won't come when Jews once again become enemies of the state."

"You couldn't have stopped them from holding the news conference?" she asked. "Or delayed it."

"It was the best timing. With the American congressman, it meant the networks would pay attention."

"Publicity to help you raise money."

Singer shook his head. "That was never a factor. Never. If anything, Tatiana's defection effectively killed the New Exodus Project. The

Russians won't deal with us, not after that news conference. I'm persona non grata in Moscow."

"So what did we accomplish, then?"

"We gave a young woman her freedom. The Talmud says that saving one life is the same as saving the entire world."

"But we didn't just save a life, Benjamin. We traded two lives for one. Summer and Feliks Hawes. Three lives if you include Jan."

"I'm sorry about it. Deeply sorry."

"It wasn't only about Tatiana Savchenko, was it? In his own way, Jan knew that. Tried to warn me. He said that there had to be something more, that there was no return on investment in helping her defect. She was a means to an end. Was he right? What was so damn important?"

Singer remained silent, and then turned and motioned to the waiter for the check. "I don't blame you for how you feel, Claire. I wanted to see you and apologize. I failed you. I let you down. I regret what happened to you and Summer. I don't regret my role in helping Tatiana escape from a soulless system."

"Benjamin," she said. "You're not answering me. I think I deserve to know. Please tell me why you went to all this trouble for her."

Singer shook his head. "We live in a flawed world," he said. "Sometimes the path to repairing those flaws is crooked. I wish it weren't so. Everyone who agreed to help Tatiana had their eyes wide open. Each of you had your own reasons for participating. Feliks had something to prove on a professional level. Rafe craved adventure and needed the money. And you, Claire, you wanted a cause bigger than yourself. You got that, didn't you?"

She didn't respond. She thought about Jan and the last time he had seen her, and what he had said—that he could take the blue from the sky for her. She thought about their brief time together—so brief that it almost didn't seem real—and how it had changed her life in ways that she didn't fully understand. She felt a sudden urge to leave, to get outside while it was still light. Claire stood, tears welling in her eyes, and told Singer in a low voice that she was going and that he shouldn't contact her again. Then she left, her head down, walking quickly through the room, eager to reach the street where no one would know her and wonder at her grief.

Epilogue

Prague

Friday, November 24, 1989

Nigel Hawes heard his name being called as he was leaving the hotel. He turned to see who it was and immediately recognized Isabelle Lavalle, a news photographer Nigel had first met three years earlier in Reykjavík at the summit between President Reagan and General Secretary Gorbachev. They had both been there to cover the talks for their respective employers—Nigel for the *Guardian* and Isabelle for Agence France-Presse.

He was glad to see a familiar and friendly face. Isabelle was in her mid-fifties, with a mane of black-and-white hair and a lovely face, her features a mixture of her French and Vietnamese ancestry. She greeted him warmly, kissing him Gallic-style on both cheeks. "Are you here to see history made, Nigel?" she asked.

"That would certainly justify my trip," he said. "After Berlin, anything is possible, isn't it?"

"I never thought the Wall would come down," she said. "Not in my lifetime. Not with such *rapidité*. Will it happen here? Who can say?

The word is that Dubcek has come from Bratislava and may appear today in Wenceslas Square."

Alexander Dubcek, the reformer who had served briefly as the leader of Czechoslovakia's Communist Party during the Prague Spring, had finished his career in obscurity in Slovakia as a minor bureaucrat in the local forestry department. He was seen as the Hero of '68, and Nigel had long wondered what would have happened if Dubcek's "socialism with a human face" had been given a chance to flourish. Would it have offered a third way between Communism and the unrestrained capitalism favored by the Tories in Britain and conservative Republicans in the United States?

"How long have you been in Prague?" Nigel asked Isabelle.

"I flew here on Monday," she said. "There have been demonstrations all week. The students started it. They had a peaceful protest march a week ago Friday—the largest since '68—and the riot police broke it up violently. The students lit candles and chanted that they had bare hands, that they were unarmed, and the police beat them anyway."

"When I saw the film of the demonstration on the BBC, I decided I needed to come," Nigel said. He had been intrigued by the bold demands made by the dissidents of the newly-formed Civic Forum: the immediate resignation of President Gustav Husak, of the Communist officials connected to the Russian invasion in 1968 and those responsible for the recent violence against Prague's peaceful demonstrators. Further, they demanded the immediate release of all prisoners of conscience in Czechoslovakia. Finally, the Civic Forum seconded the call by student groups for a general strike on November 27th in support of these demands. Did they think the regime would bend? With what had happened in Germany and Poland, was it possible Czechoslovakia might begin a transition to liberal democracy?

"I'm headed to the Square now to take some photographs," she said. "Why don't you come along? We can stop by the headquarters of the Civic Forum later. They hold a nightly press conference."

"What's the latest news?"

"I heard this morning that Milos Jakes, the Communist Party leader, has called an emergency meeting. The regime has been surprised by the extent of the pro-democracy movement, and by how popular Havel, the dissident playwright, has become."

"Have you met him? Havel?"

"I have. He's a charming man, that one. I've photographed him and the other leaders of the Civic Forum at the Theater Without a Balustrade—it's a quaint little venue. The Magic Lantern Theater Company canceled its current show there so that Havel and the other reformers could have a place to hold court."

The light was beginning to fade by the time they reached Wenceslas Square, and Nigel was glad he had worn his lined Burberry trench coat. He was staggered by the size of the crowd filling the long boulevard that made up the Square. There were people holding signs and waving flags for as far as Nigel could see. He led the way through the crowd, Isabelle following behind him, her Nikon camera hanging from a strap around her neck.

Nigel stopped halfway to the famous equestrian statue of Saint Wenceslas. He heard a roar from the crowd as a white-haired man in a gray coat and a paisley scarf appeared on the balcony of the building housing the offices of the *Svobodnoye Slovo*, the Socialist Party newspaper. Many in the massive crowd recognized him, and began chanting "Long Live Dubcek" and "Dubcek to the Castle." Alexander Dubcek beamed at the crowd and turned to embrace a younger, sandy-haired man, a gesture that elicited another roar.

"That's Havel," Isabelle said, leaning into Nigel to be heard over the noise, and pointing at the younger man.

Dubcek spoke into the microphone, his voice trembling at first, but then it grew stronger.

"I wish I spoke Czech," Nigel said.

A young woman in blue jeans and a sweater standing near them smiled and said in English: "Dubcek's saying 'the light was here before. We must act now as though the light has come again.'"

Tears streamed down the faces of many of the people around them. Others took out the keys from their pockets and began shaking them.

"It's a message to the Old Guard," Isabelle said. "They're saying it's time for them to go."

"An amazing scene," Nigel said. "Such a repudiation of the government. Do you think Husak will respond with force? A crackdown?"

Isabelle shook her head. "Gorbachev won't back him and intervene militarily. And the leaders of the Czechoslovak Army said on television the other night they won't move against their fellow countrymen. It seems Husak and the hardliners will have to accept reforms of some sort."

She checked her watch. "We should head over to the theater."

It was Isabelle's turn to lead the way. When they reached the theater, she had a brief conversation in French with a young woman at the door, who smiled and supplied Nigel with a press pass and ushered them by two volunteer guards into the building. They walked down one flight of stairs to a foyer, and then another flight of stairs to the theater, where the news conference was being held.

On the stage, Dubcek and Havel sat side-by-side, flanked by other members of the Civic Forum, fielding questions from the press. A former professor of economics, Rita Klimova, translated their responses into English. Every seat in the theater was taken, and Nigel found a place where he could stand by the wall on the right side. Isabelle moved to the front where she could take photographs.

Nigel could see that Dubcek still clung to his vision of a Prague Spring. When asked about the future of Czechoslovakia, Dubcek claimed that socialism could be reformed if the Party became more open. Havel, on the other hand, said that the word socialism had lost its meaning in the Czech language, that he once called himself a socialist but had not for fifteen years.

Nigel listened intently to the discussion between the two men, the de facto leaders of the opposition. He was surprised by how much he identified with Havel's political journey. Events over the last three years had caused Nigel to question his own beliefs. Reykjavík had been the start. While the Summit had not produced any concrete results, Nigel had learned that Reagan had proposed sweeping reductions in the number of nuclear weapons, cuts in the arsenal that some of his hawkish advisors had opposed. It wasn't what Nigel had expected. Then, the turmoil in Eastern Europe had suggested a deeper and more profound discontent with Communism than Nigel could have imagined.

Nigel's on-and-off-again girlfriend Fernanda had teased him about his shifting views. "It sounds as if you'll be quite the Tory by the time you're thirty," she said.

"Hardly," he said. "But I could support Paddy Ashdown."

"Paddy Ashdown? The Liberal Democrats?" Fernanda laughed. "That means that you're only halfway on the road to supporting Maggie. The road to hell."

Nigel was brought back to the present by the sight of a young man in jeans and a sweater crossing the stage. He whispered a message to Havel and Dubcek, who smiled broadly. Then the Forum's spokesman, Jan Urban, announced that Jakes and other leaders in the government had resigned. Havel leapt up from his chair and made the V-for-Victory sign, and then embraced Dubcek. Everyone in the theater was on their feet, cheering and applauding. The theater's stage manager appeared with a bottle of champagne and two glasses. Havel raised his glass and toasted a free Czechoslovakia.

After the press conference had ended, Isabelle joined Nigel at the back of the theater.

"I think they may actually get a free Czechoslovakia," she said. "It's like the Emperor's new clothes, the people are realizing the regime has lost whatever legitimacy it ever had. How long can it last?"

They walked back to Wenceslas Square through streets crammed with Czechs celebrating the news. Once in the Square, they found it filled with thousands of people waving the blue, white, and red national flag, cheering the announcement that the Jakes government had stepped down. It was noisy, with car horns blaring and students singing, shouting, and chanting, factory workers in overalls, a young father with his daughter perched on his shoulders, there to see history in the making. Near the top of the Square, young men had climbed onto the pedestal of the Saint Wenceslas statue, and its base was plastered with posters and photographs. A Czechoslovakian flag had been hung from the saint's giant foot, another from the leg of his horse.

"They're enjoying their triumph," Isabelle said to Nigel.

"Jakes resigning is quite a start," he replied. "Now comes the hard part. A coalition government? Or something else?"

A young man in an expensive winter coat approached them. "Excuse me," he said in English. "I overheard you. Are you journalists?"

Nigel nodded and he and Isabelle introduced themselves.

"Rafe Klima," the man said, vigorously shaking Nigel's hand, and then Isabelle's. "I live in Toronto, and I didn't think they would let me in, to be frank. I had a spot of trouble here in 1983. Serious trouble. Two possibilities for why they gave me a visa. They could be so distracted by what's happening that the process of vetting has broken down. Or the bureaucrats in the Interior Ministry see which way the wind is blowing." He paused and motioned toward a man standing behind him. "This is my cousin, Jan. He lives in Prague."

Nigel shook Jan Klima's hand. He could see the family resemblance, although Jan looked much older than his cousin. His face was heavily lined, and his hair had turned a fine white. There was a scar under one of his eyes.

"It's over for them," Jan said. "How can they stand against this? Against the people. When they opened the Wall in Berlin, I hoped this might happen."

"Jan is one of the dissidents," Rafe said. "They let him out of prison when they freed Havel. He's a painter who wouldn't follow the rules."

"No longer a painter." Jan shook his head. "I've retired."

"You're too young to retire," Isabelle said.

"Perhaps I am," Jan said.

"He just needs to get his strength back," Rafe said. "That's all."

The crowd began to chant "*Svobodu*" again and again, calling for freedom.

Jan's eyes filled with tears. He murmured something in Czech to Rafe and then turned to Nigel.

"Ghosts," he said. "There must be hundreds of ghosts, thousands of them, watching from above."

Puzzled, Nigel looked over at Rafe, who shrugged.

"What must they think?" Jan said. "Our ghosts. They must have thought this day would never come. But, thank God, it has."

Author's Note

In part, I wrote *Charles Bridge* to consider a question that has always intrigued me: what lies behind the quiet bravery of those who oppose authoritarian rule? Why are some individuals willing to risk so much in acts of resistance, to confront the Leviathan state and its agents—the informers, the secret police, the prosecutors, the wardens of its prisons and labor camps—when the prospects of success are slim and the consequences for action severe? What causes them to choose resistance?

Setting my novel in 1983 Czechoslovakia let me explore aspects of that phenomenon. The playwright and Czech leader Vaclav Havel once wrote about becoming a dissident: "It begins as an attempt to do your work well, and ends with being branded an enemy of society." While Jan Klima is a fictional character, his life follows that pattern; doing his work well—painting the ghosts he sees around him—brings him into conflict with the state. His willingness to help his cousin Rafe and Claire Markham should come as no surprise; he instinctively knows which side he is on. Nor are the consequences he will face a surprise.

The early 1980s were a difficult time for those challenging the established order in Eastern Europe and the Soviet Union. In Poland, the Communist government declared martial law in December 1981 and employed the army and paramilitary police to suppress Solidarity. The death of Soviet Leonid Brezhnev in 1982 brought former KGB chairman Yuri Andropov to power. Andropov continued the campaign he had begun at the KGB against dissidents, intellectuals, Jehovah's Witnesses, and Jews who hoped to emigrate to Israel.

In retrospect, the Soviet system, and state socialism, was on its last legs. Within the decade, Communist regimes in Eastern Europe collapsed—much like a house whose foundations have quietly rotted away and comes crashing down without warning. In Czechoslovakia, the Velvet Revolution toppled the government in twenty-four days, without violence or bloodshed. After weeks of demonstrations in Wenceslas Square, it became clear that Gustav Husak and his regime had lost any legitimacy. On the second Sunday of December 1989, Husak swore in a new government and resigned. On December 28, Alexander Dubcek was elected chairman of the Federal Assembly. A day later, Vaclav Havel became president of the country.

In June 1990, in the first free elections held in Czechoslovakia since 1946, the Civic Forum and Public Against Violence (a Slovak political group) won decisive majorities; in July, Havel was reelected as president. The shift from totalitarian repression to liberal democracy had happened with blinding speed.

* * *

Prague today is a prosperous, thriving European city. When you visit, the Cold War years seem long ago and far away. (The private Museum of Communism in Prague does paint a grim picture of the challenges of everyday life in the Czechoslovak Socialist Republic.) Nonetheless, novels are works of imagination, and I've tried to capture the atmosphere of that time and place.

I turned to Miroslav Vanek and Pavel Mucke's *Velvet Revolutions: An Oral History of Czech Society* for first-person accounts of life under Communism. Milan Kundera's marvelous novels *The Book of Laughter and Forgetting* and *The Unbearable Lightness of Being* also offered glimpses into the past. I borrowed heavily from the description of the border crossing at Ceske Velenice from Ivo Moravec's *Tightrope Passage: Along the Refugee Route to Canada*.

For the events of November and December 1989, I found Timothy Garton Ash's engaging first-person account in *The Magic Lantern* and Victor Sebestyen's *Revolution 1989: The Fall of the Soviet Empire* to be invaluable.

Once again, I'm indebted to Glenn Speer, a long-time friend and skilled editor, who read early versions of the novel and provided helpful insights. Others who offered constructive criticisms included David Billington, Jr., Christian von Dehsen, Marina Belica, Julie Flanders, and Colin Macdonald.

Any errors of historical fact or flaws in interpretation found in *Charles Bridge* are mine alone.

And, once more, I'd like to thank my loved ones—especially Maisie—for their support, understanding, and patience, and for bearing with me as I fashioned this story.

About the Author

Jefferson Flanders has been a sportswriter, columnist, editor, and publishing executive. He is the author of the First Trumpet trilogy, set in the early years of the Cold War, and of *An Interlude in Berlin* and *District of Columbia*.

Made in the USA
Coppell, TX
24 July 2021